Banished & Broken

Broken Realms 1
Jane Rose

Jane Rose Publishing, LLC

Book Cover created by Graphic Designer of Jane Rose Publishing, LLC

Published by Jane Rose Publishing, LLC

1st edition 2024

Print ISBN: 979-8-9907251-2-6

Ebook ISBN: 979-8-9907251-1-9

To the ones who feel broken—

may you find the one who helps heal your soul.

THE RUINS
THE BANISHED
TWILIGHT KINGDOM
N
W
E
S
OLYRIUM
KRYSTAL MOUNTAIN PASS
CITRINE CITY
KORIN
ALICANTO STABLES
SUNSPARK KINGDOM
SPHINX FIELDS
MAREEN
LUAR
REFLECTING POOL

CONTENTS

CONTENT WARNING

My goal in writing this book is to ruin you mentally, physically, and emotionally. I hope as you read Aliyah and the others' journey that each of the characters connect with a part of your soul and shatter it into a million pieces. I'm not going to sit here and say that this book is filled with love and romance, because frankly, that would be lying. What I can say, is that this book is filled with broken people, struggling in a broken world, trying to find the pieces to put it all back together.

As a clinical mental health professional for my day job, I feel compelled to warn you about the coming events. However, this list will only provide you *some* insight into the destruction to come. I have done my best to pick out any potential triggers, but please take care of yourself and your mental health.

This book may or may not have a happy ending. So if you choose to begin this journey into Olyrium, I pray to the Maker of above and below that you survive what is to come.

SPOILERS AHEAD Last chance to turn back now!

JANE ROSE

<u>This book contains themes around:</u>

Alcohol Use

Alluded adult content

Alluded sexual assault

Bodily trauma

Drowning

Grief/Loss

Murder

Passive suicidal thoughts

Physical Abuse

Poison

Several unhinged males

Torture

PROLOGUE

26 years ago

Blood. Screams. War raged around her like wildfire unable to be put out with just water. Across the battlefield she looked at her mate struggling to cut down the enemy in front of him after the hundreds that came before. Soldiers who had followed her lead onto the grassy field, were now slain by the masses at her feet. She hoped it would never come to this, her people's brutal dismemberment by those who did not even deserve to stand on her lands. Yet there she was. The wounds on her arms and chest were bleeding, not healing fast enough, but still she fought on with everything she had. She lifted her sword, glistening with starlight and the blood of her enemies.

With heavy breaths the queen allowed herself one last look at the sword passed down to her by the previous queen. A sword sworn to protect those who could not protect themselves. The queen did not feel like she was protecting anyone. Everything she had left behind, everyone counting on her, flashed through her mind. She knew that sacrifice would be the only way to finally put to rest this age long war.

The Great War, as some called it, had been going on for the last 500 years. Battle after battle yet no one seemed to win in the end. Countless lives lost, and for what? Power? Revenge? Did the motive matter? Was the blood seeping into every crevice of this land worth whatever reason it was spilled? The answer did not matter at the end of it all. The pain she felt right now was all she could focus on, every cut across her mate was a cut across her. Every tear down her face was a tear down his. This could not continue, but the alternative would mean letting her future go. She knew her mate would not survive, but he knew the cost of being bonded mates for as long as they had been together.

She began her incantation. The spell she spent countless hours in the library learning, hoping there never came a day she had to use it. Now there she stood, praying to the Maker for another way. The pull of the power around her surging and wracking her body with every feeling imaginable. Pain. Grief. Guilt...Peace. She let herself slip into a vision of what might have been for just one last moment.

Laying in the grass with her mate while the sounds of laughter wash over her like a calming river. Bright eyes and smiles greet hers as the embodiment of love jumps into her arms, hugging her tightly. I love you.

She opened her eyes for one last look, one last moment. Her mate's eyes met her own across the battlefield, screaming as he started to run, but knowing he would never get to her in time to stop her. It was done. She felt the threads of her bond fraying. The tether that helped her through every heartache, every joyous moment, every breath she took— he was there waiting for her on the other end. Her mate finally reached her and pulled her in close, knowing these were their last moments together. She grasped that thread one last time before it snapped. Darkness was waiting for them with open arms...

PART I:
LUAR

Chapter 1

ALIYAH

Sara throws her knife and it lands directly in the center of the post with our small bullseye drawn onto it.

"Seriously!? How can you possibly hit the center...Every. Single. Time?" I smile, laughing with my best friend who always manages to excel at everything we do.

I find my stance like Sara taught me and pull the knife from my thigh holster. It's dull and rusted on some parts, but as long as it can stab through flesh, I don't really care. I feel the cool metal between my finger tips. I bring back my arm and throw the knife towards the post. It lands just outside the ring. Frustration grips my throat and anger rages in my eyes.

"This is pointless," I say turning to Sara. She just smiles and walks over to retrieve our knives.

Sara and I met about eight years ago after she stopped a fairly grabby man from attacking me in a bar. Apparently, "no means no" didn't apply to him. Unfortunately, that was not the first time I had gotten myself into trouble. After my third time in jail for stealing bread, I was beginning to feel like it was my second home. The first being my back alley apartment in which I could barely pay the rent to afford. Hence why I had to steal the bread. If it wasn't for Sara, I would still be living in the streets.

I never knew my parents. I grew up in an orphanage here in Mareen, but ran away every chance I had hoping to find my family. I never did. The last time I ran away, I was nine, and I never looked back. The streets would become my home, but in the end I was able to pick up some pretty nifty skills along the way. Pick-pocketing, picking locks, and basically being invisible to the entirety of Luar. All the usual tools any thief would need to survive. So that is what I did: survive.

I thought about leaving Mareen and traveling to other towns to see if they could offer anything better than this dump. I never made it past the Mareen border. Every time I stood at the edge of the field, some part of me felt a pull back to Mareen. Maybe one day I will be brave enough to go on an adventure.

Sara snaps in front of my face bringing me out of my past and into the depressing reality of my present.

"You need to focus, Aliyah. You overthink your throws. You need to breathe and feel the metal in your hand before you throw it. Trust that it will go where you need it to."

"Easy for you to say! As long as I've known you, you've been good at fighting and archery and swinging a freaking sword. I'm just now getting the hang of it! What I don't understand is that you're the same age as me and yet you act like you've been training like a warrior your entire life!"

When we first met, Sara told me that she didn't grow up in Mareen, but another village on the other side of the river. Most of the villages in Luar have no connection with each other so I was surprised that Sara had chosen Mareen, of all places, to call home. I was thankful that she did.

"Oh shut up! We have been training together for the last eight years," she laughs. "You're better than you think you are if you *just let go* every once in a while."

The mud around her cheeks cracks as a smile breaks across her face. Sara and I often like to train outside the village where no one can see us. Learning how to fight isn't exactly a priority for most women here, but Sara insisted she teach me. Luar had always been a peaceful place as far as war was concerned, but the village itself was full of evil people. While I would probably never get to use any of these skills I am learning, it gives Sara and I something to pass the time.

Mareen sits on the edge of Luar and is surrounded by large rivers to the north, south and west based on the few maps the library has. It is mostly cut off from the rest of the villages, so the imports of goods are often low. Mareen itself is one of the poorest villages based on what Sara has told me. Our apartment is proof enough that the village is run down. We have no running water at the apartment so Sara and I often bathe in the nearby creek. It isn't glamorous, but it is bearable.

I look back to my best friend who is now on the ground with one leg bent, and the other out straight, stretching her muscles from training. She smiles up at me as I bring my arm across my body, stretching out my shoulder. Even with dirt caked on her cheeks and under her nails, Sara is still gorgeous. Sometimes I wonder if she is even human. Sara is a little shorter than I am and has long brown, almost black, curly hair that comes to her mid- back with ocean blue eyes that always shine with mischief.

Before she came into my life I swore I would never care about anyone. Even now I believe it hurts too much caring about people. It always leads to disappointment and heartbreak. But not with Sara. No, Sara had crept into my heart and made a home there. It never made sense to me, but when I met her for the first time we just had this instant connection. We are always in sync with each other. She is my best friend. The amount of times she had my abs cramping and almost peeing my pants laughing was too many to count. Sara is the only one who knows the dark corners of my mind and accepts me anyways. She always told me I have misty blue eyes, but whenever I looked in the mirror all I saw were gray orbs staring back at me, begging to feel something.

I toss my long, blonde braid over my shoulder. Sara had done it for me before we began training, but now it was mostly falling out in crazy strands. I got a few wins today, but she never held back and always made me work harder than the day before.

"Alright, let's be done for the day and grab some food. I think I saw the bakery put out some chocolate cake, with that peanut butter frosting you love, on our way over here earlier," Sara says.

"Okay just one last throw."

I stand and unsheathe the knife from my thigh holster and hold it between my fingers. I calm my breathing. Closing my eyes, I picture the knife embedding into the target. On my exhale, I feel a familiar spark of fire coursing through my veins; it was the same feeling I always had when Sara and I did concentration exercises. Flowing from my heart out to the tips of my fingers, the spark travels through the hilt of the knife and out through the tip. The knife sails through the air and hits dead center right next to Sara's knife, and I swear when it hits I see sparks. I blink and they are gone.

Sara beams before collecting my knife from the target. "Told you so!"

I tuck it back into its hiding spot on my thigh before jogging to catch up with her as she walks toward the bakery. She was right. The smell of chocolate cake wafts towards us, begging to be stolen. Sara looks at me with those big, bright eyes and smiles. I already know what she is thinking.

Sara and I sit by the creek as we finish our cake. I need to wash away the pungent smell seeping from every pore in my body after today's training session. Sara barely broke a sweat. She just shimmered in the light.

"You know, you didn't have to throw me into that potato cart so hard today," I huff next to her.

"I needed to cause the biggest distraction that I could! Your scream combined with the rolling of potatoes halfway down the street was the perfect opportunity," Sara giggles. I throw a glare her way before breaking into my own fit of laughter.

"The baker was so mad! I barely made it out of there alive the way he was swinging that knife around. You could have at least given me a heads up."

"You should have seen the look on your face as you fell! I would have stopped to help you up, but the baker was turning my way right as I swiped the cake from the stand," Sara continues laughing, tears coming out of her eyes.

"You're such a jerk," I say, licking my fingers to clean off the peanut butter frosting.

"And you smell like you haven't bathed in 100 years."

Sara gets up from where she is seated and begins unlacing her boots. Each of us only owns two sets of clothes. Two shirts, two pairs of pants, and one pair of boots each. All of our clothes fit too loosely on our bodies, but at this point we don't know if it was because they were too big, or because we don't have a proper food source. Wading into the ice cold river, we begin scrubbing ourselves raw to get the smell of this Maker-forsaken town off our bodies. It never works. At the end of the day, I always go to bed feeling dirty. We wash the clothes we trained in today hoping they will smell a little less tomorrow.

After we bathe, we change into our other set of "clean" clothes before laying on the grass while our other set dries in the sun.

"How come you never talk about why you left your home?" I ask Sara.

"There isn't much to talk about really. Home is where you choose to make it and my home is here with you."

"I don't think I have found my home yet," I say, picking grass in front of me.

"I know there is something bigger out there for you, Aliyah. You will know when it feels like home."

"Can you tell me something about your home?" I ask.

"It was beautiful. Where I came from had endless mountains as far as the eye could see. It had a beautiful lake that I would spend summers on with my family. There were so many different places that I dreamed of visiting back home. I never had the chance before I found myself here. Maybe one day I will have the chance to explore whatever wonders lay out there waiting for me to find, but for now I am right where I need to be." Sara's eyes flick down, while she twists her fingers together.

"Sounds like no place I know of in Luar. It almost sounds too good to be true." I could sense the sadness in her voice, but she had never talked about her home or family before so I took my opportunity to pry. "Why did you leave if it was so beautiful? Where is your family now?"

"I will answer all of these questions one day, but for now I'd like to just lay here a while longer before we have to return to that crap hole we call an apartment," Sara laughs, completely switching emotions from moments ago.

I know I need to let it go, but some part of me feels this pull to ask more. But I know for now I need to just enjoy the sun with my best friend before we have to return to reality. She was right about one thing though: home is where you make it, and when Sara is around, it feels like I am close.

Chapter 2

ENZO

"You're a dead man, Gunnar!" I yell, blood dripping from my forearm.

"Don't be such a big baby, ZoZo. It'll heal. Maybe if you weren't so slow I wouldn't have been able to slice you open like that," Gunnar laughs.

"What have I told you about calling me that?" I flash him an angry look before my rage takes over. I swing my sword with the skill and precision that has him disarmed in seconds.

"We both know you love it," Gunnar says, picking up his sword and sheathing it. He stops to run his hand down his face, wiping away the sweat from his brow. We take time each day to train in order to stay sharp. We're now both dripping in sweat from the heat of the midday sun.

"Why exactly do we need to keep protecting Luar when The Banished haven't tried to attack them in years?" he asks, turning to me.

"You know why. It's precautionary. As the Queen's Guard it is our sworn duty to protect the realms from any and all threats, even the potential ones." *We have been over this about a hundred times now.* I sit down on the ground to stretch out my muscles.

Back when Queen Dione and King Armas sat on the throne, they had an elite army, hand chosen, who were sworn to protect the realms. When the queen and king sacrificed themselves, they had no appointed heir. The throne now remains empty until someone worthy of sitting on it arises.

Since most of the elders died in the The Great War, there was no one to choose the next Queen's Guard. Most of our military dissipated after the enemy was banished, thinking there would no longer be a threat to the realms. They went back to join the armies in their home kingdoms. However, a small group remains in Korin with a plethora of duties to perform, including protecting the villages, and guarding the armories in town. My small group of friends appointed ourselves the new Queen's Guard, to hold that oath until our dying breath.

Others had given up hope and thought we were crazy for ever thinking an heir would rise to claim the throne, but we knew that somewhere out there our next queen, or king, sat waiting.

Gunnar, Duncan, Jade, and I had been inseparable since the war. We were mere adolescents when The Great War began. We went through training together as children, and fought in battle together as full-grown fae; it all felt like ages ago. Jade, Gunnar and I grew up in Citrine City training in their military academy. My father had sat on the Queen's War Council, so I was placed into the training program as soon as I was of age. After my father was killed in battle a few years before the war ended, I knew it would honor him most by taking on his responsibilities.

My father and I had a complicated relationship, especially after my mother died, but I knew he would want me to continue to serve the realms despite our history. When the time came for an heir to arise, I would sit on that war council.

Gunnar is originally from SunSpark Kingdom and has an older brother, Kaleron, and a younger sister, Liliana. He was the first friend I made at the training academy. Without him, I am not sure I would have made it at all given my— disadvantages— at the time. Even though my father was one of the fiercest warriors, I was not so lucky. It took years of training, and several mouthfuls of dirt, to become who I am today.

Jade is a few years younger than the rest of us. She joined the military academy under the worst of circumstances. When she arrived, everyone treated her like the dirt on their boots. Her time at the academy was more about surviving than it was training. Gunnar and I found a couple of other trainees beating on her one day in the courtyard. She was small, but she sure as hell put up a fight. After that, we took her into our group and helped keep each other safe. We have all been together ever since.

Duncan did not join the military until he was older. Each kingdom is required to send their second son to the military academy once they come of age, as a show of faith that they are willing to lay down their own bloodline for the sake of the kingdoms. My father told me that King Olivar of The Twilight refused to send his son into battle. He had hoped he could keep Duncan out of the military all together, but one day Duncan showed up at the training academy. We never spoke about why he evaded coming for so long. The story must be too painful for Duncan to repeat outside his own mind.

"Seems like a waste of talent just training against dummies all day," Duncan huffs.

"We haven't used training dummies in years," Jade states.

"I know..." Duncan looks up at the rest of the group before cracking the smallest smile possible. Gunnar runs at Duncan before leaping into the air attempting to tackle him to the ground. Duncan dissipates into thin air and reappears just in time behind Gunnar to snag his foot and trip him. We all laugh as Gunnar stands up and brushes off the dirt from his chest and knees.

"Seriously, Duncan?! I told you it isn't fair to use your magic in the training ring! How are we supposed to practice hand to hand combat if we are fighting against shadows," Gunnar scolds.

High Fae are all blessed with unique magic that is usually passed down through generations. Duncan's magic was a pain in the butt for training, but came in handy during battle. He has the ability to teleport which is irritating, but effective. Gunnar has fire magic, which significantly helps during the overnight journeys. Jade was not passed down an ability since she was not born High Fae, but she can predict her opponents next move as easily as a psychic can read another's mind. She knows your next move, likely before you even do.

Then there is me. I inherited the gift of telekinesis. After my time at the academy, and my father's questionable training techniques, I only use my ability when absolutely necessary. The things he forced me to do to harness my ability— I was disgusted with myself at how vile my mind had become, so I trained my body to protect itself instead.

The four of us sit on the dirt floor of the training ring for a while, stretching and chatting about going to Adryanna's Tavern later on this evening. Jade looks over at me and smiles, a light blush brushing across her cheeks. My childhood best friend and most trusted advisor. Jade's battle strategies are truly magnificent, and not to be trifled with.

I always knew that Jade had feelings for me, but one cannot compromise one's mind for love. Either of us could die at any moment and I cannot risk any distractions on the battlefield. It's hard enough worrying about the other soldier's under my command, but to worry about someone I love would be too debilitating. Love and war were never meant to mix. Not that we had to worry about that though; Olyrium is at peace, just like it has been for the last 25 years.

Chapter 3

ALIYAH

Sara had gone into the market to try and snag some food for dinner. We weren't often lucky enough to steal food twice in one day, but the risk was worth it. I make my way down the streets of Mareen kicking a rock in front of me. Rats scurry away from the sound of my footsteps and the brown water running through the gutters puts a nice touch on the glamorous village we call "home". As I open the door to our small one room apartment, our landlord, Cyrus, is waiting for me.

"Where is my money? Rent was due two weeks ago," Cyrus says, rage bubbling below the surface. If his face gets any redder, he will probably explode like a tomato.

"I've almost got this month's rent, I swear! I just need a few more hours until Sara comes back with it!" I say, looking down so he won't see the lie in my eyes. He knows I can't make rent, just like every other month. How could I when every piece of silver or gold we steal goes to feeding ourselves. I wouldn't have to steal if I had money to spare. I know what comes next. I always know.

"We both know you don't have it, just like usual. Do you know what the alternative is to paying rent, Aliyah."

Bile rises in my throat at the thought. I breathe in deep through my nose to calm my fraying nerves. I have been met with this realization more times than I can count. Unfortunately, I do know what the alternative is to not paying. *Smack.* The hit lands across my face before I can even react. The red mark blooming on my cheek will show five distinct finger markings. I hadn't moved fast enough to dodge his hand before it connected with my face. You would think with all the training I have done with Sara that I would be able to stand up to Cyrus, but it's something about him that makes me feel weak and helpless. It's like a switch flips in my brain and suddenly I am that scared girl living in the streets all over again.

"I'll go to the post," I say, between my teeth.

"That's right. Move." Cyrus points to the door.

"I don't really feel like going right now, thank you very much," I retort under my breath. I was already headed to the post so might as well make it count. I am thankful that Sara isn't here to see this happen. She had seen the aftermath of my time on the post, all bloodied and bruised up, but it would never bring me peace if she had to subject herself to actually seeing it happen. I didn't want her to have a front row seat to my pain. She would try to take my place and I would never let that happen.

Cyrus grabs my arm with more force than necessary and pulls me towards the door. My feet feel like blocks of lead as they make contact with the cobblestone. As we make our way through the alleys to the village square eyes peak out of the darkness watching me on my way to the post. I walk with my chin held high and refuse to let a single tear fall.

When we arrive at the village square, I stare at the post that sits in the center and is bolted to the ground beneath it. Hanging on the post is a whip with one long leather strap. Cyrus pushes me down to my knees and my gaze locks onto the wood before me. As I kneel in front of the post, I know that, while he can strip away my flesh, he can never strip away my dignity. A small crowd gathers around the outside of the square to watch my punishment. Cyrus, being the maniac that he is, likes people to watch so they know if they can't pay, this will be their fate. He forcefully takes my wrists and brings them around the post. It's wide enough that my cheek digs into the wood. The post is already speckled with my blood from the last whippings.

The familiar smell of cedar and copper is almost calming. Like a memory burned into my brain. As he shackles my wrists down, I begin mentally preparing for what is to come. I feel the coolness of his knife on my lower back as he cuts off my shirt. Down to one now, I guess.

"What is this punishment for?" yells Cyrus, so the whole square can hear.

"For being completely and utterly poor and not being able to pay your steep price in rent!" I say, hoping my words cut him as deep as his whip will me.

"You'll pay for that retort." Cyrus snarls.

And now it begins. One lash for every day late. Today's total would be fourteen. This is the highest it has ever been. I wondered if he didn't come for rent sooner because he knew I would have to come down here. The post and I were about to get a whole lot closer from how long I am going to spend on it today.

The first lash always hurts the worst until my body can work to block out the pain. *Crack.* One. *Crack.* Two. *Crack.* Three. After three I let my mind drift away to another place waiting for it to end. I imagine myself in that beautiful world Sara described earlier that day.

The rolling hills are covered in wheat and wildflowers as far as the eye can see. The warm breeze caresses my skin. I look up to the sky with the sun shining down on my face. I am smiling and happy. I'm wearing a long tattered dress that blows in the wind behind me. I run my fingers over the wild wheat that grows and as I look off into the distance I see a figure. Tall, with broad shoulders, and brown hair. I can't see his face though. Like something that is not yet complete. I start walking towards him. This feeling in my chest is almost glowing, brighter and brighter with each step. As I cross the distance between us I reach out my hand...

Rip. The cold metal on my lower back brings me back to the present moment. I hadn't realized I passed out from the pain. My vision is rimmed with black as my body begs me to give up. *Was my back so torn to shreds that he ran out of room to whip me?* But as cool air whips across my exposed body, I realize the lashes are no longer payment enough. I am kneeling in the mud, covered in my own blood without anything to cover my body. Tears prick my eyes for the first time on this post as he grips the back of my hair and pulls me to a standing position. My back aches at the movement and I know a fresh layer of scars will mar my back forever. Just add it to the tally of those that came before.

Cyrus's dry, crusty lips meet my ear as he whispers, "the post is too good for you, Aliyah."

His pungent breath in my face isn't the only thing causing the vomit to rise in my mouth, but I hold on, refusing to give him the satisfaction. I look around as the crowd begins departing, not wanting to subject themselves to this kind of torture. Yet they would gladly stand by while I am whipped within an inch of my life. I hear the clattering of his pants as Cyrus positions himself behind me, taking away one of the most intimate choices someone can make.

I try to get my mind back to that beautiful place, but even my dreams cannot save me from my reality this time. I close my eyes and let a single tear slip onto the wood, mixing with my blood. I bite the inside of my cheek to stop myself from crying any further. Physical pain is better than this kind of torture. Cyrus steps back from me and curses in frustration, clearly unable to fulfill his fantasy.

"What's wrong Cyrus?" I spit. "Can't manage it for someone who's almost a corpse?"

"Screw you, Aliyah. I will be back for the rest of my payment in one week. Have it or it's back on the post, but this time I'm getting Sara on here instead."

Over my actual cold, dead corpse will I ever let Sara take the post. Cyrus storms away leaving me shackled to the post, bared for all to see. I start praying, asking the Maker to protect me. I pray that some other jerk doesn't come along and try to take advantage of my current situation. Once I knew Cyrus was gone for good I let myself truly cry for the first time on this post. I knew my bones were showing through the rips in my flesh, but that was pain I could handle. That pain was familiar. But this— this was something else entirely. I had never been with anyone in that way before in my life, and to have that choice taken away by someone so vile, so cruel— it left me feeling like my soul was stained forever. Like it was my fault for letting it happen in the first place. All this because I couldn't pay rent. With these thoughts running through my mind, my vision starts to waiver in and out, and as darkness consumes me, I pray I won't wake back up.

Chapter 4

ALIYAH

Cold hands shake my shoulders as my eyelids, heavy from exhaustion, slowly open to see my best friend looking at me with worry etched all over her face.

"Aliyah, I am so sorry. How did this happen? I was only gone for a short time! It was my turn to take the punishment!" Sara thinks we take turns receiving the lashes from Cyrus, but I always make sure that when Cyrus is around she is nowhere to be found. I would never let her suffer the pain.

"It was definitely my turn," I smile weakly at her, trying to make light of the situation.

I'm not sure how she got the shackles off my wrists, but it didn't really matter. My arms feel heavy dropping to my sides, after being chained up for so long. I have no clue how much time has passed since I blacked out, but disappointment hits again when I realize I'm still alive. At the end of the day, I know I could never leave Sara to deal with the grief over losing me. Every once in a while I crack though, and ask to be taken into another world of peace and comfort, instead of the dark, damp reality of my life.

"You always do this. This isn't supposed to happen to you. This isn't supposed to be your life," Sara cries as she helps me up.

"What other life would there be for me to live?" I mumble to myself.

"Why are you not clothed? The lashings are normally just on your back." Sara looks at me with such concern, trying to cover me as much as she can. The number of lashes on my body makes it difficult for me not to wince in pain at the slightest touch. I hate seeing her like this.

"Cyrus didn't think the lashings were enough this time."

As we make our way back to the apartment I tell Sara the rest of what had happened. While she can't hold me because of the open wounds on my back, she lets me rest my head on her shoulder. Even as I walk completely exposed through the streets, I can't seem to care. The whole village has seen me bared now. There is no point in trying to cover myself.

On the walk back it begins to rain, which washes away most of the blood running down my body. Thankfully that meant I didn't have to go to the creek to rinse off, or have Sara try to find water in the village. That was just an infection waiting to happen. The last infection I had almost killed me and we used all the money we had to buy a cure for the fever and blisters that broke out along the wounds.

When we get to the apartment door, Sara uses her foot to push it open. With pain coursing through my body, my eyes wander around our apartment to distract myself. The one room has a small cot sized mattress on the floor with one deflated feather pillow on top. Our sheet is thin and itchy, so we rarely ever use it. On the back wall there is a small table that holds a single candle and the few knives we have. Towards the ceiling, there are three small windows that open towards the street. The apartment is set lower than the street level, so the rain water often leaks into our room, along with any other watery filth that villagers dump into the street.

Sara helps lay me down, face first, onto our shared bed and covers me up to my waist with our thin, scratchy sheet. At this point, the after care of my lashings has become a sort of ritual.

I lay on the bed and try not to cry for the hundredth time, and Sara finds our single needle and thread to sew up my back. She has such delicate hands when she stitches me back together like a rag doll, but the scars still become puffy and red with scar tissue. The healers in the village say it is not infection that causes this, just that some unlucky few have scars that do not heal right. Rejected by my own body.

Sara brings over the candle and sets it on the floor next to the bed. She runs the needle through the flame to sterilize it. The first poke of the needle through my skin causes me to take a sharp breath in. In and out, in and out. I try to breathe through this. Fourteen long, deep gashes in my back will take time to stitch and I pray to the Maker that we have enough thread. Sara begins to hum a tune. She sings it every time she stitches me back up. It helps calm my nerves and makes me feel safe. I let the song envelop my senses as I pass out from the pain.

Bright eyes open to a beautiful woman peering down. The soft song in her voice wraps around the air like a warm blanket. Back and forth, back and forth, swaying like a boat on water. A gruff voice cuts off the song in the wind. "Your Majesty, it's time." Panicked eyes drift away from what she was looking at. "Please just one more moment— just one more." Wetness drips from the woman's eyes as she looks back down. A loud bang sounds in the distance. Screaming begins ripping through the air like a title wave. Louder and louder. "Wake up, wake up!" someone yells. The rocking turns to frantic shakes...

"Wake up, wake up! We need to leave!" Sara frantically searches around the room once she sees my eyes opening. She carefully helps me into a shirt, once I sit up, and lays some pants on the bed. I cringe when I bend over to slip them on.

"Sara, what's happening? What's going on?"

The smell of smoke wafts in from a broken window. When did the window break? Sara is throwing things into a pack and strapping her knives to her body as she goes.

"Sara, seriously what's happening?"

"We need to leave *now*. Get your shoes on and pack anything you want to take with you."

What did I have here that I even cared about, besides for Sara? When she sees me not packing anything she simply nods and grabs my hand. I snatch a single knife off the table on the way out and slip it into my thigh holster. We ascend the stairs leaving our apartment, and on the surface, our entire village is burning to the ground.

Chapter 5

ENZO

As I sit up in bed my head pounds with regret. Gunnar and I went round for round last night, seeing who could drink more shots of amber. I thought it would be easy for me to win, but with every shot glass I emptied, Gunnar did the same. He beat me by only one when I finally hurled. After emptying the contents of my stomach, which included the numerous shots of amber and my last meal, Duncan bet me I couldn't sneak into the local armory. He said that I couldn't steal the helm off the knights uniforms on display, and sneak out without being detected by the village guards.

Being that my body processes alcohol faster than most, I eagerly accepted. I was thrilled I would be making him look foolish for thinking I was too drunk to accomplish such a delicate task. I was this close to making it, until Gunnar tripped on a loose cobblestone and fell into another standing knight suit, sending it clattering to the ground. His idiocy alerted the guards of our location and we had to make a run for it. I knew I should have refused him when he begged to be brought along. Gunnar swore he *"wasn't that drunk"* when we left. The guards are under my command and wouldn't dare try to punish me, but a bet is a bet. Needless to say I lost and now, thanks to Gunnar, I owe Duncan a favor of his choosing, to be collected at his discretion. My losing bet with Gunnar earlier meant I had to wash his soiled clothes for a week. I knew he was purposefully going to sweat as much as he possibly could in each set as to make my task even more disgusting than it would already be.

I make my way into the washroom and fill the tub with hot water. After stripping out of my pants, I sink into the tub and breathe a sigh of relief. My sore muscles begin to loosen inch by painful inch. I let my eyes slip shut for just a moment and I remember the strange dream I had last night.

Standing in a field of wheat and wildflowers, the sun is high in the sky. I feel a pull to something across the field. When I look around I see the outline of a woman's figure walking towards me. There are no discernible features, just long legs that connect to wide hips and a narrow waist, before moving out again to her full chest. But everything is a shadow. No face to gaze upon, but she wears a tattered dress that blows in the breeze along with her flowing hair. She is just a breath away. She reaches out her hand, but suddenly she is pulled back into darkness.

When my eyes flashed open this morning, I could have sworn it was real, but then I remembered what alcohol does to the brain and thought it nonsense.

Realizing the bath water is now cold, I scrub my body with a wet cloth and dunk my head into the water to wash away any dirt and grime that lingers from last night.

Stepping out and finding my towel, I wrap it low around my waist, my chest still dripping with water. I approach the reflecting glass over the basin and take a brief moment to gaze into it. What I see is nothing short of what a warrior should look like. A marred chest filled with raised white flesh from years in battle, and a broken gaze that looks back at me. A soulless, loveless, broken pair of eyes stare back at me. It's all I can think about as I exit the washroom and stride over to my closet. I avoid any more reflecting glass along the way. *You'll never need love.* The motto I tell myself over and over again. My lifestyle does not allow space for love.

Just as I am pulling on my leather pants, the door shoots open revealing Gunnar, Duncan, and Jade all rushing inside. Jade's face flushes as she realizes I am still without a shirt, even though she has seen me bare chested countless times before while training. I shake my head and huff out a breath at the sheer fact that after hundreds of years together she still can't get it through her head that we are never going to happen. I wasn't going to lose one of my best friends for a one night stand, let alone anything more— something that requires— *emotions.*

While trying to catch his breath, Gunnar says, "Sorry...to just come...barging in...Enzo, but...there has been...a disturbance..."

Cutting Gunnar off, Duncan states, "Gunnar, pull yourself together before you speak. No one can understand you when you sound like a fish sucking in air."

"Seriously boys, knock it off and take this seriously!" shouts Jade.

The three of them begin bickering about nonsense, as per usual. They ramble on about how it's wrong to tell someone bad news when you can't even breathe properly.

"Everyone just shut up," I yell over them. All sounds silence at my booming voice. "Tell me what is going on right now and say it before I hurl my breakfast at you!" I say, picking up a croissant.

"Toss me one anyway ZoZo. I'm literally starved," says Gunnar. Duncan cuts him a look and Gunnar simply shrugs and catches the pastry as it flies towards his head.

Finally, Jade speaks up. "Enzo, we wanted you to be the first to know so you can give us orders. There is a small town named Mareen, in Luar, that is being ransacked and it is nothing but chaos."

"What do we care if a human village is being burned? It happens all the time at the hands of their own people," I say.

"Right. Except the report from the SunSpark Flying Legion contains concerning content. During their rounds, they spotted more than just normal pillaging, in fact it seems the attackers aren't taking anything at all. Almost like they are just looking to kill anything that moves. There have been reports coming in all night of other villages falling to these riots, but we didn't think they were connected until now," Jade finishes.

"Well what is different about these attacks compared to the usual ones?" I ask, still trying to put the pieces of the puzzle together. I am growing impatient as they dance around the words that actually need to be said.

"It's the smell. Like rot and burning flesh— before any fires were set. In addition to finding bodies completely stripped of their skin," Duncan says gritting his teeth.

"The Kalari," I mutter. The Kalari are the filthy creatures born and bred for destruction. They are skeletons that hatch from skin-like sacks, already bonded to the Banished King. They follow his every command like the mutts they are. Kalari can appear like fae, or human, by wearing the skin of those they have slain. But you can't hide the smell of rot by covering it with a cloak of flesh. Often times the skin just sags off their bones, so I'm not sure why they bother hiding their true forms at all. Filthy creatures.

"How did they get out of the border? I thought the barrier around the Banished Kingdom was secure aside from just a few small tears here and there?" I ask.

"I'm not sure. Here is what we know, for the last few years there have been occasional holes that get ripped into the barrier, allowing just a few Kalari to get free. There have never been any riots, though. It's like The Kalari escape and then just disappear. There have usually only been about one or two small holes a month, but last night there were reports of over a dozen tears, with hordes of Kalari sneaking through," Duncan adds.

"So what are you saying?" I ask. I already know the answer, but I dread saying it out loud.

"I'm saying that I think our training is about to pay off," says Jade.

"We are going to Luar," I whisper.

Chapter 6

ENZO

The journey to Luar is as excruciating as it possibly can be. Jade and Duncan haven't stopped bickering about who got to eat the last of the croissants before we left. While the trek is only a short distance to The Bridge, the minutes seem to drag on. Gunnar slows his pace to match mine, noticing the scowl that deepens across my lips with each passing second.

"What's going through that big, ugly head of yours?" he says with a smirk.

"I'm irritated. I have been wracking my brain for months now trying to figure out how the barrier keeps getting tears. Now suddenly there are over a dozen holes. How does that make sense? I can't even hear myself think. Jade won't shut up and Duncan isn't helping by continuing to piss her off. One of these days, I swear she is going to snap and we will all be screwed," I say, with a smile that doesn't quite reach my eyes.

Gunnar takes a moment to himself, smiling, and observes the fools in front of us still bickering.

"That may be so, but they are still family and we love them all the same."

31

Family. The concept that blood runs deeper than anything, and yet these fools are not blood related to me in any way. But they are the only *real* family I have left. There is nothing I wouldn't do for them, and yet there is a part of me that always feels like there is something missing in my life.

Gunnar is the only one with a family that he still talks to and the only one who has ever had someone he truly loved. That was before we left for what would be the final battle in The Great War. After the war ended and we returned to Citrine, she had disappeared. Gunnar had gone back to SunSpark to see if she returned there, but when he showed up in Citrine, he never spoke of her again. I have no idea what happened to her and I have no interest in anything surrounding even the idea of love, so I never bothered to ask. He has taken many lovers since, but never anyone serious. I never understood how someone could be so impacted by the loss of just one woman. There were plenty of other females out there for him to spend his life with. He didn't need this one particular girl.

Focusing back on my chosen brother beside me, I smile and this time it is actually genuine. Duncan finally calls back to us.

"We are approaching The Bridge! Better hurry up or I will be forced to leave you dead weights behind!"

The Bridge between realms is nothing made of cobblestone or brick, but is an invisible portal between realms. Only fae can operate The Bridge since the war. They simply place their hand on the ground where the pillar is buried, recite the incantation, and it will shoot up from the ground.

Twenty-five years ago The Bridge was closed off to all humans. As sworn protectors of the realms, obviously we needed to be able to reach Luar, but the humans could no longer cross into our realm. While fae and humans used to fight side by side in battle, the remaining fae rulers felt that, with Citrine empty, the humans posed too much of a threat to Olyruim. The other kingdom's rulers believed the humans would seek to invade Citrine and take it for themselves. That is when the remaining rulers cast a spell so powerful, that it would wipe the minds of every human. Since that day they have no idea that fae, or Olyrium, even exist.

The Bridge to The Banished Kingdom is also sealed off, but for both ways. It would take one hell of a power surge to be able to push through the barrier without being eviscerated. Queen Dione's magic and sacrifice are unbreakable, but the price for such magic was her life.

As we approach The Bridge, Jade dismounts her alicanto, Reyla, and frees her to go graze the crystal fields until we return. Gunnar and Duncan do the same with their matched. As I dismount Ruby, my matched alicanto, I feel my stiff muscles ache between my legs. We dared not stop along the journey. We had to get to Luar before any more damage is done by The Kalari. *The bane of my existence.*

Jade is ahead of us now placing her hand on the ground. The large white pillar shoots up and a burst of energy rips through the air. We walk in silence to the column that stands at the edge of our world. The white marble is cool to the touch as we all lay our hands on the stone. I feel the hum of power beneath my palm. All we have to do is imagine a place in Luar we want to go to and it will drop us there in the blink of an eye.

"On three everyone?" I ask.

Gunnar, being the dimwit he is, responds, "On three or after three? Is it one, two, three, bridge or bridge on three?"

"You're such an idiot. It's on three," says Duncan.

"Screw off Duncan," Jade glares at him. "It's after three."

"Everyone just shut up and bridge. On three," I grumble, irritated as ever, wanting to get this over with.

"One—" Gunnar smiles, sword glinting in the sunlight strapped to his back.

"Two—" Jade rolls her eyes. Her quiver of arrows is fully stocked and ready to be fired at our enemy in mere moments.

"Three—" I mumble, battle axes strapped tight to my back.

Duncan's words are the last thing I hear before being bridged away to Luar.

"Wait, where did we decide to—"

My feet immediately drop into a huge puddle of mud as I bridge into Mareen. I look around for the others to make sure they landed safely, but they are nowhere to be found.

"You have got to be kidding me. We forgot to decide where exactly we were landing." I roll my eyes so far back into my head, it is a surprise they don't get stuck there. *Oh well.* I start walking towards the village ahead of me knowing I will find them later. We knew we were going to Mareen, just not specifically *where*.

The screams of those being slaughtered and the heavy footfalls of villagers running fill my ears. I go to step out of the mud, but the squishing of my boots makes me pause. Looking down, I take in the sight beneath me. It is not mud I landed in— it's the innards of humans and pools of their blood. Their skeletons lay not to far from sight, completely stripped of their skin. The Kalari's signature.

"Unbelievable," I mutter under my breath.

Taking off towards the center of the village, I see a group of The Kalari leaving a bakery. The windows are completely smashed and I see the patrons inside tied to chairs, mouths gagged, and The Kalari lighting the fuse of a bomb. I run towards the shop and, as I reach them, I unsheathe an ax from my back just in time to cut off the arm about to throw the bomb inside. The Kalari turn and charge at me with swords dripping red. It's four against one, but quantity over quality never works. The Kalari may have numbers, but their fighting skills are weak. All they care about is killing whatever is in front of them. They have no technique taught to them. In the eyes of the Banished King, his forces are expendable.

As I take on the enemy before me, I catch a glimpse of silver blonde hair out of the corner of my eye before it disappears behind a building. A strange pull in my mind wants me to follow it. I finish off The Kalari as easy as cutting butter with a knife. I barely even broke a sweat. I take off in the direction that I saw the hair disappear to. As I round the corner, I never in my wildest dreams could have predicted what I would find.

Chapter 7

ALIYAH

As I step outside with Sara still grasping my hand, I realize the calm, quiet village I once knew has been replaced with one of pure chaos. It's hard to tell what smells worse, the dead bodies laying on the ground, their innards hanging out of them decorating the cobblestone, or the smell of burning, rotting flesh. Blood runs down the streets, coating everything in its wake. As we try to move out of our doorway, I find myself tripping over an arm here and a leg there. People from around the village that had come to see me be beaten and assaulted now lay dead in the street. It is difficult to feel pity for them in that moment, but a life is a life and should not be taken in this way. The plague maybe, but not like this. Gutted and eyes open in horror. As I look closer, I realize that some even have their skin completely removed.

"We need to move now!" Sara pulls at my arm, snapping my attention back to her.

"What's happening?" I have to yell over all the screams ripping from those being dismembered around me.

"I don't know, but I know somewhere you can hide." Sara begins pulling me through the streets and all I can do is put one foot in front of the other, letting her guide me to where it's hopefully safe.

Left. Right. Right. Left. Left. Left. Building after building blurs by my vision now clouded with tears from the stitches in my back, pulling with every turn. Rounding the last corner, I'm out of breath and my back throbs in pain.

Sara finally looks back at me. "Stay here. Do not move or make a sound until I come and get you."

I take in my surroundings once more. The space she has brought me to is a small back corner between four buildings with only one way in and one way out. The perfect place to make sure no one can sneak up behind you while you guard one direction.

"Sara, I don't understand. Why can't I come with you? We can fight together. Make it out, *together.* Please, don't leave me. It's not safe for you either! "

"*Shh,*" Sara pulls me into a warm embrace, being careful to not push too hard on my wounds. "Everything is going to be okay. There is no time to fight our way out of this. What we need now is an escape."

"An escape? There is no way we are making it out of the village with what is going on out there."

I don't even know what is going on out there. But I keep that last part to myself since Sara is in no hurry to answer my questions.

"I think I know a way, but just stay here until I come get you. If anyone comes around that corner, remember your training, and use everything I've taught you. You have my full permission to do anything you need to in order to survive." Sara smiles before pulling me in for one last hug.

"Sara— just in case—" I begin.

"No. Don't you dare say it. I *will* see you again." Then she is off, and all I can do is wait.

My legs are starting to go numb as I stay crouched down against the wall hidden in shadows, hoping that no one finds me. I hear the screams ripping from the throats of those out in the street and I feel like a coward just sitting here. But I have to listen to Sara. Something inside me just knows that this time I need to heed her warning and stay put.

Snap. Something in the alley breaks the silence between the screams and mayhem around me. Pulling the knife from my thigh strap, I prepare to pounce on whatever comes around the corner.

A large frame comes into view. A man with knives and battle axes visible on his body glinting in the fire's light. Right before his eyes turn down to where I am crouched, I spring up. I grab the back of his neck before he even has time to react and bring it down on my knee, with a hard *crack* of his nose, making contact. I turn to move away from him. He stumbles back in surprise, but not before grasping a lock of my hair and pulling it towards him. With my head jerked forward I fall towards the ground as he trips over a loose stone, landing me right on top of him.

My thighs straddle his broad chest as I scramble to pin his shoulders under my knees. He releases my hair and in lightning speed, rolls us so I am on my back beneath him. *Son of a—* My back digs into the cobblestone drawing a sharp inhale between my teeth as fury rages in my chest. For the briefest second I see a flash of something in the strangers eyes. Concern? Regret? No, I must have imagined it because the next time I blink he is breaking into a smirk that makes me want to rip his lips right off that irritatingly handsome face.

"Well, well." His voice drips in seduction. "What do we have here? Hiding in the dark while others are out there being slaughtered by the masses, little dove?" The man's eyes roam over my face taking in my features. His hands come to rest on either side of my head as he looks down at me.

The stranger has shaggy chestnut brown hair that falls into his face as he looks down at me with rich, hazel eyes. They are practically ripping apart my soul bit by bit. Still stunned by the impact my back had on the cobblestone, I take a brief moment to soak in the male above me. His hands are almost the size of my head alone and his forearms are corded in muscle. My eyes rake over his biceps, lightly flexing as he shifts his weight above me. I let my mind drift over to his bulging chest that heaves with each breath pulling his shirt tighter and tighter to his sweat- soaked skin.

I don't dare glance at the rest of his torso, but I can only imagine what it would feel like to have it— *stop that right now*. I can't believe I almost let my mind go there for this random male pinning me to a dirty street while others are being murdered just yards away. And yet, curiosity gets the best of me. I let my chin dip ever so slightly and my eyelids hood as I take in the male above me. His body looks like it has been carved by the Maker Himself. A broad chest tapers down to a thin, muscular waist before moving to two thickly muscled thighs. Involuntarily, my mouth begins to water. I swallow quickly before reminding myself of the hellish situation I am currently in. *Get it together, Aliyah.* He may have significant size compared to me, but hopefully all my training with Sara is about to be very useful.

"How do you know I'm hiding and not one of the killers?" I reply, trying to mask the pull to him in my voice, not wanting him to know my traitorous thoughts.

"The fact that you don't smell like rotting flesh and your skin is perfectly intact on your bones," he says, like it is the most obvious thing in the world. He has that stupid smirk still plastered to his face, as if he knew I had been perusing his body not moments ago.

"I am not sure how you can smell me from all the way up there." I bat my eyelashes and heave my chest a little higher with each breath, so our bodies just barely touch. It's only for a moment, but his eyes flick down to my chest, tunic pushing up from the bottom exposing my stomach. *Sucker.* That is the only moment I need before I bring my knee up hard, connecting with his groin.

He grunts in pain, rolling off and onto his back next to me.

This allows me time to scramble to my feet and regain my footing. Darting towards the exit, a large hand clasps around my left ankle. *Smack.* My chin connects with the ground when my arms refuse to get under me in time. The taste of copper rushes my mouth before I spit it onto the street beneath me.

"Let me go!" I scream, while kicking my legs towards his face, as I lay on my stomach.

"Serves you right, little dove," he chuckles to himself, while grasping my other ankle in his hand.

In the blink of an eye, he is on his knees, flipping me onto my back and pulling my legs out and around his body. My back scrapes against the ground and red hot fire scorches up my throat from the pain. I close my fists so tight, my nails break the skin on my palms. He begins his slow crawl back up my body, pinning it down with just a glare.

The feeling of his eyes roaming over my body causes everything around us to fade away. The pain dissipates for just these few moments. I stare into his eyes that bore into mine. A small breath leaves my lips and the base of my spine tingles. Great, now even my body is working against me.

A loud boom goes off in the alley and brings me back to the present. I palm the knife on my thigh holster preparing to strike. He moves to grab my wrists, but not before I get my knife to his throat. He pauses above me, but makes no move to push the knife away. I feel a drop of his blood drip onto my cheek. He *smiles* and leans down, pressing the knife deeper into his neck, yet I find my elbow bending so as to not push it any deeper. Another drip on my cheek.

As he leans down, his face is just inches away from mine and my eyes slip shut. I feel the pad of his thumb wiping away the drop of blood on my cheek. His thumb trails through the blood, smearing it across my cheek. The feeling is similar to that of spreading paint with a brush. As he goes for the other drop, my eyes flash open and I push in hard with the knife. He winces slightly and leans back, grabbing my wrist that holds the knife. He quickly pins it above my head and sits fully on top of me. He tips his head quizzically before peering into my eyes.

"I always did love the color blue," he smiles.

"Let. Me. Go. Now," I say, with a stern look on my face. "Or you will not like how this ends."

For some reason, he gets off me and backs away three paces. Confused and uncertain, I stand and back away another three paces toward the opening of the buildings. I feel blood dripping down my spine from my open wounds and pray I haven't ripped too many stitches.

Holding the knife in front of me at an arm's length, I continue my retreat towards the street. I would rather take my chances with the killers out there than with the one eyeing me like prey in here. As I reach around to pull the tunic away from the flesh on my back, I wince when pain sears down my body.

My arm trembles ever so slightly, and my knees are on the verge of collapse. The male's eyes darken and the muscles in his jaw tick. In three short strides, he is crossing the distance between us. With almost no effort, he knocks the knife from my hand and throws me over his shoulder, like I am nothing but a sack of grain.

The world is upside down as I beat against his back with my fists as hard as I can. All he does is chuckle as we clear the buildings, and enter back into the throws of my village being ransacked.

"Put me down this instant!" I start to panic knowing Sara will be coming back for me, and I told her I would wait in that alley. *If she isn't already dead.*

I banish the thought from my mind knowing that she would never abandon me. I try to look around to at the carnage that is now my village. Shops are burning, children lay next to their dolls, rigid and cold. This place was never my home, but it is all I know. I have no interest in going wherever this idiot is taking me. With one last attempt, I move to pull a battle ax from the holster on his back. Again, all he does is chuckle when the ax won't budge.

We pass the post where I was whipped not one day before, and there lying next to it, is Cyrus. His head is torn to shreds in an all too familiar pattern and lying next to him is that horrible whip.

Chapter 8

ENZO

The female dangling over my shoulder continues to beat at my back. *Like that will do her any good.* I have no clue why I took her with me, but seeing her wince when pulling away the tunic from her body made my teeth grind, and rage cloud my mind. The next thing I knew, I was throwing her over my shoulder and walking back towards The Bridge, the village around me forgotten. I may not know what the endgame here is, but I can figure that out as I go. I am committed to this act no matter what happens now. It doesn't help that she is arguably the most beautiful— *Whoa.* Nope. Not even going there.

She is just a girl that I found, and while she may intrigue me, she is nothing more than a human. *I have no room for love,* I remind myself. Though I won't deny, seeing the blood drip from her lip and down her chin after she hit her face on the ground, did make me want to kick myself for causing her such pain. Just the *thought* of her getting hurt by my hand again makes my insides twist at an uncomfortable angle.

The sounds of approaching footsteps tear my thoughts away from her and my plans for what I am going to do next. When the scent of rotting flesh fills my nostrils, I know The Kalari have followed us with the intention of killing. The female stops kicking her legs and must notice the approaching group.

"Put me down, put me down, put me down!" she begs. I like the sound of her voice flowing into my ears.

"No." Without a second thought, I send The Kalari flying through the air, impaling them with their own swords, just for good measure.

I feel the girl go completely still and rigid against me. Normally, I would never use my powers to manipulate others, but war was different. For some reason protecting *her* was – *Ugh! Enough of this.* I block that thought out of my head as fast as it came. She means nothing to me other than an interesting little thing that I want to take back with me. Three figures clear the nearest alley coming toward us. I immediately recognize them as the idiots who came with me on this mission.

"Where the hell have you been?" I bark at them.

"Well *someone* forgot to clarify exactly where we were going," Gunnar chimes in.

"You all were too busy arguing over whether it was on three, or after three, that I couldn't even ask before you all just disappeared!" Duncan says, now wiping blood from his brow.

Jade has her eyes fixed on me and both hands are clenched into fists.

"Care to explain?"

I look at her with the same flat look I always do. "Explain what?"

"Hello! Does anyone care to help me here?" the female's clearly irritated voice fills the air.

"Oh right, her. Nothing to explain," I say, looking at Jade with a passive expression.

Gunnar and Duncan slowly circle me, eyeing her body still pinned under my grasp. A low growl rips from my throat, surprising me, when I catch Gunnar staring a little too long. He throws his hands up in surrender, and slowly backs away with a cocky smirk on his face. I don't know what came over me in that moment. For some reason, seeing another male, even my brother, looking at her in that way pulled something feral out of me.

Duncan is standing behind me now, crouching down to see the girl's face. He moves her long blonde hair out of the way before laughing. The girl is dead silent as my friends try and piece together why I have her with me.

"She's human, Enzo. What *exactly* is the plan here?" Duncan asks.

"She is coming back with us." That gets her attention. She begins kicking and screaming all over again. Her little fists connecting with my back feel more like a massage than a beating.

"The hell I am! I'm not going anywhere with you!" she squeals.

"Seriously Enzo. A *human*?" Jade says, and I don't miss the disdain in her voice. That simply won't stand. Not when someone is questioning *my* decisions.

"Jade, if you don't shut up, and help me get her back to the house, I will not hesitate to leave you here to rot with the rest of The Kalari."

Jade's head snaps back like I have physically hit her, but she turns on her heel and storms away towards the edge of town. Duncan only raises his eyebrows and whistles low before doing the same. Gunnar, however, has to push just one more of my buttons.

"So, uh, how exactly do you plan to take a human back to Olyrium? You know she can't go there, and you can't seriously intend for her to stay with us."

"I have a plan. A plan that you are not privy to, might I add." I have no plan. All I know is I am not leaving her behind.

Chapter 9

ALIYAH

"**I** am *not*, I repeat, *not*, going anywhere with you!" I scream, trying to get him to see reason. My anxiety is bursting out the seams as question after question filters into my head. *Where are we going? How come a human can't cross a bridge? I don't remember seeing a bridge in Mareen. What are his plans for me after we get there? What are my options for escape?* This group must be completely delusional if they think I am just going to go willingly with them. They can't make me go. Maybe I can try to reason with just one of them.

"*Shh.* I'm thinking," Enzo, I think his name is, says while still carrying me on his shoulder.

"I am so tired of being carried over your shoulder like some child throwing a tantrum," I grumble.

"Ah, but isn't that what you are doing? Kicking and screaming like a child? I would offer to change positions, but it seems you have an injury to your back, and carrying you like the beautiful bride you would be would only serve to hurt those wounds further, little dove," he says, sarcasm dripping from his voice.

"I am not a child, and I most certainly will *not* be your bride. But I am a human being! Perfectly capable of walking by myself."

"I guess we'll never know, will we?" Turning his head to one of the others, he says, "Gunnar, how much further to The Bridge?"

We have been walking for what feels like forever. My view from the shoulder of this giant male tells me that we are no longer in the village, but the grassy fields on the outskirts of town. I have only been out here a few times exploring with Sara, but I know for dang sure there is no bridge out here.

"I know for a fact there are no bridges out here. You are all delusional!" I yell.

"I thought I told you to *shh*. Unless you have something useful to say that contributes to the group?"

I seriously want to bury my knife into his cold, black heart.

"The Bridge is just up ahead. Another few minutes walk," one of the males calls.

I can't identify who said it, because the only view I continually have is this male's backside. I use my arms to push up on his lower back trying to get a better angle so I can see where we are going. But his torso is so obscenely large, that all I accomplish is his shoulder digging deeper into my stomach. With a huff, I decide to give up until an opportunity presents itself for escape. Then I will run like my life depends on it. *Which I am starting to think it does.* One of the males Enzo called Gunnar, I think, had asked him how he was going to get a human over the bridge.

It would be less concerning if I knew it was an actual bridge, but I am gathering that is not the case. The more time I spend on Enzo's shoulder, the more danger I realize I am in. I can't get the image out of my head of him flinging that group of humans onto their own swords without him even touching. No human can do that. I always knew there were monsters in the world, but I pictured them as snarling beasts with fangs and fur, not a male with a body carved by the Maker himself. If there were more like him where we are going, then I need to escape and find Sara fast. I say a silent prayer to the Maker who listens that Sara is alive and well, even if she is panicked looking for me.

"Almost there," the female voice says.

She instantly seemed to dislike me, for whatever reason. Talking about me with so much disdain, like she couldn't be more disgusted with the fact that I am human. She is human too, so clearly the jealousy must have come from the fact that I was with Enzo. *Like I somehow had a say in the matter.* I roll my eyes. I can still feel the heat from his hands where they clasp the backs of my thighs, keeping my legs in place.

Every so often, I notice that he draws soothing circles with his thumb on the backs of my thighs. As if soothing circles would magically calm me down. Like I would suddenly want to be whisked away to some foreign land, where he would take care of me, and I would never want again— not want for *anything*. But not me— I may not be happy here in Mareen, but I am happy with Sara. I wouldn't leave her, even in my dying breath.

Suddenly a face appears below me. A male with dirty blonde hair, cut close to his head and chocolate brown eyes, peers up at me with a quizzical look. He has impossibly tan skin for somewhere that is mostly overcast. I don't know where the heck he came from, but it certainly isn't dreary ole' Mareen.

"Why the long face, human?" he laughs. He is crouched down so his eyes can meet mine, but is walking ridiculously, all bent over, to keep pace with Enzo.

"Ha. Ha. Notice how I'm *not* laughing. If you haven't observed, I'm being carried upside down, against my will." I look at him with sharp eyes, willing them to burn a hole through his head.

"Against your will? Well now that just won't do." A mischievous smile pulls across his lips as he stands to walk behind Enzo. Right as Enzo takes his next step, the male sticks his foot behind Enzo's knee, causing it to buckle and drop to the ground. The male, still facing me, begins to laugh as Enzo growls in protest. Enzo's arm tightens around my thighs. He brings his other hand up to place it on the small of my back, helping to keep me in place.

"Knock it off Gunnar."

As Enzo tries to right himself, his grip loosens around my body, and I take the opportunity to knee him right in the stomach. He releases the grip on my thighs completely and I shove back from him. The world spins from the blood rushing back to the rest of my body. Slightly dazed, I turn, intending to make a break for it, but a large arm drapes over my shoulders and grips my throat while pulling me closer to his chest. Gunnar stares down at me with a large smile on his face and begins walking again.

"Better?" he asks.

I swallow against his hold on my throat. It isn't enough to cut off air to my lungs, but it is enough pressure to remind me not to run. I turn my head as much as I can in search of Enzo. I find him walking behind us with his eyebrows pinched in, clenched fists at his sides, and a glare that could kill. I smile up at the male next to me, using my best doe eyes, and hopefully piss Enzo off.

"Much," I say. "Thank you for coming to my rescue." I hear a scoff behind me and turn to see Enzo rolling his eyes. He has his hands stuffed in his pockets and kicks a small rock in front of him. He probably thinks I should be thanking him. *Not in a million years.*

"I wouldn't say I rescued you, I just really like pissing off the big guy," he says, glancing back at Enzo.

"I'm Gunnar by the way. Clearly ZoZo won't be letting you go anytime soon, so I figure we can get to know each other a little better."

"ZoZo?" I ask, looking up at him with a hint of curiosity.

"I swear to the Maker, Gunnar, if you say one more word to her about that name—" Enzo grumbles from the back.

"Back when Enzo was a child, he was quite small. Smaller than the rest of us, that is. Even Jade grew taller than him for a while there. Anyways, Enzo would always try to run and catch up with us, but his legs were so short that he could barely keep stride. Figuring he needed something to motivate him to keep up, we all started calling him ZoZo. It irritated him so much that he pushed himself harder and harder every day to become bigger than us all. Duncan is still the biggest, but Enzo eventually grew into that ego of his. He now holds the title of biggest pain in the butt," Gunnar says, laughing harder than he probably should.

"A title which often is passed around quite a bit," the female, I believe they call Jade, says.

Jade has shoulder length straight brown hair and sapphire blue eyes. She is about a head taller than me, but still shorter than the other males. She has a strong build that looks like she has trained for years in combat, but she looks to be no more than 30 years old.

It's clear they all have a long history with each other. I wonder if they are related in some way. Maybe that's why Jade looked at me with such disgust? She is just protective of her brother. Either that, or they are together and she feels I am stepping on her territory. It won't matter for much longer. As soon as I get out of Gunnar's grasp, I am making a run for it.

"Are all your heads filled with hot air? We are basically kidnapping this girl and none of you have even bothered to ask her name. What *is* your name?" This must be Duncan. Duncan has jet black, shaggy hair and deep emerald eyes. He is huge just like Gunnar said. Duncan's arm muscles are as big as my thigh, and he has a seriousness to him that makes me question if I should even take my next breath in his presence. He stares blankly at me waiting for a response.

"Aliyah," I say, quietly. Gunnar releases my throat, but keeps his arm draped over my shoulders. "My name is Aliyah." My voice is a little louder this time.

"Aliyah, it is a pleasure to meet you. My name is Duncan. I apologize for how these idiots have treated you," Duncan says.

"Please, Duncan. Please just tell them to let me go," I plead.

"My deepest apologies, Aliyah, but what Enzo wants, he gets. And currently he wants you to come back to Olyrium with us," Duncan says, eyes flashing down, before snapping back up. "If you don't make it through The Bridge, it was a pleasure meeting you."

Gunnar pulls me along as I process what Duncan just said. *If you don't make it through the bridge. If? Through?* What the heck does he mean by "if" and "through"? Panic creeps in and I dig my heels into the soil beneath me. I fight with all that I can, but Gunnar's grip is firm on my shoulders. Jade has run ahead a few paces and I stop fighting for a brief moment as I watch her place her palm on the ground and whisper something. I stop dead in my tracks, stunned, as a huge white pillar erupts from the ground.

Chapter 10

ENZO

Aliyah. Who knew a name could make me feel like a thousand lightning strikes hitting my heart? Saying her name is like a warm summer breeze. It's like looking up at the sun, and feeling its heat on my face. By the Maker, I can't deny it any longer. She is *beautiful.* Even covered in dirt and grime from that filthy hole she calls her village, she still smells slightly of vanilla.

Watching her attempt to fight Gunnar off is both equally amusing and— I can't even let myself go there or I will be carried away to a place I won't come back from. Especially because, in the next few moments, she may be ripped to shreds by The Bridge. I have been wracking my brain since I decided to steal her away, trying to figure out how to get her across.

Aliyah's eyes brim with tears now as she continues to struggle against Gunnar's hold. I trust Gunnar with every fiber of my being, but if he harms a single hair on her head, I will not hesitate to inflict the same pain on him. *Not that I care about her in particular,* I remind myself.

As we approach the pillar and begin laying our hands on the cool marble, Aliyah starts to plead with anyone who will listen. I can see the frustration bubbling up inside her the longer it takes for her to escape, but the fear in her eyes has my heart clenching.

"So on three or after three?" Gunnar laughs.

"We aren't going through this again. On three," I snap, a little more irritated than normal. I still have no plan for how to get her across, but maybe if she is holding on to me The Bridge will think she is one of us. I snatch her wrist from Gunnar, who just smirks at me as I tuck her under my arm. Maker she smells so good. *Focus Enzo.* Her little hands clench around my tunic and pull in desperation.

"One," Duncan begins. "Two."

A roar rips from my throat. I look down to see Aliyah sinking her teeth into my pectoral muscle, drawing blood as she pulls away. My arm snaps back from her and she takes the opportunity to slip from my grasp. Blood seeps through my shirt from the tiny holes where her teeth were, and pain that is just irritating enough to notice has me distracted from the creature approaching behind our group.

Out of the corner of my eye I see a figure running towards us. His eyes flash with the promise of bloodshed and the human skin he wears is slipping off the bones around his face. He holds a single battle ax in his hand as he approaches our group. I can smell his rotting flesh from here. Aliyah, not knowing the difference from The Kalari or a human, begins running towards him like an idiot. I storm after my girl, not wanting The Kalari to have her.

"Help! Please help me! They are trying to kidnap me! Plea—"

Her cry is cut short as the ax comes flying through the air, burying itself in her chest. I hear the crack of her breastbone. A small whimper escapes her lips, and a tear drips down her cheek, as she falls to her knees.

Chapter 11

ALIYAH

I'm dying. I'm sure of it. The crack was too loud, the blood is too much, and the pain radiating from my chest into my limbs has my head spinning. I drop to my knees as shock wracks through my body. I'm not even sure I feel pain anymore. I hear a roar rip through the sky behind me, but I'm too weak to turn around and see which beast it came from.

I am trapped in my own frozen reality. I feel each shallow breath pass through my nose and down my throat. The ground beneath me is wet, like after a fresh rain fall. I feel my pants begin to soak up the water from the soil. I can't believe I'm going to ruin another shirt. What will Sara think? She is going to think that I abandoned her! Sara is probably frantically searching for me, or has given up hope and is praying to the Maker that I escaped the turmoil that has taken over our village. Oh no— the village. How will the people who survive ever recover? I'm shaking now.

I'm close to greeting death; I can feel it. *Wait.* I am not shaking, I am being shook. Big, calloused hands are gripping my arms. I look down to see those hands wrapped around my biceps. His fingers are so beautiful. *Can fingers be beautiful?* His are. I would love to have those fingers running through my hair. I swear I hear my name, but I can't seem to figure out where it is coming from. My gaze meets caramel colored orbs staring back at me with so much concern. Tears slip down my cheeks as I stare into those eyes.

"Hi," I whisper, smiling at the male in front of me.

How could I ever think this male was anything but beautiful? I reach out my hand to caress his jaw and run my thumb over his bottom lip. He reaches up and cups my face with both of his hands, seeming to beg me to look at him. I know he is saying something to me, but all I hear is the rush of blood in my ears.

Time seems to slow as I feel his arm slip around my back. The pain of my wounds cease to exist. I'm in no pain at all anymore. His other arm reaches under my legs, carrying me like the bride he said I would be. Enzo's smell envelops me and wraps me in what feels like a warm blanket. The smell of fresh rain and teak wood. For the first time I feel simply bliss. My hand hasn't left his cheek, as I pull his face down to look at me once more.

"I think I do want to marry you," I say, just loud enough for him to hear.

He says nothing back as my body begins to sway back and forth with each of his steps. I don't care where we go anymore, as long as I can stay like this forever. I let myself rest my head on his chest. I'm so tired. Just a little nap. That is all I need. I'll feel better when I wake up. I'll just close my eyes for a minute. I let my eyelids slip shut and breathe in that scent that I hope never leaves me again. Then, I feel nothing as darkness drags me under.

PART II:
KYRSTAL KINGDOM

Jane Rose Publishing, LLC

Chapter 12

ENZO

"When will she wake up?!" I yell at the healer. "You told me she would be awake soon— that was three days ago!"

"Respectfully, General Enzo, it has been quite some time since we treated a human. I thought she would have awoken by now. The poison from the ax must have taken a heavier toll on her body than we originally anticipated. You did the right thing leaving the ax in her chest— she was lucky that her bones are not more fragile or it would have broken her in two."

The healer's words are not bringing comfort over my current situation.

"Yes, yes, I know. But when will she wake up? Are you sure you gave her enough antidote for the poison? What else can be done? I can't just sit here and do nothing!"

"Unfortunately, General, at this time that is all you can do. She needs time to rest and heal. Her breast bone has healed and the antidote given. The rest is up to her. If you don't mind me asking, how exactly did you get Aliyah here? Humans haven't been allowed in Olyrium since the war ended. She should have been eviscerated."

The thought of her being turned to dust makes my blood boil, and the mention of it makes me want to rip his tongue out. I honestly have no clue how she survived crossing through The Bridge, but I was not about to admit that to the healer. These people looked up to me as their General, and not knowing answers is not an option.

"That is none of your business. And I suggest you keep her name out of your mouth, if you wish to keep speaking at all. You are dismissed until further notice." As the healer leaves, my mind wanders back to that field in Mareen.

After the ax embedded in her chest, everything felt like slow motion. I was running towards her before her knees even hit the ground. Since The Bridge needs to be held above ground by a fae, Jade had stayed with it. That way when we needed to leave, we could in an instant.

Gunnar and Duncan had immediately swarmed The Kalari and ripped him limb from limb. I would have done it myself, but all I could focus on was Aliyah, and the gaping hole in her chest. She looked so distant from me, almost like the entire world only existed in her head.

Thankfully the poison most likely took to her bloodstream quickly, causing intense delirium, and little to no pain. The Kalari poison was a fickle thing. Only a few healers have antidotes for it since they are supposed to be locked away in the Banished Kingdom. At some point, I will need to figure out how they are getting off the island.

Jade said that tears had been appearing in the barrier for the last few years, but we had no knowledge of The Kalari plotting to take over Luar. The Twilight Kingdom is the closest to the Banished, but the SunSpark Flying Legion should have spotted any Kalari fleeing.

I know they can't be crossing over The Bridge from the Banished Kingdom because we made sure their pillar was permanently damaged. *Were the other kingdoms slacking with their patrols?* Krystal

Kingdom's military has been sparse since the war, but maybe it was time to start recruiting, again. At least I know I could trust our own soldiers to bring me accurate reports.

But for now I need to fix Aliyah. *She told me she wanted to marry me.* I know she was just delirious from the poison, but hearing those words fall from her lips was— I don't even know what it was, but it was glorious. I have suddenly never wanted anything more in my life. Yet, I know that once the poison is out of her system she will come to her senses.

She will never love me, especially once she finds out that I really did kidnap her, and I that I have no intention of letting her go. Especially now. Seeing her lie in my bed, with her head on my pillow, I need her to stay. If only so the scent of vanilla never leaves my sheets.

I stand from the chair I was sitting in and walk toward my bed. Her blonde hair spills across the silk pillow cases, her chest rising and falling. She slowly breathes in and out. The only motions telling me that she is alive are her steady breaths, and the occasional flicker of her lashes on her cheeks.

I suppose I should make the most of my time while she is still sleeping, so I let myself pad over to the side of the bed. However, my feet suddenly stop moving. The tunic the healer put her in, at my request, when we arrived is cut deep so he can keep an eye on her wound.

When the healer recommended I leave her shirt off entirely, so as to not spread infection, I nearly ripped his eyes out. No one will see her in such a state without her conscious permission.

I take in the huge scar, running from the top of her breastbone, down to where it ends just at the crest of her rib cage. I couldn't protect her. I wasn't there in time. I'm taken back to that moment on the battlefield when I saw my queen fall and there was nothing I could do to stop it.

Failure and disappointment. The two feelings I let sit in my heart for what felt like forever. I wouldn't let myself fail her again. Aliyah deserves better.

A throat clears in the doorway and Jade steps into the room.

"How long do you plan to stay here with her?"

"As long as she is asleep, I will be by her side. And then for any days she allows me after that."

"She is mortal. *Human.* She doesn't deserve to be here. She belongs with her own kind. You brought her into *our* home. I think you should return her to where she belongs."

"Jade, I don't give two craps about what you think. She stays until I otherwise say so. Now get out."

Jade turns on her heel with a huff and storms out. Screw her. She has no idea what I am feeling. But she is right about one thing, Aliyah is human. Our realm was not meant to keep her, yet I cannot bring myself to let her go.

I don't dare lay down beside her, for fear that I will never want to get back up, but I do allow myself to sit on the edge of the bed. I reach for her hand, if just to feel it in mine for only a moment more. When she wakes up, I am going to ask her everything about herself and pray she will want to stay.

I let out a heavy sigh, and place her hand in my lap. As I turn to look at her face, I study the lines and curves of her cheeks and nose. Her full lips are just begging me to kiss them. I want her to know what it is like to kiss me. To show her the kind of love that I only dream of having. But I know that will never be.

I am incapable of being loved, so instead I allow myself one kiss of her forehead, just so I can feel her skin on mine. Just this once, I scold myself.

As I lean down to kiss her, my hand trails up to those beautiful blonde locks and I move to tuck a stray hair behind her ear. Her skin is warm and soft like butter, but as my fingers crest her ear my entire world stops.

When I push the hair back, her once rounded human ears are gone, and the tips of my fingers brush over her newly pointed ones. *Fae ears.*

Chapter 13

ALIYAH

I think I'm hearing voices in my head. My ears are ringing as they adjust to the sounds around me. I try to lift my hands to cover them, but they feel like lead at my sides. Everything is so loud that I pinch my eyebrows together, hoping that will block out the sound. My skin feels like it is on fire, but at the same time is being wrapped in cool silk. I slowly crack my eyes open and the blinding light coming through the windows makes me snap them shut again. My head is pounding and I feel like I've been trampled by a thousand oxen. The voices are filtering in from somewhere, but there is no one in the room around me. I pry my eyes open and allow them to adjust to the light. I try to sit up, but the pain in my chest is excruciating.

Where am I? This looks like no place I have ever been to, so it is certainly not my village, or my apartment. The room is a moderate size, nothing too fancy. The biggest difference I notice is that I'm not wrapped up in scratchy sheets and laying my head on a flat pillow. No, the sheets I am laying in are silky and soft. There are four pillows surrounding my head and they are all stuffed perfectly.

Okay Aliyah, focus back. What is the last thing I remember? I remember screaming— *Enzo.* He was trying to take me across some bridge that isn't a bridge at all. I have the faint taste of copper in my mouth. *The bite.*

I bit Enzo before escaping his grasp! There was this man who was running towards us, but his face was distorted and looked like his skin was a candle's wax dripping down his bones. He was supposed to save me, to take me away from those crazy people trying to kidnap me. But then he— my chest!

I sit up in bed so fast and I wince at the pain that follows. My eyes fly open and stare down to where, I am sure, the ax is still embedded. How could I have survived that? I have no memory of anything that happened after the blade cut through my breast-bone. I look down at my arms in front of me and marking my right forearm is a scar in the shape of a moon with a star in the middle. Who had carved this into my body? I've never had this before. Enzo must have done something to me! Now I'm trapped here with no knowledge of where I am or what he wants with me and I am getting carved into like a piece of wood!

Panic begins to creep up my throat. Bile threatens to fill my mouth. It's like I can still feel the ax in my chest. *I can't breathe. I can't breathe. I can't breathe!* I start to push the sheets off with my legs and claw at my throat like maybe if I rip holes in my neck I can get air in faster. The door flies open, hitting the wall behind it, threatening to shatter the door into pieces. Enzo takes up almost the entire doorway with his shoulders.

He races over to the side of the bed, a look of worry etched into his face. *I must have been pretty bad off if he is giving me such a concerned look.* He moves to wrap his arms around me. *I want him to hold me.* But reality hits that he kidnapped me. He brought me here in the first place. If I hadn't been in that field that ax would have never gone into my chest, almost killing me.

"Stop," I command, trying to settle my breathing.

Gasps come in and out too fast. My chest burns with each inhale as my newly formed scar stretches to accommodate the strain. Enzo freezes, pain crossing his face for a brief moment before setting his lips into a firm line.

"What can I do?" he asks gently, but you can hear the edge in his voice.

"You— can— take— me— back," I say, between gulps of air.

My hand is on my chest now, feeling the skin beneath my palm. I look down to see a raised, pink scar marring my chest. *Add it to the others.* I just want to go back to Mareen. I need to find Sara. I pray she is still alive. I don't need Enzo, I need Sara.

I'm here. I must be losing my mind because I can hear her voice in my head like she is just in the other room.

"Please, just take me back. I need to find my friend, I need to find Sara," I say, tears threatening to spill from my eyes.

Enzo has the audacity to look hurt, like he is surprised that I want to leave him after he kidnapped me.

"Please," I say, again. I tentatively reach out my hand and grasp his. Heat radiates up my fingers from his touch. His eyes flash wide for a moment at the contact, and I debate pulling away. I need him to trust me, though.

"I'm assuming you saved me from the ax in my chest? Thank you. But I am ready to go back to Mareen now."

"I can't do that, little dove," he replies, quietly. The tears spill over my cheeks, but I wipe them away quickly.

"Stop calling me that!"

Overwhelming anger takes over my body and I start to rush out of bed. As soon as my feet hit the ground and I am standing in front of him do I realize that the *only* thing I am wearing is this overly large tunic. It is cut so deep you can see the entirety of my new scar.

Enzo's jaw ticks and his nostrils flare. He reaches a shaking hand down to my chest and lightly runs his fingers over the scar there. I didn't even realize I was holding my breath, until my lungs begin to burn. I exhale slowly and wonder why I am not cutting off his hand right now for touching me. As he reaches the bottom of the scar, he lets his eyes slip shut and his head hangs low like he is ashamed. Enzo drops his hand and takes two steps back. For some reason, I immediately miss his touch on my skin. *Pull it together, Aliyah.*

"You aren't going anywhere like that, and I can't let you leave anyways." Enzo's eyes won't meet mine.

"I'm not sure if you noticed, but I didn't exactly have any time to pack. Please, for the last time, just take me home and we can forget all about this." My eyes are clear of tears now, and have been replaced with frustration at his complete lack of empathy for my situation.

"Here." He crosses over the room to a dresser, and begins sifting through clothes. He appears so comfortable in this room, almost like it is his own. *Crap, what if this is his room?*

He tosses a pair of loose linen pants at me that appear too small to be his. *Maybe they are Jade's.* I roll my eyes.

"Thank you. I love getting to wear another female's clothing," I say, my voice dripping in disdain.

"I would never keep another female's clothes in here, or anywhere else near me for that matter. The washroom is in there." He points to a small room attached to this one. "You can clean up and come down stairs," he grumbles, as he exits the room. Why do I feel a sense of relief when he said he wouldn't keep another female's clothes in here? They could still be together after all.

I pad over to the washroom and stop dead in my tracks the moment my feet touch the cold stone floor. The room is beautiful beyond any imagination. There is a white marble tub that sits in the middle of the room, with two wash basins to the right and a gorgeous reflecting glass hung on the wall above. I am enthralled with the stall that sits on the opposite side of the basins. It has walls of glass that look to be frozen over and knobs on the wall.

I pull the tunic over my head and let my hair flow down my back as I gaze at myself in the reflecting glass. It has been ages since I have really seen myself. My empty, gray eyes stare back at me. Dark circles rest under them, clearly indicating a lack of nutrition and sleep over the years. I know I am going to regret this, but I need to see the damage. I pull my hair over my shoulder and turn so my back is to the glass. There upon my back are fourteen freshly pink scars, and over a dozen more white ones, all raised. *I'm a monster.* Only Sara has ever seen my back and I'm going to keep it that way forever.

Shaking my head, I walk over to the glass stall and turn one of the knobs. From above me, water showers down from hundreds of tiny holes in the ceiling, raining down on me like a waterfall. The water is so warm and soothing that I tip my chin up to the sky and allow my eyes to fall closed, as I just simply exist in this moment.

I stand there for what feels like eternity, letting the water wash over me. I haven't even used soap, and yet I feel like this is the cleanest I have ever been in my life. Along the far wall are rows and rows of soaps and liquids for washing. I take my time, sniffing each and every one on the shelf and select one that smells like vanilla and honeydew.

As I lather the soap in my hands, I rub it on my skin and rinse it off. Then I repeat it about three more times before I finally feel like I have scrubbed myself clean. I may be going back to Mareen, but I sure as hell am going to smell a lot better than I did before. As I reach up to start cleaning my hair, my fingers run over my— *my ears.* What in the heck happened to my ears!? My fingertips gently brush over the shell of my ear, realizing that the tops of them are pulled into sharp points. I jerk my hands back and quickly wash and rinse my hair. Stepping out of the stall, I find a cabinet of fluffy white towels, wrap one around my body, and twist my hair into another.

I race so fast out of the stall that I almost slip and fall on the tile flooring. My feet slip and slide as I skid to a stop in front of the reflecting glass. With my hair now out of the way, I can clearly see my ears. I turn my head from side to side, noticing the sharp points at the top of where my rounded ears used to be.

Anger boils in my veins so hot that I reach back and slam my fist right into the glass. It shatters all over the basins and onto the floor beneath my feet. I don't even feel the sting of the cuts on my knuckles as I storm out of the washroom.

As I walk back to the bedroom, I don't even let myself take it in. There is no time. Enzo owes me a *huge* explanation. Not wanting to put on my old tunic that is cut way too deep for my liking, I cross the room to the dresser that Enzo got the pants from, and pray that there is a smaller tunic inside. I find my tattered undergarments on the chair next to the dresser. I pull them on and open the dresser hoping to find something more fitting.

Unfortunately, I don't find one, so I just pull out the first one I grab from the drawer and slip it on. It smells like fresh rain and teak wood. It's huge on me, so I roll up the sleeves and throw on the pants that were left for me. Thankfully these fit. I let my hair down from the towel and give it a good shake before running my fingers through the strands to get out any tangles. I take one last deep breath before flinging open the door and making my way downstairs. *Time to get some answers.*

Chapter 14

ENZO

The female standing at my front door looks so familiar, yet I can't seem to place her in my mind.

"Enzo, you seriously don't remember me? In all your years, you remember every dumb thing that Gunnar does, but you don't remember me? Do you hate me that much?" A look of pain flashes across her face as she tries to peer around me and into the house.

"How do you know Gunnar? In fact, how do you know me?" I ask.

"Sara?"

A small voice comes from behind me. I turn to see Aliyah coming down the stairs. *Is she wearing my tunic?* Just the thought of her in my clothes short circuits something in my brain. I step out of the way, just as Aliyah comes up behind me. The smell of vanilla and honeydew invade my senses like an unwanted house guest as she passes by. I shake my head to clear the fog that is *her* out of my brain. Aliyah's blue eyes go wide as saucers and tears spill from the corners.

"Sara, oh thank the Maker you are okay!" Aliyah runs at Sara, and both of them go tumbling down into a pile of limbs as Aliyah clutches to the girl's torso like it is her only lifeline. *I wonder what it would be like for her to see me that way.*

As they stand up laughing, brushing dirt off their clothes, Aliyah turns to me. She has a huge smile on her face and her eyes light up like a hundred fireworks are going off inside her head. There are no lines of worry on her face, no fear present in her demeanor. She looks—happy.

"Enzo, this is my best friend in the entire world, Sara. This is who I was trying to get back to!"

She pulls Sara into the house and walks over to the living room. She walks so confidently around the house, one could almost assume this is her home. A sharp burst of air shoots through my nostrils as I shake my head and cross my arms. *She will always just think of you as the male who kidnapped her. She will never love you.* I try to clear the thoughts from my mind. The constant reminders that I have heard over and over again. I am no one to be loved. Sara and Aliyah sit down on the couch in the living room and immediately begin talking.

"Tell me what happened back in the village?" Aliyah asks, worried lines returning back to her face. I frown at the loss of her smile. It made the room brighter somehow.

"After I left you, I was on my way to find something to help us get out of there. I was stopped by a horde of those filthy creatures and had to fight my way back to you. When I got to the alley you were gone. I looked everywhere, but couldn't find you. Mareen is— Mareen *was* burned to the ground. There is nothing left."

"You have one person you can thank for me not remaining in that alley," Aliyah's eyes darken as she looks past Sara and nods her head in my direction. I shrug; I was just protecting her. Why couldn't she see that? Screw the rest of the village, all I needed to know in that moment was that Aliyah was coming with me.

Sara turns to me. Anger is etched into the lines of her face, but I'm not sure if it is directed at me or the situation.

"How did this happen? How did The Kalari get to Mareen? How did they get to Luar?" Sara asks.

"I have no idea. There have been recent— wait, what did you call them?" How does Sara know about The Kalari?

"The Kalari. Enzo, focus. How did they get into Mareen? I thought they were banished for good. We shouldn't be dealing with this, again."

I stood there, completely speechless. "Sara," I asked tentatively. "How did you get here?"

"We both know how I got here, Enzo. I told you, I know who you are. You and Gunnar, even Duncan and Jade. And you know me too, you just can't pull the cobwebs from your brain long enough to remember." She rolls her eyes at me. Aliyah shifts behind her, clearly uncomfortable.

"Sara, what are you talking about? How did you get here? How did you find me? What are The Kalari? How do you know Enzo?" Aliyah rapid fires questions at Sara.

"Ali, you are my best friend. We always said that we would be there for each other. No matter what, right?" Sara asks, hesitantly.

"Of course. Sara what's going on?" Aliyah begins to look scared, and every part of me wants to walk over to her and take her in my arms. I stare at Sara, trying to place her. Things start to clear in my mind. *I remember now.*

"Aliyah, I'm fae. I was born in this land and was sent to Luar to protect you. I'm your Soul Guardian."

Chapter 15

ALIYAH

"**I**'m sorry, I must have blacked out there for a second. You're my *what?!*"

What is happening here? Why is my world continually being flipped upside down, over and over again, and still I am no closer to getting the answers to the millions of questions floating around inside my brain?

"Your Soul Guardian. Someone who is bound to you from birth by an ancient spell. A Soul Guardian's only purpose is to watch over you and to protect you until their dying breath or until you find your mate and the bond snaps in place." Sara looks at me, eyes brimming with tears, willing me to understand what the hell is happening.

She reaches for my hand, but I pull away. For the first time, I am looking at her, actually looking at her, since she arrived and I see the points of her ears, and a scar in the shape of a sun on the inside of her left forearm. How did I not notice any of this before just now?

"No, that can't be right. We only just met eight years ago. I haven't known you since birth. How would that even be possible? Were you bonded to me when you were a baby too? How can a baby protect another baby? We are the same age, Sara. Furthermore, I am *human*. At least— I think I am." I reach up brushing the tips of my ears. The sharp points still feel foreign to the touch. "You can't be my Soul Protector or whatever the heck you called it because humans don't have those," I say.

"Ali, listen to me. You were born during the war, The Great War, as many know it. During that time, many were going off to fight. By that point in the war, I was several hundred years old. I happened to be in Krystal, seeing Gunnar before he left, and an older woman brought you to me. She asked me to watch over you and asked me to be your Soul Guardian. I wanted to ask her why she chose me, or why you needed a Soul Guardian to begin with, but all the woman said is that you were important and that I would most likely never see her again. She performed a simple, yet very powerful ritual that bonds your soul to mine. Before she left, she gave me instructions to take you to Luar and only come back when you were ready. Then she was gone. When we got to Luar, I was so scared I was going to raise you all wrong, so I left you at that orphanage. I thought you would be better off with someone who knew how to raise children. I tried to stay away. I watched you from a distance for years, but that night when that man tried to attack you, I couldn't just sit by and do nothing anymore."

Sara reaches for my hand again and this time I let her take it, if only to feel the comfort of something familiar.

"So, you just left me there? All those years on the streets, starving, being beaten for stealing, and countless nights in the cold, you just sat by and watched? I spent my entire childhood alone, Sara. I had been to jail time and time again. How could you possibly think that was better for me?"

Anger flares in my chest and I suddenly snatch my hand back. How could she do this? This entire time she was pretending like eight years ago was the first time she had met me. In reality she knew I was fae. She knows who my family are...*my real family.*

Hurt flashes across her face, and part of me wants to apologize for snapping at her. I feel like I don't even really know who I am anymore. How can I trust that my friendship with Sara is real and not just because of this Soul Bond thing? But there was one thing I was right about my whole life: no one wanted me. Not even my own mother wanted to keep me. She pawned me off to some fae girl to be my freaking Soul Guardian, and yet I still spent my entire life with no one.

"Ali, please, I am so sorry I didn't tell you sooner. I just never thought we would be back here. I thought we would be living in Luar for the rest of our lives. The woman who performed the Guardian Ritual had given us a human glamour so that we would be safe living there. Though— it must have faded when you passed through The Bridge." She reaches for my arm to run her fingers over my newfound scar.

"I don't care!" I yell. "I don't care that I was glamoured, or carved into as a baby so that our souls could be bonded forever or whatever crap you're telling me right now. How can I trust you? How can I know that our friendship is even real?"

Ali, every laugh, every tear, every wound I stitched for you, was real. You are my family, too. There it is again!

"Why can I hear your voice in my head, Sara?" I start crying all over again, gritting my teeth together with frustration.

"That's our Soul Bond, Ali. We will have it until you find your mate and accept their bond or I die. Then our Soul Bond will be severed, and your mate will take over the role of protecting you. I can speak into your mind, and you into mine. That is why in Luar you always felt such a connection between us. Now that we are back in Olyrium, we have our full bond, without the glamour."

Enzo, who had just been standing there this entire time doing nothing to help me understand, finally speaks up.

"I haven't heard of a Soul Guardian in ages. Last I knew they were all killed during the war. From what I know the tomes that held the spell to bond Soul Guardians were lost."

"My mother was a Soul Guardian. When I left for Luar with Aliyah, my parents had already gone off to battle a few years before. If there are none left— I hope it was a swift death."

My heart is breaking for Sara. I don't know if it is the Soul Bond or not, but it's like her grief is my grief. I hate that she lied. That she left me in that awful place because she was afraid. But she is still my best friend. And in this moment she needs me as much as I need her. I move closer to her and wrap my arms around her. I let my eyes slip shut. *I've forgive you.* I push the thought out of my head, hoping that she heard me.

I feel her small sob against my chest. I never knew my parents, so I have no one to grieve, but Sara had known hers and never had the chance to say goodbye. I am not sure which is worse. Right now Sara is my only family, and she needs me.

I hear footsteps coming from the back of the house, and as I open my eyes, I see Gunnar, Jade and Duncan come into the room. I let Sara go and stand up, pulling her with me.

"I'd like to stay awhile, if that is alright with you? I think I would like to see where I come from, and decide whether or not I'd like to stay permanently. Will you stay with me?" I whisper to her.

"'Til the end," Sara smiles softly, wiping the tears from her eyes. Her back is turned towards the group as she collects herself.

"Everyone," I say. "Since Enzo is so hell bent on keeping me here against my will, I figure we should try and get to know each other better. This is Sara, my best friend, and as I have just found out, my Soul Guardian. If you touch a hair on her head, I will personally see to it that you don't have hands anymore." I say, smiling, turning her around.

As she turns, Gunnar's jaw hangs open before a giant smile crosses his face.

"Saraphena?" he asks, as he moves to cross the room, before Sara meets him halfway.

"I never thought I'd see you again," Sara says, tears welling up in her eyes.

"You left without even saying goodbye. Why are you back now?" Gunnar says, not with anger, but genuine confusion.

"You kind of missed the whole story, but, yes, I did leave without saying goodbye. Words cannot describe how sorry I am, Gunnar. I didn't want to leave," Sara looks back at me, "but I had something come up. I understand if you're angry at me, and I don't expect to pick up where we left off. I know it has been twenty-six years. I'm sure you have someone else in your life now that you love."

"Saraphena, my love. There is no one but *you*. Welcome home."

Chapter 16

ALIYAH

"**G**unnar?!" Sara and I sit on Enzo's bed after she shared heartfelt welcome homes with everyone.

I try not to think about the fact that I am sitting in Enzo's room again, but he didn't exactly have a spare room for me to stay in, let alone one for Sara. However, with recent realizations, she may just be staying with Gunnar. I am bouncing up and down on the bed with excitement. "Tell me everything!"

"Well there really isn't much to tell," Sara says, as she starts to blush from her checks down her chest. "Before I left to go to Mareen with you, Gunnar and I were in love. We aren't bonded mates or anything like that, we just started out as a fling and it grew to be more. I honestly never thought I would see him again.

When Gunnar was heading off into battle with Enzo, Jade, and Duncan I thought I would see him if he returned, but then that woman found me. I had no idea what happened to him after I left, and a part of me hoped he had died. I knew it would break his heart to come back and find me gone. I was sure that he thought I left him by choice, but the woman wanted me to go and not say goodbye to anyone or leave any clues as to where I was going, so I never knew what happened to him."

I can't imagine what that must have been like for her. Guilt starts to build in my chest. It's my fault that she had to leave all those years ago and my fault that she never got to say goodbye to her love, or to her family for that matter. *She left everything behind for me.*

It's difficult for me to wrap my head around the fact that Sara didn't actually come from another village in Luar. When Sara told me about the village she grew up in, there was a part of me that always knew it could not have been somewhere in Luar. Now that I know Olyrium exists, I understand her description so much better. I laugh to myself.

"I think based on the response you received downstairs, he is happy you're back," I smile at her, trying to push any negative thoughts that try to creep into my mind about her lying to me all those years.

"I think so, too. So what is this deal with Enzo? He just decided to kidnap you and now he won't let you leave?"

"Enzo is seriously starting to get on my last nerve. First he just took me from that alley, even though I was screaming at him to put me down. Then he goes and gets an ax buried in my chest. Then—"

"He *what?!*" Sara stops me. "You had an ax in your chest? Are you okay? How could he let this happen? Oh my Maker, how could I let this happen! I am your freakin' Soul Guardian for Maker's sake! My entire job is to protect you and I left you in that alley thinking it would be the safest for you!"

I try not to laugh as Sara spirals.

"Sara, it isn't your fault. You didn't expect me to get taken away by some overbearing brute. I'll tell you, though, I put up one heck of a fight before he ultimately won. It's only because he has size on me. If I had been one second quicker," I smile.

"But you're okay now right?"

"Just added another scar to the collection. Nothing out of the ordinary. They can't kill me that easily!"

"Maker, you are crazy. No more axes to the chest, okay? Promise me." Sara holds out her pinky finger.

"No more axes to the chest, promise." I lock my pinky with hers. "I think it's time I saw something outside these four walls. Let's go see what kind of trouble we can get into around here."

Chapter 17

ENZO

"So, do you want to talk about it?" I smirk at Gunnar.

His eyes shine a little brighter at the mention of her. "Talk about what?"

"Saraphena, obviously," Duncan says, rolling his eyes and crossing his arms over his chest.

"Ohhhhhh, yeah that! It's no big deal."

"No big deal?" I question, walking across the room towards him and taking a seat on the couch. I clap my hand on his shoulder. "The girl you love comes walking into our house twenty-six years after disappearing, hoping you were waiting for her, and it's 'no big deal'?"

"That pretty much sums it up, yeah," Gunnar smiles. "I really did miss her, though."

"Now it all makes sense why you were never in any serious relationships since we came back from the war," Jade comments from the kitchen.

"How could I ever get into anything serious after I found the girl of my dreams? Some part of me prayed that she was out there somewhere, waiting for me too, but I didn't want to get my hopes up. I guess the Maker does listen to our prayers."

I hear the stairs creak as I turn to see Aliyah and Saraphena bounding down the stairs. She looks the happiest I have seen her since coming here. Granted, she arrived almost dead and has been asleep for three days. That would put anyone in a sour mood. Something in my chest squeezes at the sight of her smiling and laughing.

"So, what's next?" Sara asks, walking over to sit by Gunnar. Aliyah looks at me like she wants to come sit next to me, but turns away, thinking better of it, I'm sure.

"I want to see *everything*. Also, is there any way I could find out who my parents are? Even if they aren't alive, and I pray that they are, I'd like to know where I come from, at least," Aliyah asks, hope filling the air around her.

"I think that can be arranged." I smile at her, thankful that she has resigned to staying here with me. I can protect her now. I will always protect her. She may have a Soul Guardian, but it never hurts to have two people looking after her. Maybe if we had both been there that ax never would have made it into her chest. I grimace at the memory.

I move from the couch and take her hand, leading her towards the front door. When I open it, she inhales sharp and her eyes go wide as takes in the village.

"Holy— Where...where are we?"

She stands there, mouth agape, looking out over the bustling streets of the village. All the vendors are out today, selling anything from jewelry to flowers, furs to glassware. People are bargaining over prices and trading other items for what they need. Korin has done well for itself since the war. The recovery efforts took years to build everything back, but in the end we were left with the perfect little village to live in. Our group used to all live in Citrine as part of their military, but after the war, we decided to stay together and get a cottage of our own, right in the heart of the village.

Duncan was worried about having privacy, living in such a busy part of town, but the amount of weapons we have stored in this house means no one would *dare* come in without our knowledge. We often have to leave the village to train, however, because using our abilities this close to the population could end very badly. Gunnar had already destroyed one firework stand several years ago, trying to impress some children, and was banned from using his magic inside the village square.

I begin walking hand in hand with Aliyah around the outside of our home. I am surprised she hasn't pulled out of my grasp yet, but I'm not going to say anything about it. We pass by several vendors and she is in awe of everything they have to offer.

"Tell me *everything* about this place!" She beams up at me, excitement lining her eyes. *I never want her to look at me any other way.*

"This is the town of Korin. Our home away from home. There are three kingdoms in Olyrium. Each kingdom has a queen and king, along with their own military, but all the training is done here in Krystal at the military academy. All the kingdoms are completely unique to themselves, but each serves a purpose for the others. First, there is SunSpark Kingdom that has ever glowing rays of light. The sun never sets there, but simply changes shades as the day goes on. The Queen of SunSpark provides seeds to the other kingdoms to grow crops.

"Then there is Twilight Kingdom where the sky is either filled with shades of dusk, or the darkest of nights with a million stars lining the sky. Twilight used to provide the fiercest warriors, built to withstand any element due to the subsequent training they received after leaving

Krystal's academy. They basically go through years of torture to become unbreakable."

Aliyah hangs on every word I say, intently listening so she doesn't miss anything.

I continue, "then there is Krystal Kingdom. Every mountain is made of crystals ranging from blues to greens, purples to black. Citrine City, where our king and queen used to reside, is made from crystals far more beautiful than anything else in Olyrium."

Second only to Aliyah, but I keep that part to myself. Her eyes shine with so much innocence. This is the world she would have called home. She is practically bouncing out of her skin as she turns to take in every angle.

"We are surrounded by huge, crystal mountains and the walkways are formed from ivory crystals. Lush green moss grows instead of grass here, and there are almost no trees. At night the moon's light bounces off the crystals and fills the sky with ribbons of light that extend past where the eye can see."

Watching her explore this place— seeing it for the very first time— it almost makes me think that she could truly be happy here with me and my chosen family.

"What does Krystal Kingdom provide?" she asks.

"Krystal provides the most handsome males, of course." I bump her with my shoulder as we walk, and she elbows me in the stomach.

"So, where is the absolute best place you like to go in Korin?" She beams up at me like I am her whole world. *I wish I was.*

"How do you feel about drinking?" I smile.

Chapter 18

ALIYAH

Adryanna's Tavern is by far the most interesting place I have visited in my entire life. The outside looks like a small brown cottage with stone siding and a tiled roof of gray and red slats. The windows appear to have some sort of frost over them, but upon closer inspection I see that it is just grime from the patrons inside. As we walk in the front door, I am met with the stale air of fae, sweat, and ale. Music fills my ears so loudly, I practically have to scream to get anyone to hear me.

"This place is amazing!" I say.

Fae of all sorts are dancing in the middle of the tavern with their hands thrown in the air or spinning with a partner to the music that comes from the front of the room. A small band plays there with so many interesting instruments. I will have to ask Enzo what each of them are later. The fae females have on the most interesting outfits that would never pass for appropriate in Luar. Their tops are made of sheer fabric and rhinestones cover their chests. Their backs are completely exposed, save for the chains holding the fabric to their body. They wear skirts with sheer long strips that barely cover anything as they move their bodies to the music. Most of the fae males only wear tight tunic pants and no shirt. For how hot it is in here, I don't blame them for wanting to dress lightly, but I suddenly feel very under dressed.

"They could wear the most glamorous gowns and sparkling jewels in all the realms, but they would never come close to how beautiful you are," Enzo whispers down next to my ear.

A soft smile graces my lips at his compliment. My feet stick to the floor with each step I take towards a table in the back. Gunnar and Jade have grins spreading from ear to ear as they greet the fae around them like they know each other well. This must be their usual table, because when we approach it, the fae sitting there immediately get up.

A tall red- haired fae female comes over to our table. She is beautiful in every way possible. Full hips, a large chest, and eyes that are almost too big for her face that hold irises of deep purple. Her dress is made from the thinnest of materials, showing off her voluptuous figure. It's cut low, barely covering her chest and a slit so high, her hip bones show, showing off her gorgeous shoes made of purple rhinestones. She smiles at Enzo and something uncomfortable pains in my chest at the sight. She has no right to look at him, Enzo is— *whoa*, hold up. Enzo is not *mine* in any way, shape, or form.

"Adryanna you look ravishing as always," Enzo smiles up at her.

As he brings his eyes back towards the table, they land on me and his head cocks to the side with a questioning look in his eyes. I didn't even realize it, but I am staring straight at him, with my lips pulled into a firm line, and my brow is furrowed. Enzo breaks out into a grin, before reaching over and taking Adryanna's hand, and presses a kiss to her knuckles.

I shove my chair back harder than I intend to and it slams against the ground behind me. Every eye turns to look at me from the table and embarrassment immediately crawls up my neck.

Ali, are you alright? What happened? I hear Sara's voice in my head and I feel myself becoming angry again. No, not angry— *jealous.*

I'm fine. Let's go dance, I say, back to her.

I have never been more thankful to be able to talk to my best friend without anyone hearing us. Sara gets up and grabs my hand, dragging me onto the dance floor. So many others surround us now that, as we make our way to the middle, I keep getting bumped into by someone dancing. When we make it to the middle of the dance floor I close my eyes and just feel the music pulsing through me. I just want to feel free for one night.

Are you having feelings towards Enzo? Sara asks.

That snaps my eyes open, as I look directly into Sara's gaze. She has a cocky smirk on her face and she glances to her left. My eyes follow, and I find Enzo watching me with a satisfied smile on his stupid face.

No. Absolutely not, I say back. I don't want to talk about Enzo anymore.

I just want to drink and enjoy this place. A server comes over to us with a handful of drinks in small short glasses. Over the music he yells, "compliments of Adryanna! On the house!"

Sara and I both smile and grab one of the small glasses and tip it back, taking it in one gulp. The smooth liquid fills my mouth and my taste buds light up. It tastes of honey and lavender as it slips down my throat. I grab another...and another...and another until the whole tray is cleared and Sara and I are giggling uncontrollably.

I close my eyes once more and let the music wash over me. I feel hands on my hips as someone comes up behind me. *Something feels wrong.* I turn and find a fae male with a slimy grin on his face. He runs his hands down my thighs and back up pushing his fingers under my tunic. Bile rises in my throat, and I see Sara's eyes go wide before forming thin slits. She clearly feels my discomfort through the Soul Bond we share. She moves to push him off me, but I hold my hand up and flash her a smile before turning back to the male. She gives a curt nod before backing up a few steps.

"Hey there. I don't think I've seen you around here before," the fae male shouts. I feel his hot breath on my ear as he leans in to talk to me. "Want to go somewhere a little more private?"

Thoughts of Cyrus flash into my head. *Screw that.* I grab his hand, and spin him so his arm is twisted at an odd angle behind his back. He cries out in pain, but it's drowned out by the music around us. I kick the back of his knee and he drops to the floor in front of me. Out of the corner of my eye, I see the crowd parting as someone walks through, but I am solely focused on this dirt bag.

I lean down so my mouth is right next to his ear to be sure he hears me. "I would rather eat glass, than go anywhere with you."

He struggles in my grasp as I lean back and place my foot in between his shoulder blades and push as hard as I can, while still holding onto his wrist. The snapping of tendons ripples up his arm. Disgust claws at the base of my neck. I know what I did was wrong, but what he was about to do was worse. A sneer spreads across my face as I look down at him crumpled on the floor, clutching his shoulder.

He stands to run away before turning to me. "You're crazy! I will kill you for that!"

I note each of his features and notice the ring on his pinky finger, that way I can identify him later if he tries something else. He takes off through the crowd and I turn to face my best friend who stands there, arms crossed and smiling like a fool before bursting out in laughter. I join her and place my hands on my knees as my stomach starts to hurt from laughing.

"Maker, Aliyah you are *sick*," she says between laughs, and hands me a drink from a passing server.

We both tip it back in unison, and laugh some more before we keep dancing. I am so caught up in the song that I barely register when *he* comes up behind me. I turn to face him with a scowl on my lips.

"I'm surprised you were able to peel your eyes off Adryanna long enough to come out here and dance with me." I grit my teeth and look up at him as I continue swaying my hips to the music. His dark gaze roams over my body starting from my eyes, down my neck, holding for a brief moment on my chest, before coming back up to my eyes.

"The only thing my eyes have been stuck on is you."

I ignore his comment and turn towards Sara again. Gunnar has joined us on the dance floor and Sara is twirling in his arms, smiling like the last twenty-six years didn't even happen. I look around to find Duncan still sitting at the table sipping from his ale with a grim look on his face. I wish he would come out here and have fun with us. Jade is in the back with a male, kissing him in a dark corner. *So maybe she isn't with Enzo after all.*

Looking back up to Enzo, I still find him staring at me with a small smile on his face. He doesn't dance at all, but just stands there like a statue. I'm not sure if it is me or the alcohol fueling my next decision. I take a step towards him so that our chests are just a breath away. His eyelids hood as he looks down at me and I swear there is a flicker of heat in them. I reach out and place my hands on his chest and let them roam around his torso while I bend my knees and sway my hips in a rhythmic pattern. I slip one hand under his shirt and my fingers immediately find carved out abs, flexing beneath my touch. I lock eyes with him and his smile has faded, leaving a completely impassive face.

I turn and press my back to his chest and reach up to wrap my hand around the back of his neck. I lay my head back on his chest and turn so that I am looking up at him. I give him my biggest doe eyes and bat my eyelashes before smiling the biggest smile I can muster. We begin swaying to the music together and Enzo wraps his hand around my hip.

A sharp breath leaves his lips as the only crack in his otherwise stoic demeanor. I turn to face him and lay my head back on his chest as the music slows down around us. Couples join the dance floor around us, swaying back and forth to the music. I hear the beat of Enzo's heart and he rests his chin on the top of my head. I move my hands up to his hair. It feels so soft to the touch and I want to pull so badly. I have to stand on my tip toes, but I bring my mouth to his shoulder and plant small kisses up the side of his neck before stopping with a kiss right under his earlobe.

I feel a low growl pass through his throat by the vibration on my lips.

"*Aliyah,*" he murmurs under his breath.

I pull away and smirk before beginning to turn around. In what feels like less than a millisecond, I am being thrown over his shoulder and he starts walking out of the tavern. *Not this again.*

Chapter 19

ENZO

My dove is going to be the death of me. She is kicking and beating at my back, again and again, just like when I first brought her here to Olyrium. I can't help but laugh as she stills in my arms.

"Wow," she says, in a hushed breath.

Aliyah is looking towards the stars, seeing the crystal's colors dance off every building and into the sky. I set her on her feet. Her head is tilted towards the sky in awe.

"It's— *magnificent.*"

"I couldn't agree more." Her eyes find mine looking down at her instead of the night sky. Her cheeks flush from more than just the alcohol and she smiles up at me.

"Thank you. Thank you for showing me this."

"Of everything in Olyrium, Krystal's night sky surpasses them all."

She stumbles, most likely from the number of drinks she had, and falls into my side. I wrap my arm around her waist to steady her. The scent of vanilla fills my senses and I almost reconsider what I am about to do.

But I cannot let her actions in the tavern go unanswered. With that in mind, I scoop her up onto my shoulder once more and smack her butt as she yelps from the impact.

"You were playing a dangerous game in there, and it cannot go unanswered."

"What are you going to do to me, ZoZo?" I can practically see the smirk on her face.

"I'm going to make you suffer the way you made me suffer in there." The tone of promise fills my voice. My blood is already sizzling at the thought of what I have planned for her.

I storm into the house and kick the door shut behind me. Aliyah's breaths have become rapid as I walk up the stairs to my bedroom. I throw her onto the bed and she scrambles back towards the headboard.

"Ah ah. Come back down here." She hesitates.

Defiance flares in her eyes, but she obeys, just like I knew she would. She moves her body back down the bed towards me.

My eyes catch the top of her scar along her sternum, and regret sits heavy on my own chest. I clear my head from those thoughts, because tonight is not about what has been done, but instead, is about everything I am going to do to her.

When she reaches me, she sits back on her heels, waiting for my next instruction. I kneel down before her and reach for her legs. She brings them around so that each leg is on either side of my body. I slowly unlace her boots and slip them off.

"Relax, Aliyah."

I feel her squirm beneath my touch. I move so that my knees are in between her legs on the bed. *Okay, maybe this was a bad idea.*

I can smell the scent of her even under all her clothing. My nostrils flare in response. *Keep it together Enzo.*

I run my fingers over the top of her legs and feel her shift beneath me. Her eyes fall shut as I lean down and plant a soft kiss to her lips. Tingles immediately spread over my lips and it feels as though fireworks are exploding inside my head. I pull away from her. I need to just take her in at this moment.

"Enzo…" she whispers and *hell* if I don't want to give in right now. But there is work to be done. I'm sure a few more kisses won't hurt. I lean back down and run my hands through her hair. The soft locks run through my fingers like the finest silk. Her lips are sweet like the vanilla she smells like. I can't seem to get enough of her. She is intoxicating.

My fingers find their way down her shoulders and I feel just how large my tunic really is on her. That simply won't do. I am confident that Jerico will stay open late for me to swing by and pick some things out for her. She wiggles on the bed in anticipation. It *almost* makes me feel bad. I pull away from her and start backing away towards the door.

"Enzo?" she questions.

"Now we are even," I say. I step out of the room and lock the door behind me. I slip the key into my pocket for safe keeping. I don't want anyone walking in on our little game. But I have business to take care of.

"Enzo you bastard!" I hear her yelling on the other side of the door. She bangs on the door and jiggles the handle trying to get out. That will do her no good. I can't risk her leaving while I am gone. She may not want to stay with me, but she isn't going anywhere until I say otherwise. After our kiss, I know that any thoughts I had of letting her go will never cross my mind again.

Chapter 20

ENZO

Back at the tavern I find Gunnar dancing with Saraphena, while Duncan leans against a far back post with his arms across his chest, and face in a scowl. Since the day I met Duncan, I don't think I have ever seen him with a genuine smile on his face. Whatever happened to him in Twilight must have broken him completely.

Sometimes hearts get shattered beyond repair. It takes a lifetime to find all the pieces again, let alone the time it takes to put them back together. Duncan deserves to find someone who loves him, despite whatever has happened in his past.

I remember the look on Gunnar's face when we returned to Citrine to find Saraphena gone. He was a shell of himself for weeks. He wouldn't train, barely ate anything, and almost never went outside. A few years had passed before he started to seem like his old self again.

After that Gunnar spent years drowning himself in females and alcohol, which was a blast, but I knew he was just trying to mask his real feelings. I thought it was idiotic to pine away for someone for so long, especially after they left you. But now that Aliyah is in my life...she is in every thought, every breath. She lives in my soul...she *is* my soul. But unlike Gunnar, I don't plan on ever letting her go. I step up next to Duncan to watch Gunnar and Saraphena dance.

"I need to speak with you," I whisper yell over the crowd.

Duncan turns to face me now, nodding his head to the side, indicating for me to follow him where it's more quiet.

"Who do we need to take care of now?"

I gasp and throw my hand to my chest like it pains me to hear his words, an exasperated look on my face. "I am *hurt* that you think we are jumping right to hurting someone!"

Duncan cocks an eyebrow and tips his head with a smirk, "Okay, so what did you need to speak to me about?"

"We need to find the man who was touching Aliyah tonight and dispose of him," I say. I won't deny that I am not exactly looking forward to doing this, but I have to do this...on principle. She did not want that male touching her and he did not respect that. I cannot just let that go.

"Uh huh. And why exactly do we need to hurt this man for touching Aliyah?" Duncan smirks at me.

How could he even ask such a ridiculous question? Aliyah is *mine* and mine alone. I want to replace every cell on her body that was touched by that poisonous urchin of a male.

"I don't answer to you Duncan. The male needs to be taught that he does not touch someone without their consent."

Duncan stares at me for a fraction longer than I like. "I'll see what I can find out. Wait here."

Duncan stalks off through the crowd and out the front entrance. I know he will produce results. He always does. Adryanna comes up next to me and snakes her arm through mine.

"So, the pretty blonde girl, huh?" She wiggles her eyebrows at me.

"Don't start with me, Adryanna. Have you seen Jade since we left?" I look down at her, but I can't help the smile that pulls at my lips at the thought of my little dove struggling to get out of my room back at the house.

"I knew it! Our own little ZoZo, *in love!*" She squeals.

"Unbelievable, Gunnar! If I find out he told anyone else about that nickname, I'll string him up by his toes and bleed him dry," I yell. I *hate* that nickname. "I am *not* in love, Adryanna. Aliyah is just...intriguing."

"Oooooo you must be *deep* in love if you are deflecting like this! I knew from the way you watched her across the dance floor. She has your heart already."

"That would require me to have a heart to give."

"You say you are heartless, and yet I know that Duncan is off right now looking for the man that doesn't know how to take no for an answer. If you need the back room just say the word. Scum like that deserve what is coming to them. Anyways, last I knew, Jade took off after you and Aliyah left earlier. I haven't seen her since."

"Keep an eye on Gunnar for me, yeah? When it comes to females he tends to get in about as much trouble as he is worth. When Duncan gets back, send him to the back room. I'll be waiting there. Oh and Adryanna, if you see Jade, tell her I will see her in the morning."

She nods and takes off towards the bar while I make my way to the back room. I have preparations to make. I pause and turn back, signaling her to come back over.

"Something else I can help you with?" she asks.

"Find the tailor and tell him to stay open late for me. I need to pick up a few things."

"I'll let him know. For the record, a male who buys a female clothing might send the message that you actually *care* for her." Adryanna winks at me before disappearing into the crowd.

Not long after I pour myself a drink and set up the back room for our plans does the door come crashing open. The piece of crap male from earlier is a heap on the floor, wailing in pain. *He doesn't know the meaning of pain— yet.* Duncan strides in after him, clearly having thrown the male into the door to open it.

"Found him a few bars over telling his friends about the blonde haired girl he hooked up with in the back room here," Duncan reports.

"Interesting." I walk over to where he remains lying on the floor, squatting down to eye level. I fist a large section of hair before whipping his head back so hard I hear his neck crack.

"I don't remember it quite happening that way. What about you Duncan? Do you remember it happening that way?"

Duncan simply grunts and shakes his head before turning to close the door. Immediately the male begins screaming at the top of his lungs. For what I have planned for him, I let him get it all out before he can never scream again. I close my eyes while still gripping his hair and try to block out the sounds of terror. Memories of my childhood flash through my brain. I try to ignore them and focus back on the task.

"Please— *please*— I take it all back! I'll tell them that I lied! I swear I didn't know she was with you!" The male begs like his life depends on it. Oh wait— *it does.*

"Unfortunately for you, it is a little late for that. See it isn't just about the fact that she is with me, or even the fact that you touched her, it is the fact that you touched her without her *permission.*" I emphasize the last word.

I know that my little dove can handle herself just fine, but it is the sheer fact that she didn't want his touch and he disregarded her wishes.

Yanking him up by the hair, I drag him over to the chair behind the mahogany desk and shove him down. I don't even bother restraining him because he won't get very far even if he did try to escape. Plus, he won't be living long enough to try.

"I'd like to get this over as soon as possible so please stop screaming and do as you're told. I have a little bird that needs to be let out of its cage back home." I smile down at him thinking of my dove.

"Listen to me— *please.* I will do *anything* to live. Let me apologize to her, to everyone!"

My insides twist at the thought of him speaking to her ever again. The last thing this male will ever see is my face, and he will never think of her ever again.

"Duncan," I say, letting him know I am ready to begin.

"We are going to play a little game," I continue. "A rather unfair game, if I might add. See in the end— you lose every time."

Duncan walks over to me rolling out the soft cloth filled with little pockets containing several different styles and lengths of knives. I turn back to the fae.

"Pick one."

"Wh–what?" he stammers.

"Pick one!" I yell. I'm getting impatient. Tears start to fall from his eyes. I roll mine in return.

"Fine, I will pick one for you."

Picking up a medium length knife, I twirl it around in my hand. In a fraction of a second, I embed it through his arm and into the armrest below. Blood curdling screams rip from the fae as he uses his other hand to clutch the handle. It is so deeply embedded into the chair that there is no way it is coming loose any time soon.

"Now isn't this just a blast?" I say sarcastically. "Duncan, your turn. Pick a knife."

"No more, please— *please!*" he begs.

"Ugh. I hate when they cry." Duncan walks over with a flat look on his face.

He picks up a smaller knife that is perfect for pairing fruit. Duncan grabs the fae's hand still clutching the knife handle in his arm and bends it back at the wrist.

"I promise this will only hurt— well, a lot."

By the time Duncan is done with his turn, the fae's finger bones are now visible from the bottom side of his hand and his muscles are flayed into ribbons. Duncan moves to bend the right hand back and does the same to that hand as well.

"There. Now no part of him has ever touched Aliyah," Duncan says, as he jams the knife into the top of the fae's left thigh. "Hold this for me, would you?"

I can't help but smile at the notion that my brother thought of the same thing I did not minutes ago.

"Alright let's see. It's my turn again I think! Which to choose, which to choose?" I sing-song. "Ah! Remind me, what was it that Aliyah said to you? What was it that she said she would rather do than go anywhere with you?"

"Ali—" He begins, but I cut him off with another knife being jammed into the top of his left collarbone, so it is sticking down vertically.

"Don't you *dare* say her name. Your mouth is not deserving of her name to grace it. Now try again. What did she say to you?"

"The lady— she said— she said she would rather eat glass than go anywhere with me," he finally mumbles out through his sobs.

"Ah yes! Now it is coming back to me. It seems only fitting that the punishment she would so willingly dole upon herself, be the final piece to end your worthless life. I don't enjoy doing this to others, you know? I'd much rather be home right now with my dove, but instead I'm here. I'm here having to teach a valuable lesson on basic decency. A lesson I have a feeling you were not taught previously."

"How unfortunate," Duncan says, flatly.

"Duncan, our friend here looks positively parched. Why don't you go get him something to drink? Something to help clear his throat, maybe." I look at the male, thankful that this is almost over.

Duncan exits quickly. I should ask his name, but honestly, I don't care. He begins begging and sobbing even harder knowing what is coming to him. I barely register the sounds anymore.

I let my mind drift to thoughts of my little dove. I wonder if she has thought to reach Saraphena through their Soul Bond or if she is still struggling to break out of my room. It doesn't seem likely that she has given up; my dove doesn't quit easily.

Duncan comes back into the room and hands me a small tumbler. The fae's eyes go wide and he starts shaking in the chair trying to get up. I simply stand and place my foot between his legs on the edge of the chair to keep it in place. Resting my elbow on my raised thigh, I look down into the cup.

"Drink," I say, holding out the cup.

"Wh–what? No."

"Yeah, that isn't really an option. *Drink.*"

I can feel myself growing impatient. It's going to take him an eternity to do this and I don't want to spend any more time away from her than I need to. I am *itching* to get back and see what she has gotten herself into.

"Please— I— I can't. It— I'll die."

"You can't possibly know that for certain. Now, drink."

The dirtbag hesitates as he reaches for the cup. Opening his mouth as wide as it can go, I hold his chin down and place my other hand on his forehead so he can't close up at the last second. Unfortunately, his hands are slipping all over the place, unable to hold the glass. *Dramatic much?*

"Duncan, help the man out, will you?"

Fat, wet tears drip out of his crap brown eyes and mingle with his blood on the floor. The first gulp is down his throat as Duncan pours little shards of glass into his mouth. Blood shoots out of his mouth as he tries to work down the pieces.

When the cup is empty, the male sits there, motionless, blood dripping from the corners of his mouth with his head still tipped back. His screams still ring in my ears causing a headache to come on.

"Somehow, I feel like the world is a better place without him in it," I say. I need to make it over to the tailors before it gets too late. "Duncan, tell Adryanna we need a clean up crew in here. Inform her it is for hazardous material."

Duncan leaves and I take one last look at the fae. His blood still drips in little splashes on the floor. I want my dove to know she never has to worry about him ever again, so I take a piece of him with me. As I walk out of the room I tuck my souvenir into a bag, and collect my knives, before slinging it over my back. I lock the door from the inside and close it. Adryanna has a key and knows that hazardous material means getting a crew that will be discrete.

I make my way through the crowd still partying the night away, completely unaware of what happened in the back room. As the bell on the door rings signaling my exit, I take in a breath of fresh air. Turning left down the street, I make my way to the tailors.

"Jerico!" I call, opening the door.

A short, older fae comes scurrying out from behind one of the racks. He stands as tall as my hip and has short gray hair that matches his silver rimmed glasses. He has a tape measure around his neck and pins stuck along the sleeve of his shirt.

"General Enzo, welcome! Adryanna told me of your request and I am pleased to say that I have several wonderful selections for you. Follow me."

Jerico leads me through the small shop, but not stopping at any of the racks. When we get to the back room, he has an entire rack filled with different colored tunics fit for a female and several pairs of leather pants.

"Thank you, Jerico. Please pick out some tunics and pants you think a female, with an affinity for being stubborn, would like."

"Yes yes. Wonderful!"

"Do you have any special item's in stock today, Jerico?"

"Right this way. I have a special selection of pieces that are one of a kind. I am certain that a female special enough for you to be picking out clothes will enjoy," he smiles.

I grunt in response and follow him to a shelf several rows down from the tunics. There are so many colors and materials to choose from. "Leave me."

Jerico scurries away to finish packing up the other clothing. I scan the shelves that are filled with lavish jewels and extravagant pieces of jewelry. There are crowns, rings, and bracelets, but one item in particular catches my eye. It's perfect. I pick it off the shelf and call out for Jerico.

"Do you have a box I can put this in?" I hear some shuffling and things being knocked over before he rounds the corner. He is holding a large maroon box with a silver ribbon attached, in addition to a small black box with a gold clasp. He hands it to me and shuffles back to his task. I turn and place my selected item into the box. I put the lid on and walk back to where Jerico is finishing folding several tunics and a few pairs of pants.

"All set for you, General. I do hope the lady likes them."

"I am sure she will be quite pleased, as am I. Thank you for your help," I say while tucking the folded clothing into the box, before shutting the lid. I place it on a nearby table and tie the ribbon on top. The bow is off centered and one side is longer than the other. I undo it and try again, but this time it is twisted and lopsided. I undo the bow again and growl in frustration.

"Ugh! Thats it. One last try and then I quit," I mumble to myself. I tie the ribbon, but this time one of the tails is on the opposite side of the bow and the ribbon is crumpled and twisted. How can I be a warrior, yet I can't tie a stupid bow? *Unbelievable.* I roll my eyes and tuck the box under my arm. She is just going to untie it anyway.

I wave to Jerico on my way out and thank him again for staying open late. I drop a large bag of gold coins onto his desk and exit through the front door. As I make my way back up the street, I can't help but smile at the thought of giving Aliyah my gift. Adryanna's words ring through my head, *'a male who buys a female clothing might send the message that you actually care for her."*

I shake my head at the notion. I can't have her in that way, but I don't want anyone else to have her either. A gift is just a gift, that is all. I run this saying through my head over and over as I make my way home. No matter how much I tell myself I don't care, there is a small part of my heart that glows at the thought of her enjoying my gift.

As I open the front door, the house is silent. Everyone must still be out. I walk up the stairs and take the key from my pocket. I take a moment to listen for any sounds on the other side of the door, but I hear none. As I open the door slowly, a creak sounds from the hinges. Aliyah is fast asleep on the bed. The soft rise and fall of her chest brings an odd sort of comfort to me. I watch her there for a moment before moving to place the box on the dresser. I think of going to lay on the bed, but think better of it. I don't want to wake her because if I do I'm not sure I would be able to show the restraint I had earlier.

I walk around to her side of the bed and pull the blanket closer to her chin. She shifts in her sleep, but her eyes never open.

"Enzo?" she asks in a sleepy voice.

"*Shhh,* go back to sleep. I'm here now."

She lays back down and I move to place a small kiss on her forehead before stopping myself. Her blue eyes softly open and gaze up at me.

"Will you stay with me?" Aliyah's soft voice caresses my skin.

"Not tonight, little dove. Get some rest."

I pull the covers up over her body and lean down to place a kiss on her forehead. I'm sure just one more kiss won't kill me. Her scent of vanilla and honeydew fill my nose and I inhale deeply. I grit my teeth against the urge that washes over me to stay with her. I clench my fists and let out a restrained breath. Backing away from the bed, I make my way out of the room and downstairs to the couch. *Maybe that kiss will kill me after all.*

I come down the stairs and Jade, Saraphena, Gunnar, and Duncan come plowing through the door. All of them appear very drunk and are knocking things over as they make their way into the living room. Only Saraphena looks like she could be sober.

"Maker, you all are way too loud right now! Aliyah is sleeping upstairs," I grit my teeth at their continued noise.

"Oops! Sorry ZoZo," Gunnar laughs. He pulls Saraphena down into his lap on the couch. Jade and Duncan sit on the floor, stumbling on their way down.

"I want to take Aliyah to Citrine tomorrow," I say.

"Yes! Absolutely yes!" Gunnar practically yells.

"I think that is a great idea." Saraphena places her hand over Gunnar's mouth as she speaks. "We can leave first thing in the morning. I will make sure they are sobered up by then."

"It's set then. We leave for the alicanto stables as soon as Aliyah wakes up. Now get out of my room for the night." I make my way over to where Gunnar and Saraphena sit. He scoops her up into his arms and makes for the stairs. Jade and Duncan follow, tripping over a few steps on the way up. I shake my head at their foolish actions.

I lay there on the couch willing myself to sleep, yet I can't take my mind off the woman upstairs. The last thing I remember is the look on her face when I first showed her Korin. She was so happy in that moment and part of me hopes it was because of me.

Chapter 21

ALIYAH

Who the hell left the curtains open?! Light beams into the room and my head pounds at the sight. I push the heels of my hands into my eye sockets, causing little white dots to splotch over my vision. I don't remember falling asleep last night, but I suppose all the screaming took it out of me.

I am furious with Enzo right now. I look around the room to see if he came back in here last night, but I see no signs that he may have slept in here. The bed next to me is cold and untouched. A feeling of disappointment washes over me. A vague memory comes back of him tucking me in last night, but I can't be sure that wasn't just a dream. Why does he irritate me one minute, and yet make me crave him the next?

Shifting to the side of the bed, I stretch my legs out and feel my bones pop and crack. My eyes fall on a large box on top of the dresser. That definitely was not here last night. A small note is placed on the top of the box.

For all the things I wish I could say,
And for those who will never speak again

~ Enzo

A gift? Enzo doesn't seem like the kind of male who gives gifts. Pulling the deep red box into my lap, I untie the silver ribbon wrapped around it. I laugh to myself when I see how unruly the ribbon had been tied. Enzo must have tried to tie it himself. When I lift the lid to see what's inside, all I can do is stare. In the box are several pairs of leather pants and over a dozen fitted tunic shirts. What catches my eye however is a small black box with gold clasps and a golden rose etched onto the top. I pull it out and set it to the side. Sifting through the clothes, I realize they are made of the finest materials and most expensive leathers. I could never afford to buy anything this nice. I may have bathed and put on some of his nice clothes, but under all that lingered what I truly was back in Mareen. *Poor.*

As I shuffle the clothes around to see everything Enzo had picked out, something catches the light and pulls my attention. There at the bottom is an item with an attached note.

P.S. This one was for you

Part of me should be horrified at what I find. Instead, a smile pulls across my face and joy erupts in my heart. There at the bottom of the box sits a golden ring with two small dragons forming a circle on the top and small splotches of blood crusted to the metal. *The man from the bar.* This was his ring. The ring I had memorized so that I could remember if he ever tried anything ever again.

My heart warms as I pull the other small box into my lap. Opening the clasp, inside sits a small pendent on a silver chain. The pendent is a tiny silver ax. Normally I would be upset at the reminder of that day in Mareen, but I can't help but laugh at the irony that I will now always have an ax hovering over my chest. I actually catch myself laughing out loud at the notion.

Pst. Are you awake? Sara's voice drifts into my mind.

Yeah I am, why? A few moments later the door is flying open and Sara is running into the bedroom and diving into the bed with me. As she gets under the covers, I place the box on the nightstand.

"What's in the box?" Sara beams at me.

"Just some new clothes." A blush creeps up my cheeks thinking about the gift.

I show Sara the new necklace. She did not think it was as funny as I did, but instead gave me a disapproving look that Enzo would make such a joke. I thought it was hilarious. In some strange way, a despicable male and an ax to the chest is what brought me here in the first place.

"You seem chipper this morning," I say, wiggling my eyebrows at her. "What did you and Gunnar do last night after Enzo and I left?"

"Oh, so it's Enzo and you now, huh?"

"Shut up and don't change the subject!" I giggle.

It feels nice to have this morning with my best friend. So much has changed since leaving Mareen. We used to sit in our apartment or by the river and talk for hours, but now we are sitting in the nicest home I have ever been in, surrounded by plush pillows and males who buy you new clothing without even asking.

"Gunnar and I had a chance to really reconnect last night. I think we are going to be alright after all." Sara is absolutely blushing from her neck to the tips of her pointy ears.

"Really?! I'm so happy for you, Sara. I knew it would all work out!"

A gruff voice cuts off our conversation.

"Good morning, Aliyah. I trust you had a restful night's sleep?" Enzo's body takes up the entire door frame as he stands there with his hands in his pockets.

Can you give us a minute? I push into Sara's mind.

Something tells me he needs more than a minute. Sara flashes me a smile before scooting off the bed.

"I will be downstairs packing up some food if you need me."

"Packing up food? Where are we going?" I ask, as Sara scurries from the room quickly, while glancing back and giving me a huge smile.

"You'll see," she sings, as I hear her footsteps going down the stairs.

Enzo comes over to the side of the bed where I am laying and sits down by my feet. He places a hand on my shin, and even under the blankets I can feel the electricity from his touch.

"Thank you," I whisper, as I look down at my hands while I wring my fingers together.

"For what?"

"For my gift," I say, in an even quieter voice.

Enzo reaches out and grabs my chin with his thumb and forefinger before he brings my eyes up to meet his.

"Little dove, I can't hear you when you talk with your face to the floor."

Finding some confidence, I manage to lift my chin on my own.

"I said thank you for the gift. It is the nicest thing anyone has ever done for me." To my surprise, I even smile at the end. I scoot closer to him on the bed. I place my hand on his, and see his pupils dilate and nostrils flare for the briefest of moments.

"I understand why you gave them to me, though. I know the clothes I wore in Mareen weren't exactly fashionable. I'm sure you must have been horrified to see such disgusting pieces of fabric touching all your nice things," I say blushing.

"Me leaving last night had nothing to do with a piece of fabric, though I am happy to rid you of them," he winks at me.

"I suppose I won't be needing them anymore. Now that I have such nice things, that is."

"No, you won't." He trails his fingers down the collar of the tunic I'm wearing. The feeling of his fingertips brushing my collar bone sends tingles straight down my spine.

"The necklace is absolutely hilarious. Sara didn't think it was as funny as I did, but I love it. Thank you."

His fingers continue their exploration, wrapping his large hand around my neck. My eyes fall shut at the contact and my heart beats faster. I can feel the blushing creeping up my neck where his hand sits.

"I wanted to make sure you never forget what brought us together and the battle ax was always my favorite weapon. It used to pain me thinking about that moment in the field, but now I know that without that moment, I wouldn't know what I know now." Enzo's breath caresses my ear. I hadn't noticed that he had leaned forward, only inches away from my face.

"And what exactly is it that you know now?" I'm breathless. Enzo places a small kiss to the side of my neck, just under my ear.

"I know that—"

Enzo is cut off by the door opening. I quickly pull from his grasp and scoot back on the bed, separating myself from him like I have just been burned. I may as well have been with how my skin sizzles from his touch.

"We are ready to leave whenever you are," Gunnar smiles.

"Thank you, Gunnar, but next time, knock before you come in so that I can refuse you from entering," Enzo grits out.

"Noted," Gunnar smirks before leaving and closing the door behind him.

"So where are we going that Sara needs to pack food?"

"Last night I talked with the others. We have decided to take you to Citrine City."

Something shifts in the air and a sense of unease sweeps over me. I don't want to go anywhere new right now. I just want to stay in this room. There is so much more in Korin that I want to see before I leave. Almost as if he senses the change in my body language, Enzo reaches over and pulls me into his lap, wrapping his strong arms around me. Every fiber of my being both lights up and instantly calms at his presence.

"What is Citrine City?" I ask.

Enzo places his hand on my knee. I try to push out of his grasp, but my mind just won't let me. My heart feels this pull to him. I can't seem to tear myself away.

I relax in his hold, and he loosens his grip on my knee, but does not remove his hand. He moves his thumb in those soothing circles again as he answers my question.

"Citrine City is where Queen Dione and King Armas ruled before the final battle when they both died. It has been abandoned since their deaths since they had no known appointed heir, or a child who could take the throne. It has a library there filled with books. One of them specifically contains citizen records. Since we are working to figure out who your parents are, we figure that is the best place to start. It is only about a half a day's ride to get there, so we should be back here before nightfall."

I try to focus on his words, but my mind is fixed on those small circles.

"You mean I might finally know who my parents are? Are there even records for the fae that came from villages and not from the city?"

"The book we are looking for is enchanted by a spell that records every fae ever born, along with their lineage, so if we find your name in the book we should be able to trace it back to who your parents are."

Needing to stop the situation from going any further, I push off his body and get as far away from him as the room allows. Even across the room is not far enough to escape the heat that radiates off him.

"I should probably get ready to leave. I don't want the others waiting on me too long."

Something in Enzo's gaze has my legs carrying me back across the room. I stop in front of him and lean down so our lips are just a breath away from each other.

"Thank you again for the gift."

His hands find my hips and rest there. I bring my hand up to cup his jaw. I lean in to kiss him, but at the last second I turn and press a kiss to his cheek before turning as fast as I can and sprint towards the washroom.

Heavy footsteps are behind me, but I am just quick enough to slam the door before he reaches me.

"I am a very patient male, my dove."

"It's a good thing fae are basically immortal, because that is how long you will be waiting, *ZoZo*."

ENZO

Aliyah walks ahead of me as our group makes their way to the stables. While normally I would be angry at her for this morning, I can't help but smile at the way she is absorbing every detail of the town around us. Korin is beautiful, but it is nothing compared to Citrine. Her curiosity for this new realm is contagious. I catch myself looking around and admiring the crystal mountains that I grew up with.

I never truly noticed their beauty until she walked into my life. She makes me...*feel things.* Her use of the name ZoZo this morning almost made me break down the washroom door and force her to say it again. Hearing that nickname fall from her lips has caused it to to grow on me, which is wildly infuriating. I will never admit that to Gunnar.

Aliyah is wearing the new clothing I bought for her. The black leather pants hug her curves perfectly and the tunic she wears fits much better than mine, allowing her to show off her full figure. Her hair is pulled back into a single braid and Saraphena has tucked a few light blue flowers into the weaves. She is breathtaking. I see the silver chain peeking out from underneath the collar of her shirt. I smile at the thought of her wearing my gift.

Jade comes up next to me, looping her arm through mine. My mood instantly turns sour. I try to casually unhook my arm from hers. A small look of hurt flashes across her face. Part of me feels bad for her, but what I would have felt for Jade is *nothing* compared to what I feel for Aliyah. No other woman will ever compare to my dove.

"So what *is* going on between you two?" Jade asks.

"That is none of your business, Jade," Duncan chimes in from behind us.

"It was a simple question, Duncan! Don't get your panties in a wad. I just want to know who it is that we are letting into *our* home for what seems to be the foreseeable future."

"Aliyah is— Aliyah is everything to me. She will be allowed to stay with me for eternity if she wishes."

I speak in a more hushed tone so that Aliyah doesn't overhear our conversation. Jade huffs out a breath and shakes her head as she quickens her pace to get ahead of me.

"Freaking males. They are so blind to what is right in front of them," she mutters under her breath.

"You know Jade loves you, Enzo," Duncan says, walking to catch up with me.

"Every female in the entire realm could love me, but there is only one female's love worth having."

"Take it from me brother, guard your heart. In the end it only gets broken. Love always ends with them leaving you, either by choice, or by death. All you can do is pray you go first, so you never have to know what it is to live without them."

"You sound like you're speaking from experience?"

"My father killed my first love just for being with me. She was not High Fae, but it didn't matter to me. Once my heart was hers, I knew I would never find love again. I had wrongly assumed the responsibilities of the crown only fell to my oldest brother, Aramot. He is set to become the next king of The Twilight, or at least the last I knew. I haven't heard from my family since I left, nor do I wish to. When my father refused to send me to the military academy here in Krystal, I was thankful. I didn't want to leave home at such a young age. I didn't think it was fair that a child had to leave their home just to prove loyalty to Olyrium. As I got older and fell in love, I thought I had escaped that fate forever. After she died, there was nothing left for me in Twilight. That was the day I decided I was never going back."

King Olivar. Duncan's father and King of the Twilight Kingdom. I had heard he was a vicious and cruel man. Who wouldn't be living in a place of constant darkness? Your heart and soul would have to be black in order to survive. Duncan never told me about his first love. While I am horrified at what took place, I am thankful that it brought Duncan to us. I hope he can find happiness one day.

"I'm sorry, brother. I promise you one day, I will help you get revenge on your father. In whatever way you see fit.

"For his sake, I hope he is already dead."

Chapter 23

ALIYAH

After we leave the cottage, we start walking along a field of crystals. Every direction I turn there are small crystals growing out of the ground in an array of colors and shapes. In the distance, large crystal mountains loom over us. Green moss weaves in and out around the crystals creating a grass like look. As the sun shines down, light bounces through the crystals and paints the ground several different colors. Seeing the sky lit up in ribbons of color last night was magnificent. Our path is carved out of marble winding through the fields of crystals and I see several small birds picking at the little crystals on the ground.

"They're adorable! Can I pick one up?" I ask Sara.

"I wouldn't. They prefer to be left in peace to eat, but we have something even better coming," she smiles at me.

As we approach some stables my nerves begin to flare in excitement. Korin is beautiful, but the anticipation of finally finding out who my parents are has me ready to see Citrine.

I glance back at Enzo and my smile falters when I see him linking arms with Jade. I quickly turn back around, not wanting to see the two of them together. I don't know why she bothers me so much, but it's like my feelings for Enzo are being threatened. I thought Enzo and I might have been something, but then I see him with Jade or Adryanna and I'm not sure. I know they are best friends, and I am sure there was something between them, either in the past, or even...*now.* Maybe he flirts with all the females he meets. I don't let myself go down that road any further. I have enough to worry about right now.

So what happened with you and Enzo after I left this morning? Sara says to me, while giving me a little shove with her elbow.

She had been walking with Gunnar when we started, but I think she could sense my restlessness through our bond. I am happy that her and Gunnar reconnected. I knew Gunnar would forgive her for leaving once he knew the truth.

Literally nothing. I thought with a laugh. *Do you know how we will be getting to Citrine?*

You'll see. She winks at me before taking my hand. Jade huffs past me muttering something under her breath. What got into her? I turn to see if Enzo has done something to piss her off— *hopefully*— but instead I find him deep in conversation with Duncan. It was like he didn't give two craps that Jade was upset. Okay, now I kind of feel bad for her.

When she reaches the stables, Jade opens the door to reveal stalls filled with the strangest creatures I have ever seen. My mouth hangs open and my eyes go wide looking at the giant bird-like creatures.

They have huge bodies that are covered from head to literal tail in brightly colored feathers. They have a short, S- shaped neck, but broad bodies that look wide enough to hold one fae, maybe two. Their legs are long with huge talons at the end. Their eyes shine solid gold with no visible pupil.

"Their beaks are— crystal?" I ask, astonished by the sight.

"Yes, and their bones are made of crystal as well. While one might think that makes them fragile, magic runs deep in their blood making them virtually indestructible and perfect for covering long distances." Jade speaks as she strokes one of the birds heads. She looks calmer now.

"Can they fly?" I ask, taking in their massive wings.

"Unfortunately, due to their bone density, no. But they are incredibly quick on their feet and can carry heavy loads," Gunnar chimes in.

"What are they called?" I ask, still in awe of the creatures.

"Alicanto. They are extremely loyal to their owner and can be hostile towards strangers, so keep your distance. Their feathers turn the color of the crystals they like to eat," Sara says, smiling.

Duncan, Gunnar, Jade and Enzo each walk up to a stall. Gunnar walks up to an alicanto with dark blue feathers.

"This is my matched, Azure. His feathers are blue because he primarily eats azurite crystals," Gunnar smiles.

"Mine is Reyla. She is dark purple because she loves amethyst." Jade strokes the bird's head softly before wrapping her arms around its neck.

"Name's Onyx. He eats Onyx," Duncan states flatly.

I giggle a little too loudly at the irony that he would pick such a literal name. The black bird's feathers ruffle at the name and Onyx pushes the top of his head into Duncan's chest looking for affection. Duncan lets out a small sigh and places his forehead to that of the bird's and closes his eyes. I suddenly feel bad for laughing.

"And this is Ruby. She primarily eats jasper crystals, so she will appear red. I think it is because she is a fiery little thing though. She is extremely threatened by other females in my life, so it might be best to stand clear of her." Enzo winks at me with a smirk. As I make eye contact with the alicanto, I swear I see her eyes fall into slits in an *I dare you* look.

"So which ones will Sara and I ride?"

"That isn't really up to us. The alicanto choose their rider. That's why Ruby is so protective over Enzo. Some alicanto are more hospitable than others. But Ruby loves me, don't you baby girl?" Jade says, walking over to Ruby and petting her on the neck.

My teeth instinctively grind together at the fact this animal is *so* protective and yet she can walk right up and touch it. I go to open my mouth to tell her to get her hands off the freaking bird but as I do, Sara's voice fills my head.

Don't do it. She isn't worth it. What she doesn't understand is that she can touch Ruby because she does not perceive Jade as a threat to her relationship with Enzo.

I audibly exhale the breath I didn't even know I was holding as my eyes shift away from Jade, and onto Enzo. His head tips to the side with a quizzical expression when he notices my body language shift. Quickly breaking eye contact, I spin around the room.

"So how does an alicanto choose me? Do I need to find its favorite snack or something?"

"I wish it were that easy," Sara says, looking at me with a soft smile. Gunnar comes up next to her and takes her hand. Her eyes glisten as she looks up at him and tears brim her eyes.

Are you okay? I ask into her mind.

Yes and no. I used to have another matched back home in SunSpark. Their lifespan is only about 200 years and he was turning 187 years old when I left. I thought I would be with him until the end. Just getting a little sad thinking about how he died without me even getting the chance to say goodbye.

I'm sorry. Nothing can ever replace him, but any of these big birds would be lucky to have you.

I watch her and Gunnar walk to the other end of the large stable, headed to a flock of alicanto. They squawk and screech at her approach. Enzo comes to stand next to me, his hand brushing mine lightly. He lets our hands linger together.

I watch as Sara approaches an orange one. It flaps its wings viciously at her and screeches in her face. Gunnar laughs before pulling her hand in another direction of the flock. She reaches out next to a bright yellow one, placing her hand lightly on its crystal beak.

A bright light radiates out from under her hand and the bird flares its wings before dropping its head low to the ground. Sara follows suit, dropping her hands to her sides and bowing before the bird.

"It's a sign of mutual respect," Enzo says, while watching Sara and Gunnar. "They are now a matched pair. His loyalty to her will be undying, even more than Gunnar, who I am sure would easily lay down his life for her. I suspect he won't be losing her again."

He shifts his eyes to look down at me, and I break my gaze away from the newly matched pair to look back at Enzo.

"Let's get you matched so we can head out."

Enzo grips my hand with a little more force than necessary, but it feels comfortable all the same. I like the feeling of his calloused hand in mine. He brings me over to the opposite side from where the others are standing, spending time with their matched. I walk up to a green one, glancing back at Enzo to make sure he is still there. The alicanto glares at me as I approach. All I saw Sara do was reach out and touch their beak. How hard could it be?

As I reach out my hand, the green bird snaps at it and I jerk my hand back towards my chest, clutching it tightly as a gasp slips out. *Okay, maybe this is going to be scarier than I thought.* Enzo glares at the bird and it turns to take off running, clearly not looking for a fight.

"That one was no good anyways. Clearly he doesn't know what he is missing being matched to you," he says with a wink. "Let's try over here."

He walks me over to another flock that has huddled together. I find another shade of red alicanto and reach my hand out again. It squawks and scrapes its foot on the ground before running at me full speed. Enzo grabs my bicep and pulls me to the side just in time, as it goes racing past.

"Well then. That was...kind of scary," I say, as I break out into a fit of laughter.

Enzo can't help but crack a smile, too. Something comes over me and I just can't stop laughing. The sheer fact at what my life has become is comical, at best. I am standing in a realm made of giant crystal mountains, with a fae male who I couldn't have even dreamed up, trying to find my parents who turned out to be fae themselves. My best friend in the entire world is actually my Soul Guardian, and now I am trying to get matched with an overgrown bird.

Once I regain my composure, I look up at Enzo who is now standing right in front of me.

"That was the most beautiful sound I have ever heard," he whispers. He reaches out his finger to wipe away the tears that had dripped down my cheek while laughing.

We stand there for a moment, just looking into each other's eyes, searching. Suddenly something huge slams into my back pushing me forward into Enzo, who catches me in his arms as they wrap around my waist. I have to strain my neck to look up at him from this position, but his eyes widen slightly before sliding closed like he can't even bare to look at me and he releases a tense breath. I right myself and straighten my spine, too proud to admit that I was thankful he always seemed to be there to catch me.

I turn to see what pushed me into him, and before me stands the largest alicanto in the whole stable. The beak has swirls of deep red and blue that transition on to its feathers.

The feathers appear to be deep blue, but as it shifts its body, they turn to a deep red almost like an illusion. The head has gorgeous wisps of feather- like material that curl up towards the sky. Her wingspan is huge as she stretches. Her eyes are a deep silver shade. After what happened before, I am afraid to reach out and touch her in fear that she will leave.

"I've— I've never seen one like that before," Jade stammers, as she walks over toward us, mouth agape.

As she draws near, the alicanto turns its head to face her and its eyes form slits, before it squawks loudly at her, and flaps its wings to brush up dirt in her direction. Jade coughs and waves her hands in front of her face to clear the dust that was kicked up.

"What the hell, you stupid bird!"

"Hey! Don't call her stupid! She clearly just doesn't want you to come any closer," I snarl.

The bird turns her body back towards me, waiting. She sticks out her neck as if to say, *'it's okay'*. I tentatively reach my hand out, praying to the Maker that the bird wants to match with me. I try to ignore the tremor that ripples down my arm.

She places her beak under my palm and bright white light shoots out from around us. I hear the others yelling and telling each other to close their eyes, but it doesn't seem bright to me at all. All I see is my matched. The light fades and the bird bows deeply in front of me. When I go to bow in turn, the alicanto shoots out its wing to stop me from bending over at the waist. I push its wing away from my abdomen and try again, but the wing holds firm.

"Why won't you let me bow for you?" I whisper.

"This type of alicanto are rare, Aliyah," Enzo says. "I have only ever known one other to be in existence."

"Do you know who it's matched was?" Sara asks tentatively. Enzo looks at her with a stitch of worry in his brow.

"Queen Dione," Enzo answers. Everyone shares a glance at one another.

"Well what does that mean?" I ask. The tension snaps as Enzo continues explaining.

"The changing of her feathers indicates that the ore she eats has that same ability to change color in different light. It only forms on one mountain around here, which is probably why I haven't seen one in ages. I am surprised to find one all the way in Korin though. Those crystals only grow on the border of Krystal near Twilight Kingdom, which is what makes their properties so rare. The darkness in Twilight and the light of Krystal form a very rare crystal. There should be no reason why she came all this way from the border."

Enzo's face looks worried, but it quickly fades as Duncan claps him on the back rejoining the group.

"What are you going to name her? How did you know it was a her by the way?" Gunnar asks.

"I— I'm not really sure? I just kind of had a feeling that it wouldn't be a male."

Sara, why did the bird get upset at Jade? She has no romantic threat to me and the bird. I laugh a little in my head at the thought.

She probably just sensed that Jade is a little salty. Fair enough.

"I am going to call you Mirage, since your feathers seem to want to change colors," I say, stroking the top of her head.

"A beautiful name, for a beautiful alicanto," Sara says, stepping up next to me.

She reaches out to stroke Mirage's feathers on the neck, and it lets her touch her willingly. *See, definitely just thinks Jade is prickly.*

I give Sara a side glance and smile.

"Whatever, can we just go now? I want to get there and back before nightfall," Jade says, tapping her foot impatiently.

Suddenly all those nerves from before come flooding back in. Today is the day I find out who my parents really are.

Chapter 24

ALIYAH

The journey to Citrine City is shorter than I expected. Whether from how fast Mirage runs, or the fact that I spent most of my time watching Enzo. *I guess I'll never know.*

We had passed over flowing rivers deep enough that we all got wet, but not so deep that the alicanto couldn't cross. The water had glistened almost as bright as the crystal mountains surrounding us. This is the farthest I have ever been from Mareen. I don't think I ever want to go back now. Seeing what this world has to offer I know now that Mareen is my past. This world was meant to be my home and I want to see everything it has to offer.

"We are almost there," Jade yells back to us from atop Reyla. Jade has had this irritated look on her face ever since Mirage flung dirt at her back at the stables. I can still see bits of dust clinging to her clothing. Her alicanto is absolutely beautiful— too bad Reyla's owner has an ugly personality. I roll my eyes at Jade's tone. This is supposed to be a fun trip. An exciting trip. Yet here she is throwing her metaphorical wet blanket of a personality all over it. *It's fine, everything is fine.* I remind myself.

You better wipe that death glare off your face before she notices. My best friend's voice fills my mind and it snaps me right out of my bad mood.

Why does she have to be so irritating all the time?

Gunnar only spoke of her past a few times when we were together. I don't know the full story, but I know that she didn't have the best childhood. She was lucky to find this family after what her parents did. Her parents were traitors to the throne. When the war had reached SunSpark, her parents sold information to the enemy. When the queen found out about their treason, her parents were hung in the square. Being a child, the queen spared her, but she was to serve in the military as penance for her parent's crimes. People treated her horribly there, knowing what her parents had done. I know she can be difficult to deal with, but try to give her some grace.

Ha. Grace. Sara says that like I don't understand what it is like to do horrible things just to survive. I try to shake off the negative feelings inside me. If Sara had never dropped me off at that orphanage, maybe I would have had a better life.

No. I scold myself for even thinking that. Sara never asked to be anyone's Soul Guardian and those were difficult times she was living in too. Sara had to leave her family, her home, and she had to give up a chance at love. I look up and spot Sara and Gunnar laughing together and I see the love that lines their eyes. At least I could give her that again by staying here. My heart breaks a little as I look over at Enzo.

His caramel colored eyes bore into mine. Tears start to brim in my eyes. *I will never know love like that, even if I wanted it.* Enzo was handsome, kind— he deserves someone better than me. He has led armies, fought against countless enemies, and fought alongside queens and kings. What do I have to offer him? I am a nobody. From what Sara described, my mother was a pauper who dabbled in witchcraft. I am *nothing*.

Back at the stables when Mirage matched with me, I had a glimmer of hope that I could be something more at the mention of the queen. The look on everyone's faces sparked the tiniest flicker of hope in me that maybe I had some connection to her. But that would be ridiculous. Why would she have given me away if I was their only heir? She would have kept me here, in Citrine. She would have wanted to keep me safe herself. Which is why I know I am nothing more than who I was in Mareen— *an orphan*. Someone who has no one to call family. No place to call *home*.

A single tear spills over and drips down my cheek. Shame drowns out all other emotions. I feel numb. Like I am outside my body watching myself shrink into nothing. Maybe I did die. Maybe I never recovered from that ax in my chest and this is all just a dream. Maybe—

"Aliyah...come back to me," a low voice speaks and his face comes into view before me.

When had we stopped moving? When did I get off Mirage? Enzo's strong hands are clasped around my shoulders as he lowers himself to eye level with me. My mind feels clouded.

"It's time to come back to me now." He brushes his thumb over where the tear fell, wiping away the remnants of my pain. I blink a few times and shake my head. The world snaps back into focus, and there he is before me.

"Thank you, but I'm fine now." I pull away from his touch.

"Aliyah, wait." Enzo goes to grab my wrist to turn me back to him. "Why are you pushing me away?"

"Enzo, please," I beg, tears brimming in my eyes again. "I can't push away something I never had."

"Aliyah, just wait."

I turn to walk back towards Mirage, to finish the journey that ends with what I've known all along.

"Little dove, you've had me since the moment I first laid eyes on you. I may not have known it then, but I know how I feel now."

Frustration boils in my veins. I stomp back over to him and stop so close we are almost touching chest to chest.

"How Enzo? How can that be true?" I practically yell. The others are approaching behind me, probably wondering why we stopped.

"You are a warrior! You have seen battle, fought armies and won! And what am I in all of that? What have I accomplished? I am a broken soul scattered into a thousand pieces that will *never* be put back together again. No matter what we find in that freaking book, I will always be—"

Enzo's lips crash with mine. His hands run up my arms and into my hair, pulling back slightly to deepen the kiss. My eyes fall shut as the sensation envelops every sense. My hands grab onto the collar of his tunic in desperation.

If this is to be our last kiss before he accepts the truth of who I am, then I will imprint every second of this kiss to my memory to cherish for all eternity. For just this moment, it's just us in this field of crystals. For just this moment, it feels like he loves me. Enzo pulls away and leaves me completely breathless, chest heaving and lips tingling.

"You are *everything*, Aliyah. Everything and so much more," he whispers, so only I can hear.

"Woohoo! Get it ZoZo! Kiss that girl! Show her who is in charge!" Gunnar shouts and claps his hands together behind us.

I turn to see Sara jumping up to stop his hands from clapping as he raises them above his head just out of her reach, and hollers louder now.

"Gunnar, stop! Leave them be! You're ruining the moment!" Sara whisper-shouts to him.

Duncan has a smirk plastered across his face and arms crossed over his chest. Jade just rolls her eyes and her fists clench at her sides. I still have no idea what I have done to make her so angry at me, but I will try to give her grace like Sara said.

I turn back to Enzo. "Why— why did you do that?"

"You were spiraling. I figured you needed a hard reset to turn that beautiful brain of yours off."

"Enzo, we can't. There is no 'us' here. We can never be together." I step away from him before he can say anything else. I walk up to my best friend, needing her comfort.

"Let's go," I say, grabbing her hand. "Where are the alicanto?"

"We decided to give them a break and graze for a while. Citrine isn't too far of a walk left anyways. It is just around this crystal formation. Come on, you can walk with me the rest of the way."

"I don't know what I would do without you, Sara, I hope you know that. I am sorry you can never be mated while being Soul Bonded to me. I'm sorry this burden fell on you, but I'm not sorry I have you in my life. I hope one day we can find a way to break our bond so you can be truly happy."

"Who said I wasn't truly happy now?" Sara gives me a shoulder bump and a wink.

I know she is trying to lighten the mood, but I've seen how she looks at Gunnar. I know she will never be able to be truly happy with him until I am out of the picture. If I could find someone to break the bond, I would. I know that I will never find a mate or accept the bond. I'm too broken for anyone to really love me. They might love the person I am on the outside, but once they realize what is on the inside— I can't face that rejection. I give Sara a side smile and start walking. It's time to find out how much of a nobody I really am.

Chapter 25

ALIYAH

As we round the crystal formation, which I thought was large to begin with, a giant, glittering, crystal palace stands before me. Its tall spires are pointed sharp at the top, and there are hundreds of them.

There is a long bridge that crosses over water that looks like pure aquamarine crystals with barely any ripples on the surface. The bridge is made of white- washed stone before ending at two ginormous doors made of pure crystal with hues of pink and pastel purple. The light cascading on the castle is almost ethereal. Behind the castle, crystal mountains go on for miles, protecting it from any who would wish it ill. In another life, I would have been honored to live in such a place.

"It's beautiful," I say, with a gasp to Sara. She smiles brightly next to me before tugging me along towards the front doors. They glimmer in the sunlight and I almost have to cover my eyes from how glorious the castle is.

"Come on! I want to show you something," Sara says.

My legs can barely carry me fast enough to keep up with her. Her stride is full of determination and excitement carries her faster than I can keep up with. Inside the front doors lay two grand staircases that line the walls to my right and left.

Straight ahead of me there is a corridor that opens up into what I assume are other hallways to parts of the castle. The steps are of shining purple crystal, and I am surprised I don't slip, as Sara pulls me up the right staircase.

"Seriously Sara, where are we going?" I yell, while laughing at her excitement.

I don't think I have seen her this excited since we stole that chocolate peanut butter cake back in Mareen. A smile graces my lips at the thought of times that seemed much simpler.

As we crest the top of the stairs, my breath catches in my throat. The entire second floor in front of me is wall- to- wall windows from floor to ceiling. The view from up here goes on for what seems like forever.

The sun is getting low at this point, causing the light to reflect off the castle and painting the sky above in colors I swear I have never seen before in my life. It's such a shame that no one lives here now. What a waste of a view. Maybe one day the castle will be restored and a new king and queen will take their place here.

"Aliyah!" Sara says with a grumble.

I hadn't realized she wasn't holding my hand any more. I turn to see her waving me down while she stands in front of a door on my right.

The hallway is filled with door after door, but it is the paintings on the wall that catch my eye. Depictions of great battles, men in full suits of armor, and fae running with their alicanto. As I walk through the hall I imagine that this must have been what Citrine was like before it was abandoned. A painting of a masked ball shows fae in different colored dresses dancing while smiles grace their face.

I slowly walk in front of a portrait of what I assume is the previous Queen Dione. I stand gawking at the beauty that was the queen. She is wearing a deep purple dress with sleeves of mesh cloth adorned with rhinestones that I swear still twinkle in the light.

She has long strawberry blonde hair and big grayish- blue eyes. They look like they hold such love and adoration for her kingdom. Like she was proud to be their queen. On her head sits a crown of rose gold with crystals the color of the sky ribbons during sunset. Her warm smile looks so familiar.

I shake my head and turn towards the door that Sara went through. As I turn to look over my shoulder, I swear the eyes of the queen are watching me. I slip through the door and find Sara waiting on the other side in a giant throne room.

"Jeez! You scared the crap out of me!" I jump.

"Sorry, I didn't mean to. Are you alright? You look like you've seen a ghost."

"Yeah, I'm fine. The painting in the hallway of the queen is— gorgeous."

"I know right. She was beautiful. I only had the pleasure of bowing before her a few times, but she wasn't just a queen, you know? She was a fierce warrior and enchantress. She fought in that last battle Gunnar went off to. Right before I left—" Sara trails off, her eyes still looking full of regret at the memory.

"How did she die?" I ask.

I start to move around the room, taking in each and every detail. In the entrance way of the room sits a large round table with multiple chairs and maps strewn about. Miniature pieces depicting warriors and ships are scattered over the maps. This must have been where they came up with battle strategies.

I run my finger across the giant table and note the collection of dust that has piled up on my finger. *What a shame, something so beautiful should never be discarded like this.*

As I look around the room, I spot two chairs that sit a few steps off the ground on a dais. One chair is made of tall pastel crystal clusters that jut towards the sky and the other is equal in height, but is made of darker shades of crystals.

This must have been for the queen and king. Behind the throne's are more floor length windows so you could look out across the vast mountains. I bet the view of the night sky is gorgeous in here.

"I honestly don't know what happened to her. After I left I never had contact with Olyrium again. If I could have contacted them, I would have told Gunnar twenty-six years ago why I had to leave him."

"She sacrificed herself."

Enzo's voice fills the space with power and ease, commanding our attention. It's no wonder he is a General now.

I hadn't heard him come in, I was so distracted gazing around the throne room. Sara excuses herself to go find Gunnar and shuts the door behind her. I walk up the few steps to the dais and run my hands over the crystals. I thought it would be cold to the touch, but it is surprisingly warm.

"What do you mean? Sacrificed herself how?" I say, turning to take a seat on the pastel colored throne.

Enzo stops dead in his tracks and stares at me with a strange look in his eye, but continues on with his explanation.

"I was there that day. When the queen sacrificed her life, and the life of her mate, to save everyone. I was just a soldier then, nothing more than another body on the battlefield. I saw what she did and that kind of sacrifice— that isn't the kind you can come back from. We all knew that Queen Dione was also an enchantress, but we didn't know it would cost her as much as it did. She was an incredible leader and she would never send her subjects into battle without being there to lead them herself. But she saw how many lives were being lost.

"She was the kind of queen who would rather lay down her own life than watch others die in her name. King Armas knew the risks of being mated to someone for that long and what it would do if she gave up her life. I had watched as he crossed the battlefield to get to her so in their last moments she wouldn't die alone. When she spoke the incantation to send The Kalari and their leader to that desolate island, it took everything left in her. Every drop of magic she had went into that spell."

"That's— horrifying. To love someone so deeply that your lives are literally tied together even to the point of death."

"It was a great honor for our king to die by his mate's side."

"I'm not sure anyone could ever love me that much," I mutter under my breath, as I look down at my feet.

"Aliyah." Enzo kneels before me on the throne. His hand cups my cheek and I instinctively lean into his touch.

"You will be loved far more than you can ever comprehend in this lifetime."

"How can you know that? My own mother didn't even want me. Why would anyone else?" A tear slips down my cheek and lands on the crystal throne.

"I just know," he says looking at me with what almost looks like love in his eyes.

My glassy eyes meet his as he gives me a soft smile before standing and grabbing my hand to lead me out of the throne room.

"Enzo." He stops walking and turns to me. "Please stop saying my name like that."

"Like what?"

"Like at the end of it all I'll still mean something to you."

Chapter 26

ENZO

How could she possibly believe anything otherwise? I wish I could tell her what she is doing to me, but I fear she would push me away further. But it was right there...it was right on my lips when she said no one could ever love her that much. So much that they would die for her. *I* would die for her. And I would find her again in the next life and prove to her in every lifetime that she is worthy of love greater than anything in this realm. My little dove is changing me. My heart feels like for the first time I could make room for love in my life. That voice in my head, telling me that no one would ever love me, has been quiet lately. In fact, ever since I found her. If I couldn't say that, I would just have to settle for showing her...for now.

"Can I show you something?" I ask, trying to bring some joy back into her eyes.

"I suppose," she sighs.

"Follow me, and don't say a word after we leave this room."

"Lead the way," she smiles softly.

I lead her from the throne room and back into the hall. We pass the endless wall of windows and into the hallway on the other side of the far staircase. I catch Aliyah turning her head to take everything in as we go. If only she could have seen this place in its prime. We turn down a hallway on the right with a dead end.

"Umm. You know there is nowhere to go from here right?" Aliyah giggles.

"Shhhh, I don't want the others following us."

I hear their voices carrying up the stairs asking each other where Aliyah and I could have gone off to. I know we are supposed to be in the library looking at the tome to find out who her parents are, but we are going to have to stay overnight in the castle anyways, so we might as well explore.

"When Jade, Gunnar and I were children visiting the castle on breaks from the academy, we would play hide and seek in these halls to pass the time. I was always found first because I was the weakest, as you are aware," I say, with a grumble on that last part. "We would play for hours, and in order to beat them, I had to get creative."

I knock on the wall a few times hoping that the tunnel is still intact. When I hear the hollow sound bounce back, I know I've found the right panel. I press in on the panel and it pushes back out with a click revealing a hidden tunnel behind it.

"Come on, it's in here. It's going to be dark, so hold my hand and stay close. It's a short walk."

"A short walk to where?" Aliyah's voice bounces off the walls echoing back at us as I pull the panel closed behind us, shrouding us in darkness.

"Somewhere with plenty of fun things to choose from."

Gunnar's voice is just outside the tunnel now. "They probably just snuck off to pretend like they aren't into each other again."

I quickly push Aliyah up against the tunnel wall and press my body into hers. I place my hand over her mouth, leaving just enough space for her to breathe out of her nose.

Her body is so close to mine and I can feel her pulse quicken with each passing moment. I stand with my leg between hers, so our bodies are as close as they could possibly be. Her chest heaves with each breath and I feel the rush of air coming out of her nose and onto my hand. The tunnel is completely black, so I can't see her, but I know her eyes are wide as saucers. I lean in so that my mouth is just a hair away from her ear.

"Does hiding away in here with me make you nervous, little dove?"

She says nothing because my hand is still covering her mouth, but I can't guarantee that she won't make a sound, so I keep my hand there.

I run my tongue over the shell of her ear and she trembles beneath my touch. I feel her shift, trying to put space between us. I nip at her ear and she jumps at the feeling.

"If I move my hand, will you promise to keep quiet?" I whisper.

She nods her head, and I slowly lower my hand, but I make no move to give her body space. A breath passes and then my lips are on hers. Our lips crash together in a tangle of teeth and tongue. Her mouth opens so easily for me and my hands instinctively go to her hair. Her hands clasp around my neck and she drops her weight onto my thigh, still between her legs.

I pull away from her and the sound of our heavy breaths fill the air around us, echoing off the walls.

She starts to protest, but I quickly cover her mouth again with my hand.

"I thought I told you to be quiet?"

I hear her mumble something under the palm of my hand. Given her tone, I know that she said something snarky back to me. I can almost hear the eye roll she surely gave me.

"As much as I would love to continue, I don't want them to be looking for us for too long."

I step back and drop my hand from her mouth. I take her hand and lead her deeper into the tunnel. She doesn't say a word the rest of the walk.

Chapter 27

ALIYAH

Hey! Where are you guys? I ignore the sound of Sara's voice in my head.

She knows I would reach out if I was in any sort of danger. I trust she could find me if she really needed to. Enzo holds my hand tight as we navigate through the tunnels. Even though we are far away from the entrance to the tunnel, my mind is still back at the entrance pressed up against those stones.

I had needed him. I needed Enzo in that moment and, yet again, he left me wanting more. This is the worst game I have ever played. Enzo turns one last corner.

"Here we are. Ready?" He asks.

I don't respond. I'm not sure if I am *allowed* to speak yet, so I just stand there.

"You can speak now, Aliyah. We are far enough away from the entrance that no one will hear you."

"Ready is a relative term. I could answer it better if you told me more specifically what we were doing down here."

"Where is the fun in that?" he says, as he pushes open a rock like door.

Before me is a large room made of solid stone, with multiple nails jutting out, holding up huge broadswords. Some that are almost as long as me. Enzo stands in the doorway as I walk into the middle of the room.

Lining the room are tables that hold quivers, arrows with long feathers attached to the ends, bows of various lengths and my favorite thing of all. An entire wall of throwing knives. There are at least twenty different sets of knives, all with differently designed hilts. Some have swirling designs, some have what looks like flames licking the handles, but the set that catches my eye are completely different from the rest. They have hilts that are made of red, yellow, and orange feathers, encased in a clear glass.

"Those are gorgeous! Who do they belong to?!" I squeal.

"This is an old weapons bunker from when Citrine had an active military. Now they just sit here, waiting to be used. If you like something, then it is yours."

"Really? The only throwing knives I have ever had were the ones that Sara and I found in the trash back in Mareen. They sucked for fighting, but they allowed us to practice well enough."

"Who taught you how to throw?"

"Sara did. When she first met me she offered to teach me some self defense. When I took her up on the offer, we slowly progressed to fighting with knives and eventually worked on throwing them. Mainly just at standing targets, not actual people."

"Probably a useful tool to use when someone is trying to kidnap you," Enzo winks at me.

I snicker back at him, and continue walking around the room, inspecting all the different designs on the hilts.

"Aliyah, are you angry at me for bringing you to Olyrium?"

"I was at first. Getting an ax buried in my chest wasn't exactly on my to do list that day." I smile back at Enzo running my hand over the necklace hanging around my neck.

"I'm sorry about that, Aliyah. I never intended for that to happen. When I took you from that village I had no intention of causing you more harm."

"Hey now," I say, walking back over to him. "No one ever tries to get someone they care about killed. Sometimes accidents just happen, but you made up for it by bringing me here and healing me. You could have left me in that field to die, but you didn't. Plus, that ax only brought us closer together in the end."

"I would *never* leave you behind, Aliyah." His hands come up to grasp my wrists. He tugs me in closer to him than before and drops his forehead to mine. His eyes shut as his head makes contact with mine and for a minute, it's peaceful. No trying to figure out where I came from, no feelings of being a nobody. Because in this moment, it feels like I really am everything to him.

So I let myself have this moment.

I run my fingers through his hair and behind his neck as I pull him down into a deep kiss. Our lips and tongues crash together in desperate need to release every bad thought running through our heads. His hands find the back of my thighs and he lifts me up. My legs instinctively wrap around his waist as he starts to walk.

My butt hits a table and he sets me on top of it. He stands between my legs, hands in my hair now and the push and pull of our bodies just feels right. His lips are plush and he smells like fresh rainfall. I don't want this moment to end, but I know I can't let it go too far either.

Despite what he may tell me, I want a better future for him than me. He deserves that much after all he has been through.

It's going to break me when I have to let him go in the end, but sometimes letting go means giving them the freedom they deserve. But for now...I'll just enjoy whatever time I have left with him.

As we exit the tunnels, my lips are still tingling from his kiss. I'll never forget that feeling. Enzo laces his fingers with mine as he closes the tunnel door and turns to head back to the main hall. A soft smile crosses his lips.

"Where the hell have you two been?" Jade rounds the corner and Enzo's smile drops immediately.

"None of your business, Jade," Enzo snaps.

"Hey, it's okay. He was just showing me some of the history of this place. It's beautiful, isn't it? Who knew crystal could be made into something so enormous and yet still feel like home somehow?" I smile at Jade.

She gives me a strange look, almost like she is wondering why I'm being nice to her. She doesn't deserve to be snapped at, even when she makes it really freaking hard to like her.

"Well, it's officially dark now which means we can't go back tonight. While you two were off gallivanting around the castle, we found rooms down the hall to sleep in for the night. Enzo, your room is next to mine and Aliyah, yours is at the far end of the hall on the right. Sara and Gunnar are across from Duncan, who of course wanted a room to himself. Dinner is ready in the kitchen. Thankfully I thought ahead and packed some extra things just in case. See you all in the morning." Jade turns to walk away.

"Jade! Hey, hold up a second." I turn towards Enzo and say in a whispered voice, "I'm gonna try and fix things with Jade. I'll see you in the morning, okay?"

I lean up on my tiptoes and press a quick kiss to his cheek before turning and running after Jade.

"Hey! I said wait up. I want to talk."

"About what?" Jade snaps.

"Look, I think we got off on the wrong foot. I'd like a chance to just talk. Would you like to grab some food from the kitchen and find a place to just sit, you and me?"

"I already ate."

"Oh okay, well maybe we can just talk then?"

"Fine. Meet me in the lounge room after you get your food."

She turns down another hallway on her left and disappears into a room. I count the doors slowly in my head and remember the room she went into. Third door on the right. Got it. Okay, now to find the kitchen.

After stopping at my room to make sure I knew where it was, I make my way down the staircase on the left and walk through the entry way towards the back of the castle. I am still reeling at everything around me. I walk down one hall on my right, but find no kitchen. Most of the rooms are empty or with white sheets covering the furniture. As I make my way back down the other hallway, I hear the sound of dishes clanging together. Following the sound, I find Enzo standing in the kitchen plating some food for himself.

"Anything good?" I ask.

Enzo turns around and has a mouth covered in white powder. "Aliyah, I didn't expect you to be here. I thought you were with Jade?"

I can't contain my laugher as Enzo holds a jelly filled pastry in his hand and white powder dropping onto the floor collecting with the dust. "You know, for someone as strong and scary as you, the white powdered lips really take away from your whole warrior vibe."

Enzo quickly takes the back of his hand and wipes off his lips. Setting the pastry down, he leans against the counter and crosses his arms. A smirk develops on his face.

"I'll have you know that many warriors still enjoy pastries. We are only fae after all." Enzo can't contain his smile even though he is trying so hard to be serious.

"I'm just surprised you allow your self such delicacies," I wink at him.

"Oh, little dove, I indulge in several fine delicacies. Though I'm finding I am having a hard time trying to stave off certain cravings for the things I really want."

I feel my cheeks flush and my ears grow hot at his confession. Not wanting him to have the upper hand, I walk over to him with confidence. I know the dangerous game I am playing, but somehow I just can't help myself.

"You missed a spot," I say, taking my finger and brushing some of the powder off his face and onto my finger. I stare into his eyes as I place my finger in my mouth. As I swirl my tongue around my finger, I hallow out my cheeks as I suck the remnants off.

Enzo's demeanor snaps in two as he closes the distance between us. His mouth finds mine in an instant and I can still taste the sweet jelly on his lips. Enzo picks me up and walks me over to the island in the middle of the kitchen. Before he sets me down food flies off the table, discarded and forgotten. Enzo's lips never leave mine as he lays me back on the table. My hands caress over his muscles bulging as he holds himself up over me.

He breaks our kiss only to say, "You are both the best, and the worst, craving I have ever had. Though I feel, no matter how hard I try, I will never be satisfied."

He plants kisses down my neck and my leg curls around his placed between mine. I need him closer. Suddenly our clothes are putting too much distance between us. I need to feel his skin on mine. I scramble to pull his tunic over his head. He shifts his arms with ease to pull it off the rest of the way. I didn't remember feeling them before, but as I take in his chest, he is marked with several scars. I let my fingers run over them as his eyelids hood and his breathing becomes erratic.

"Aliyah," he groans.

My eyes meet his again and when they do, he moves to pull my tunic over my head.

"Stop."

Enzo immediately ceases his plans and moves to get off the table.

"I'm sorry. I'm just not—"

"There is no need to explain. If you don't want to do this with me, I understand."

"It isn't that," I say looking down. "I just— I have never had sex with someone by choice. That decision was taken from me and I'm just not sure when I will be ready to try again."

As I lift my gaze to him, fury burns in his eyes. "Aliyah—"

"Please don't be mad. I promise it isn't you. I don't mean to make you upset, I just can't get the feeling of what happened to me out of my head. Every time I think about going further, I start to panic."

The anger immediately fades from his eyes and concern replaces it. "Aliyah, little dove, I am not mad at you. I am sorry if that was the impression you saw. I am mad that the decision was taken from you. No one should have their decisions stripped away. Is this man still back in Luar?"

"He was, but he got what he deserved in the end."

"Good," Enzo visibly relaxes. "I will take whatever you want to give me. We go at your pace."

"Thank you. I wish I could get there one day with you, Enzo. I just don't think— I should go find Jade. I am sure she is waiting for me."

"Even though she doesn't act like it, Jade needs someone like you in her life. She will come around."

"I hope so," I say jumping off the counter. "Thank you, Enzo. It means more to me than you know."

I give him a soft smile and walk over to him. Running a hand down his chest, I feel the raised flesh there. His chest rises and falls slowly under my touch. "One day, I'd like to hear about how you got these."

"One day, I'll tell you everything you want to know." Enzo smiles down at me and I shift onto my toes to plant a kiss on his cheek. I let my hand linger on his jaw as he turns his head to kiss my palm.

As I walk out of the kitchen, part of me feels regret for starting something with Enzo that I couldn't finish, but the other part of me feels comfort knowing that I have the time I need. Cyrus has haunted the corners of my mind, planting doubt that I would ever find a male who is patient and kind.

Enzo is not Cyrus. I need to stop letting a male from my past control my future. I stop in the hallway and turn on my heel back to the kitchen. I stride in with a new sense of determination to take back control of my life. I'm tired of letting Cyrus continue to chain me to that post, even in death. With Enzo, I finally feel free.

"Enzo," I say walking into the kitchen. He turns just as he is pulling his tunic back on.

"Aliyah, I thought you were going to find—"

I run over and leap into his arms, knowing that he will catch me. I wrap my legs around his torso and my arms around his neck and give him a deep and passionate kiss. His hands find my thighs to hold me up and a groan ripples up from his throat. When I pull back and open my eyes, there he is just staring back at me.

"I don't want anyone to have control over my choices ever again. I can't know what is in our future, but if there ever comes a time when our fates are sealed together forever, I know I will be ready for that next step with you." I give him the biggest smile I can and wink as I jump down from his arms. This time when I leave the kitchen I feel empowered, and for the first time, I feel in control.

Chapter 28

ENZO

"And where were you for so long?" Gunnar says, as I enter his room.

"Where is Saraphena?" I ask.

"Washroom, why? What's up?"

I run my hands down my face and can't help but let the smile pull at my lips.

"I don't know what she is doing to me, but I'm afraid I might be falling in love with her."

Gunnar gets up and walks over to a large table in the room and pulls a water sack out of his bag. But as he pours it into two glasses, an amber colored drink pours out instead.

"Leave it to you to bring alcohol on this trip," I laugh.

"Someone has to bring the fun to this group. Between Duncan's general personality, Jade's clear hatred for Aliyah, and your somber vibe, it's a rather depressing group." He laughs, turning back to come sit on the couch that is placed in front of the huge fire.

"Gunnar, how did you tell Saraphena that you loved her for the first time? Like how did you know that she felt the same way about you?"

"Enzo, it's me. Of course she was going to love me back." He smirks at me, and takes a sip from his drink.

"Gunnar shut the hell up. Give me a serious answer."

"You're right. I'm sorry. She just had this— look. That's when I knew."

"This has been wildly unhelpful." I go to stand and leave.

I knew I never should have gone to Gunnar. In love or not, he can't answer anything with helpful information. Bless Saraphena's heart as to how she finds the patience to put up with his crap. As the door shuts behind me I hear Gunnar yell for me to stop, but I'm already gone.

I knock on the door across the hall, hoping for some helpful answers. Duncan's face fills the doorway as he cracks open the door. He is in nothing but his sleep pants.

"Can I come in and talk to you?"

"No. I'm sleeping." Duncan's eyes are still blinking away the sleep that fills them.

"Duncan, you're literally standing right in front of me, clearly not sleeping. I'm coming in. I need your advice."

"With Aliyah?"

"What? No! Why would you immediately assume it is about Aliyah?" I say a little more defensively than intended.

"Enzo. How do I say this?" He thinks for a moment. "You kiss her in the field. I see you staring at her when she isn't looking. You brought her here in the first place when you swore you'd never come back to this castle after it was abandoned, and then you disappear for over an hour, most likely in the tunnels. So you tell me. How did I guess it was about Aliyah?'

"Fair point. I'm coming in." I push the door open with my hand and storm into the room. Duncan just chuckles to himself and shakes his head.

"So, what can I help you with?" he asks.

I know this is a risky topic for Duncan. We have never asked him about his love life before. Mainly because every time we try he just shuts us down. After what he told me on the way here, I get why. I honestly don't think I have seen him even touch another woman.

"Your first love—" I start.

"Get out." Duncan's face is stern. His arms cross over his chest and he walks towards the door to open it.

"All I am going to say is this," he starts. "Is she worth it? Is Aliyah worth the feeling of dying inside every time you think of being without her? Is she worth feeling like you can't take your next breath without her? Ask yourself those questions first before you even think about opening your heart to her. Now get. Out."

I go to leave his room but stop in the doorway.

"Duncan," I say turning around. "What if I tell her how I feel and she doesn't feel the same way?"

"I can't tell you that, brother. Only you can truly answer if she is worth taking that risk."

In his own way, this was the most helpful conversation of the night. There is no way I am asking Jade for her advice on this, so I will just have to settle for Duncan's response. I exit the room without a word and the door slams shut behind me. Standing in the hall, I find myself thinking over Duncan's words. As I enter the washroom in my room, I strip myself of my dirty clothes, wash them in the basin and lay them out to dry. Those questions repeat themselves in my head over and over. As I ready myself for bed and try to get comfortable for the night, the answer to those questions settles into my chest with ease.

Absolutely. Aliyah is worth *everything*.

Chapter 29

ALIYAH

I think Jade is screwing with me. I counted the doors right. I know it. Yet she was not in the room that she originally went into. When I went into the room it was completely empty and dark. There wasn't even any furniture in there.

It was hard enough finding the kitchen on my own, but now I can't seem to find my way back. I retrace my steps and get back to the main hallways. I turn down the one I know she said were where our rooms are for the night. Maybe she went back to her room? I knock once. Twice. Three times. No answer.

This son of a— Sara comes out of her room and spots me in the hall.

"You okay? What are you doing outside Jade's room?"

"That witch told me the wrong room. I'm just trying to patch things up with her seeing as she freaking hates me right now." I fling my arms up in the air in frustration.

"I don't want to hate you, but it's easier than liking you." Jade's voice fills the space and Sara ducks her head back in her room.

Sara, you coward!

Love you! Her sing-song voice is followed by a soft laugh.

"Jade, I didn't mean to say that. I just thought you gave me the wrong room."

She stands there holding two glasses, and a bottle of what looks like wine. Great, now I feel like even more of an idiot.

"I didn't tell you the wrong room. The room you saw me go into has a tunnel that is a faster route to the wine cellar. I figured we could drink and talk. You haven't had wine until you have had fae wine."

"Jade, I'm so sorry. Okay let's just start over again. Here, let me help you with that. You lead the way." I go to grab the wine from her hands, but she stops me.

"I don't need anyone's help. I've got it. Let's just sit in my room."

She pushes open the door and steps inside, motioning for me to follow. She climbs into her big bed and places both glasses down on the side table. She pours two glasses while I look around the room.

It has a beautiful white stone fireplace that has a roaring fire burning. The mantle is filled with beautiful crystals and before the fireplace sits two huge plush chairs that look softer than anything I have touched before. I run my hand over the fabric and I was completely right.

I take in Jade's huge four- poster bed. It has a black frame and gold silk sheets with a comforter made of fur. I don't know how she plans to not just slip right out of bed with all that silk. Also, how did she find such clean things in an abandoned castle?

Jade hands me a glass of the wine and I take a sip. Notes of strawberry and blackberry slip over my tongue with an explosion of bubbles that follow. It is one of the best things I have ever tasted.

"This tastes amazing! Thank you. So listen, I know that Enzo bringing me here was not what you wanted. I think Enzo bringing me to Olyrium at all was not what you wanted. But why do you hate me so much?"

"I don't hate you— I mean, I do, but not for the way you think." Jade huffs out a sigh before continuing.

"You make Enzo happy. Happy in a way I have never seen him. Happy in a way *I* could never make him. But they are my family. They are *all* I have left."

So she did have feelings for Enzo. I want to ask her about their relationship, but clearly it is a sore spot.

"Jade, I am so sorry. I didn't know you had feelings for Enzo. I don't mean to threaten your relationship with any of them. I never wanted to come here though— it wasn't exactly my choice."

"I know that, but if anything that makes it worse, because Enzo *chose* you. We went into that village to protect the humans, to protect everyone, and yet, when we left, he refused to leave without you. Even when you were lying half dead in that field with an ax sticking out of your chest, he refused to leave you. I had my chance to be with Enzo, and he didn't choose me back."

I place a hand over my scar instinctively at the thought. She continues her story.

"Our whole lives we were trained to look at who was worth rescuing and who wasn't. You were basically *dead* Aliyah. What made you so worthy of saving?" Jade stares at me with tears brimming in her eyes.

"Nothing. Literally nothing. I am nobody, Jade. I have no worth in this life, or any life after this. I have no clue why Enzo thought I was worth saving. But I am here now and I can't change that fact."

"I know. And I'm trying to adjust. My parents made choices that marked me for death." I think back to Sara's words about how her parents betrayed their kingdom. "They didn't want me, you know? I was worth less than nothing to them. They especially never wanted a girl. My father always wanted a son to groom in his image. Imagine his surprise when out popped a girl instead. I was always his greatest disappointment. No matter how many times I proved to be the perfect strategist following in his footsteps, I always fell short. When they betrayed our kingdom, they didn't think twice about how that would affect my life."

I stare back at Jade as tears drip into her wine cup.

"I am so happy you found this family, Jade. Enzo and I can't be together in the future, anyways. He will go on to do great things. And I will find this book in the library tomorrow and confirm what I already know. In Olyrium and Luar, I am nothing more than an orphan. Enzo can't be with someone like me."

"Aliyah, regardless of what we find tomorrow, you will still be everything to him. I want us to be on good terms, I really do. But you need to understand one thing. If you hurt him, I will not hesitate to put a blade in your chest. If you break up this family so help me—"

"I won't. I will do everything in my power to not break up this family. I promise." I walk over to where she sits on the bed and hold out my pinky to her.

"What the hell are you doing?" She looks at me quizzically.

"It's a pinky promise. An unbreakable seal that I take *very* seriously," I laugh.

"Does it have magic that makes it binding?" She gets more and more skeptical.

"No, Jade, there is no magic. It's just fun."

"I don't like it. I don't want any bonds with you. Just don't hurt Enzo, okay?"

She stands to grab the empty wine bottle. *Jeez this girl is making it really hard to like her.*

"Fine," I say dropping my hand. "So, where is this wine cellar? Looks like we are going to need a lot more wine to work through this."

Five bottles of wine later, and many, many steps to the roof, Jade and I are on one of the tallest rooftops of the whole castle. I am standing at the edge, overlooking the mountains. I am way drunker than I thought I would be, or frankly even should be, but I am having the time of my life.

"I'm on top of the world!" I scream out into the distance.

My wine sloshes over the side of my glass and dumps into the air below. *Dang, that's a long drop.* I step back a few steps and plop down next to Jade. I fling my arm around her shoulders and lean my head down on her shoulder. She drops her head on top of mine and sighs.

"You're right. I think we just needed to put our past behind us and move forward. I need to stop thinking of it like you are taking Enzo away, but maybe I'm gaining the sister I never had," she says to me while smiling.

"Seeeeeee. I totally knew we were gonna be besties the whole time. I just had to get past your terrible personality!"

"I'm going to act like you didn't just say that and chalk it up to the wine."

We stare out into the starlit sky taking in the ribbons of color. Jade and I talk for hours after that about our life, our trauma, and what we wished our lives could have been. We watch the sun come up together and the stars fade, along with my drunken haze.

"Are you ready to go in?" Jade asks.

"Can't we sit here just a little longer? I'm not sure I'm ready to find out who my parents are just yet. Let's just pretend a little longer."

"I am sure that Enzo is already tearing apart the castle looking for you. Let's get going so we can get back home."

Home. Is that was this place was now? I have never known what home feels like, so I have nothing to compare it to, but I think I'm starting to understand.

Chapter 30

ALIYAH

I'm nervous. I say to Sara through our bond.

Don't be, she says, grabbing my hand.

We stand outside the library doors. Everyone else is inside, but I wanted to bathe and try to look presentable after last night. I thought the hangover would be worse, but honestly, I feel okay this morning.

I feel some relief knowing that Jade and I are in good standing with each other now. She asked me not to hurt Enzo, and I intend to keep my promise to her to the best of my ability. No matter what happens here today though, I hope Enzo will stop looking at me like I am everything to him. I want to be so badly, and I know that he has told me differently, but Enzo has lived, for what I assume, has been a few hundred years, and will most likely live a few hundred more. Plenty of time for him to forget all about me. I know it isn't fair to him, but maybe I can keep him just a little longer. The feeling of disappointment pangs in my chest knowing that our stolen moments in the shadows will have to end at some point.

Until that day comes, I'm going to make the most out of the time we have left together. One day, duty will call him away, or he will find a woman of higher station that will give him a family of his own. I want to tell him how I feel, how I truly feel, even if it kills me in the end.

Enzo deserves to be loved. I don't have much to offer him other than a cracked heart and a body scarred beyond repair. But maybe, just maybe, that would be enough for him. I can't ask him to give up his station, but maybe he would be open to keeping me around until another opportunity arises.

Sara pushes open the library doors and gives me a reassuring look. As we walk hand in hand into the library, we see the others lounging on some chairs in the far corner. Enzo rises when he sees me coming in and walks over towards me.

"I've got her from here, Saraphena. Thank you," Enzo says, taking my hand in his.

Sara walks over to where Gunnar sits and hops into his lap, giving him a kiss on the cheek, before taking a book from the side table and opening it up to read with him. Jade gives me a soft nod paired with a smile that I somehow feel I don't deserve, but accept anyways. Duncan, as always, is just sitting there staring into the roaring fire, expressionless.

The library is by far the biggest one I have ever seen. As much as I love reading, there weren't many books, if any, back in Mareen. When it came to stealing things, the choice between food or books was pretty clear.

The walls of the library are filled with every book imaginable. Shelf after shelf that create a giant maze throughout the room. One could easily get lost in here for hours and never be heard from again. On either side of the fireplace, from floor to ceiling, is just books. The tallest shelf is at least four stories high. There are vines that stretch around the shelves with crystal flowers growing out of them, preserving the flowers forever in full bloom. I think I would be okay getting lost in here forever.

Enzo leads me through the stacks and over to a stand with the realms largest possible book sitting on top of it. We are out of sight from the others, so I take the opportunity to speak with Enzo.

"Enzo, wait," I start. He looks at me with his head slightly tipped to the side in question.

"What's wrong?"

"Look, I have no idea what I am going to find in this book. A few days ago my entire life was completely flipped upside down. I found out I was never really human at all. I had an ax buried in my chest. I have a Soul Guardian that I am lucky enough is my best friend. And—and I know we don't have a lot of time left together before things change between us, but I'd like to stay with you for as long as you allow me to."

I look down at my feet, afraid to see his face. Silence. I am met with complete silence.

"And, look, I know that you are going to go on and do amazing things that probably require some fancy princess to be by your side, leading armies, or whatever it is that you do when you're not spending time with a low life like me. But I just thought that maybe you could settle for someone like me for the time being. I know I'm not a princess or anything, but—"

"Aliyah, if you chose to spend forever with me, I would never want for anything again," Enzo says. He lifts my chin and places a soft kiss on my lips. My body melts at his touch and my heart sings like a thousand choruses. "No matter what we find in here, it will not change a single thing about what I feel for you."

"Is it bad if I don't want to learn about my lineage now?" I ask, smiling softly. "What if knowing is worse than not knowing?"

"If I have learned anything in the last few moments, it's that knowing is far better than not knowing," Enzo smiles.

"Okay. Let's do this." I turn to the book and Enzo steps up behind me wrapping his arms around my waist and places his chin on my shoulder, looking over the book.

"What exactly am I looking for? This book is huge. It will take me hours to go through it all."

"It's enchanted, little dove. Open the book and place your palm on the blank page. It will sense who you are and find your lineage for you. Just trust the pages."

I do as he says and crack open the book to a blank page in the middle. I place my palm on the page and wait. Nothing happens. No tingles, no bright, blinding light. Not even a single drop of ink appears on the page.

"I don't understand."

"Huh? That's weird. Maybe the book hasn't been used in so long that it just needs an extra moment." Enzo's eyebrow kicks up in question.

Suddenly the book bursts into flames before me. I jump back as heat flares beneath my palm, just in time before fire engulfs the entire book completely turning it to ash.

Chapter 31

ENZO

"What the hell is going on back there?" Saraphena yells, turning the corner to find Aliyah and I completely dumbfounded at what just happened.

Footsteps come crashing around the corner as everyone files in between the shelves to see. They all just stare at the pile of ash before us.

"I— I don't know what I did?" Aliyah says.

"It isn't your fault. It must have been spelled or something to destroy itself, but why?" I add.

"Are you alright?" Jade comes up next to her and places a hand on her shoulder, just as the first tear slips off Aliyah's chin.

"Why is it that for every step closer I get to finding out who my family is, I end up taking ten steps back?" Aliyah turns, as Jade pulls her into a hug.

I glance over at Duncan and Gunnar who both have wide eyes at the sight of Jade hugging Aliyah. She sobs quietly on her shoulder, and I give a shrug before turning back to them.

"Look, we will figure it out. Maybe the book only works for someone who is High Fae? There are two other kingdoms we can visit to try and see if anyone knows who your parents are. Maybe you aren't even from Krystal Kingdom! You do have golden blonde hair— maybe you are from SunSpark. After all, that is where Saraphena and Gunnar are from," I say, oddly optimistically.

"Exactly! The whole reason I was even in Citrine was to spend time with Gunnar before he left. Maybe that woman was doing the same!" Saraphena has a soft smile on her face as she looks at Gunnar.

"I don't know. Maybe this is a sign that we should just leave it be. Maybe I'm not meant to find out. Let's just go home and forget about all of this." Aliyah looks defeated as she talks.

"Gunnar," I turn to my friend. "How would your family feel about a visit? It certainly has been a while."

Gunnar groans. "They would be thrilled, unfortunately. Liliana would die to meet Aliyah and see Saraphena again. She has been writing to me for some time now about coming home to visit. I guess now is as good a time as any."

"Who is Liliana?" Aliyah asks.

"Lil is my younger sister. I'll tell you all about her on the way," Gunnar says, smiling at her.

"Look I appreciate everything you all are doing for me, but honestly I don't see what would help me in SunSpark."

"Well it's funny you should ask, Ali," Saraphena perks up. "Each kingdom was blessed with an item to help aid their people. In Krystal, it was the enchanted book of lineage, which is now burnt to a crisp. Hopefully it wasn't that important."

Duncan continues, "Twilight Kingdom is said to have a piece from a shooting star that fell from the sky and can grant wishes. Last I knew, it hadn't been seen in ages. So I wouldn't rely on that helping us."

"SunSpark has the Reflecting Pool. Technically, only a High Fae can use it, but I am sure that we can convince the king and queen to let you use it. All you have to do is float in the waters and it shows you a glimpse of either your past or future. It is a finicky thing, but can be useful in situations like this. It might not show you your past, but it is worth a shot, I think," Gunnar says.

"Well, what are we waiting for? Let's get moving. Nothing like taking a child of Twilight and going to the brightest freaking place in all the realms," Duncan grumbles.

We all laugh as we move to exit the library. As we all begin walking, I notice that Aliyah has stopped and is staring at something in the far corner of the library. I follow her line of sight to where a light is beaming through some of the shelves.

"What's over there?" she asks.

"The queen's sword, but to be honest I have never seen it glow like that."

As we round the corner, the sword beams bright light between all the shelves. Aliyah walks up to it and runs her hand over the gold stand. The light immediately fades, but a hum of magic lingers in the air.

The sword points down, hovering over a gold stand with crystallized grass growing beneath it. It is made entirely of clear crystal with a gold hilt, inlaid with turquoise gems, and floral engravings. The hilt points towards the ceiling, and the iridescent bubble around the sword ripples as Aliyah reaches her hand out to touch the sword.

"You won't be able to—" I'm cut off by my own astonishment as Aliyah lays her hand on the flat of the sword.

"No one has been able to touch that sword since it showed up here after the battle."

"What do you mean it showed up here?"

"Honestly, we really don't know. After the queen sacrificed herself, it just disappeared from the battlefield, and when we returned here afterwards, there it was. But that bubble around it has never been penetrated before. Can you remove the sword?"

Aliyah goes to wrap her hand around the hilt, but when she pulls, nothing happens. It stays in place and the bubble snaps back again as she removes her hand.

"Why can't I remove it?"

"I wouldn't take it personally. Many have tried and all have failed. I think it is really only meant for the queen, so it will forever be preserved here for an owner that will never come back."

"Well, that's probably for the best. That sword is huge, and I have never practiced with one, so I would probably just end up hurting myself in the process," Aliyah laughs. I swear I will never get sick of that sound.

I take a step towards her and move her to face me. I run my palm over her chin and she turns her head into my hand to place a kiss on my palm.

"Thank you for not giving up on me," she whispers.

"I know things are new between us, but from the very start I knew I didn't want to live in a world without you. So it is I who should be thanking *you*."

"Will you tell me more about the SunSpark Kingdom on the way? I don't want to look like a fool in front of anyone."

"Of course. It is about a three day ride to The Bridge to SunSpark, so we will have plenty of time to talk, and maybe even train a little. I can teach you how to wield a sword, if you're interested?"

"It's a deal. But can we use the throwing knives at some point too? I'm afraid I'm getting a little rusty. And I'll never hear the end of it from Sara if I lose all my training while we gallivant around looking for my family," she laughed.

"That first time we met, you put up quite the fight. I don't think a few days off and an ax to the chest is going to slow you down."

"Dang right!" she beams. "Come on, we have to find the others before they leave without us."

"They wouldn't dare."

Chapter 32

ALIYAH

As we find our way out of Citrine, Jade has already rounded up the alicanto for our journey. They look well rested and ready for the trip, but I'm not sure I'm ready. I feel like we are chasing a lost dream.

So much of me hopes that I am back in Mareen and all this was some nightmare and I'll wake up on our bed, back torn to shreds, cursing myself for waking up.

Enzo gives my hand one last squeeze before walking towards Ruby. The alicanto and I have an understanding since meeting each other— I won't go near her and she won't go near me. I'll wear her down though, I just know it.

I smile to myself at the thought. Who knew an overgrown bird could be so protective of its rider?

I walk over to Mirage and scratch the feathers behind her wing. She ruffles in response, turning her head to push into my chest right over my scar.

As I run my hands under her feathers, I feel some raised flesh in long strips. *How did I not notice these before?* I move to lift her wing to get a better look, and she pulls away slightly from my touch.

"I guess you're a little broken too, huh girl?" I whisper. "That's okay. We can work on healing together."

"Ready to go?" Duncan asks, mounting Onyx.

"All set," I say, hopping on Mirage. The rest of the group starts off heading south, but I stop and take one last look at the glittering crystal palace before me. I feel a pang of sadness as I look back at the landscape. Something pinches in my chest.

I'll be back, don't you worry.

Great— now I'm talking to a castle. I roll my eyes and give Mirage a little kick, trying not to be harsh now that I know she has those scars. She takes off running towards the others who are almost out of sight now, but standing right across the bridge are Ruby and Enzo.

Out of nowhere, tears start to brim in my eyes and I'm not even sure why I am crying. I quickly wipe them away before Enzo can see.

Of course he notices anyway. "You alright?"

"Yeah, just the wind. I'm not used to being on something so fast. She is making my eyes water. I'll race you!" I say, whizzing by him at full speed.

Ruby takes off, immediately passing by us, but Mirage only takes it as a challenge and picks up her speed. Before I know it, my tears are gone, and my laughter flows in the wind behind me as I leave one home behind in search of another.

Hope flares in my chest at the possibilities that wait for me across the SunSpark border. But hope is a dangerous thing.

Please let me find what I am looking for.

We stop to rest just as the sun is setting.

"We are done for the night everyone," Jade calls back.

She seems to be the unassigned leader in this group, because she has been making all the calls about which direction to take, when to stop, and even when to eat. I swear she is going to remind us to freaking blink one of these times. I try really hard not to get annoyed, especially because we are on such good terms.

"Let's set up the tents before nightfall and, if you're feeling up to it, we can train. We can show you what we've got, and you can show us what Sara has been teaching you. If memory serves, she is a pretty decent fighter," Gunnar smirks at me.

"*Pretty decent?* That's it? I put you on your back more times than I can count!" Sara shoves him in the shoulder with a huge smile on her face.

"Baby, you can put me on my back as many times as you wish," he winks back at her.

"Oh shut up. You know what I mean!"

"I don't know," Gunnar says in a sing- song tone. "You may have gotten a little rusty all those years in Luar training with mere humans."

"Then let's go! I'll even sweeten the deal for you! Whoever can put their tent up the fastest gets to throw the first punch!" Sara yells.

Duncan and Jade are already setting up their canvas tents and attached rods, rolling their eyes as they listen to Gunnar and Sara bicker back and forth.

"Do you need help with that? The rods can be tricky." Enzo walks over to me with a soft smile on his face. "Or, you can always share with me, you know, since we don't want to waste any more time setting up camp when we could be training."

"Oh, so just because I might be slightly slower at putting up a tent, I automatically I have the *privilege* of sleeping in your tent? No thanks, I'd rather share with Mirage than share with you," I wink at him.

As I unroll the canvas tent and attach the rods together, I get set up before Enzo even has a chance to finish his own. He doesn't know it, but I know the fact that he was staring at my butt whenever I bent over slowed him down significantly. Since he is so easily distracted, it should be a breeze beating him in training later.

Gunnar finishes after Sara and makes a joke about how she needs all the help she can get after twenty-six years away from him, but I think that just makes Sara even more mad.

"Alright, Aliyah, since this is your first time fighting in Olyruim, I figure you should probably know what you are up against— just in case we run into any trouble along the way," Gunnar smiles at me before taking his stance.

"And exactly what kind of trouble would I run into? I haven't seen anything out here except us."

"Sara, you didn't tell her?" Jade questions, with somewhat of a stern look on her face.

Sara doesn't back down easily though. "No, I didn't. She wasn't ready to hear it and, frankly, I didn't think it was a problem until the day you all showed up. There had been no reports and no suspicion in Luar they were even outside the barrier until that day."

"You should have told her the moment you arrived in Olyrium. I know it has been quiet in Krystal, but who's to say that will continue?" Jade is practically yelling now, as she approaches Sara.

"Why didn't you all tell her? You all were more danger to her than anything else out there! Five minutes with this group and she got a freaking ax to the chest! Plus, even if I had told her, the humans had no clue the fae even existed so she would have looked like a crazy person if anyone ever overheard us!"

"Enough!" I yell, and step between them, pushing them back with my arms.

I glance over at Enzo and see his face visibly hurt at the reminder that I was with him when that ax hit me.

"Tell me about what? Is this about The Kalari? We talked about it briefly at the house in Korin, but it got overshadowed by finding out you were fae this whole time. Why don't the humans know fae exist? Maybe if they did we could all work together."

We all take a seat, putting the training on hold for now.

"There have been reports that The Kalari have been breaking out of the Banished Kingdom through tears in the barrier," Jade starts. "We don't know how, but the day before the attack on your village, there were reports of multiple tears that just appeared in the barrier wall. We have a few reliable soldiers from the SunSpark Flying Legion who still patrol the barrier, along with occasional passes over Luar."

"Unlike in Krystal, SunSpark have sphinx as their matched. The soldiers use them to fly around the barrier a few times a day to make sure it is still intact. In months prior, there had been maybe one or two holes open up at a time, but this day, for some reason, was worse than normal. We have no clue what caused it. As for why the humans don't know we exist, they did, once. But the humans posed too much of a risk to Citrine. They had lost enough in the war fighting with fae against the Banished King. It was just easier this way," Gunnar finishes.

Apparently I wasn't the only thing getting torn up that day before I left Mareen forever. I shutter at the irony.

"So why haven't we heard about any more attacks?" I ask.

"We haven't received any reports of new tears since that day. The Bridge to the Banished Kingdom was broken years ago, and the only pillar to their island is located in Twilight Kingdom. You can only use The Bridge closest to the kingdom you wish to go. There haven't been reports from SunSpark or Twilight that they have seen any of The Kalari fleeing anywhere on ships. It is like they just vanished," Duncan adds.

"Look right now there are no signs of trouble. We should take that opportunity and train while we can. Aliyah we need to see what skills you have gained during your time in Luar, and the rest of us need to stay sharp. The SunSpark Kingdom may be my home, but that doesn't mean there aren't enemies of the throne there. While the people of Krystal want to keep the Citrine City throne empty until an heir can be appointed, or one magically appears, that doesn't mean the other kingdom's agree. We need to be ready for anything. That is why we train. That is why we fight. For the *future* of the Krystal Kingdom," Gunnar says standing and pulling Sara up with him.

"Enough talk of war. Right now let's just fight. Gunnar, show her what you got," Sara winks.

Chapter 33

ALIYAH

Gunnar takes his stance in the makeshift ring we created by moving some crystals around. The sun is setting behind us, casting that gorgeous ribbon of color into the sky illuminating our session.

The alicanto have wandered off to graze so we just enjoy our time in the setting sun, with a warm breeze blowing my hair back as I watch Gunnar and Sara move in a dance of aggression and passion. They move so fluidly together; she throws a punch and he ducks. He moves to sweep her legs and she easily evades before planting a swift kick to his chest. As Gunnar falls, his palms light up with flames and he hurdles a ball of fire directly at Sara.

"Sara!" I yell, and jump up— right as she dodges the flame. I stand there with a look of complete shock on my face. My jaw is hung open and Sara freaking *smirks* at me.

"You have *powers*?!" I spin around to face Enzo.

"Just keep watching, little dove," he smiles up at me.

Keep your eyes on me. Sara's voice fills my head.

Then suddenly she just disappears. A gasp leaves my lips as I look around and she has completely vanished.

"Oh my Maker," I whisper under my breath.

Where did you go?

Suddenly, Gunnar goes flying forward with a grunt, flames snuffing out as his palms hit the dirt. Sara reappears out of thin air, a smile on her face, and glances over at me.

"Pretty cool right?" Sara says.

Gunnar takes this opening to kick out the back of her knee making her fall next to him laughing as he pins her on her back.

"Gotcha!" he exclaims.

"Yeah, yeah. You got me, but to be fair I didn't pull my blades which you *know* are my best weapon. I wanted to give you a fighting chance," she laughs, and her eyes shine looking up at him. He leans down and presses a kiss to her nose before getting up and reaching his hand down to help her up.

"Alright, who's next?" he says.

"Jade, care to let me have another chance at beating you?" Duncan asks.

"Fine, but let it be known that you are going to lose, like always," she says, standing up and taking her place in the ring.

I sit down in between Enzo's legs and he wraps his arms around my waist, laying my back on his chest. The sun is set now and the night sky is filled with a huge, full moon, giving us plenty of light to keep going. Gunnar gathers a few medium size red crystals and places them in a small pile in front of us before placing his fire- lit palm on the pile. It bursts into flames and stays lit as he pulls his hand away, leaving a fire burning in front of us.

"Fire crystals," he says plainly, before sitting down next to Sara. As Jade stretches for a few moments, Sara leans over and whispers to me.

"How awesome was that? I haven't been able to use my powers in years and it feels so good to stretch those muscles again."

"Why was that literally not the *first* thing you told me when we got here?! That was amazing! I wonder if I have any powers!" I whisper back.

"I guess we will find out soon," she says before turning her gaze back to Jade and Duncan.

"Don't embarrass yourself too much, Duncan," Enzo calls.

Duncan ignores him and throws his first punch towards Jade's head. She blocks it easily and lands two hits on his exposed ribs. Duncan grunts and spins to swing his leg wide at her back. Jade evades again, catching his leg and sweeping his planted foot so he falls to his back, pinned.

"You give up yet?" she asks.

"Not in a million years."

Duncan goes to head- butt her, but she moves out of the way just in time. She lets him up and they reset their stance.

"Why isn't Jade using any powers?" I ask Enzo.

"She is. Keep watching."

Jade moves to throw a punch, but Duncan dissipates before her, then reappears right behind her, blade drawn and swinging right at her ribs. Right before he is about to connect with her, she turns and has a knife I didn't even see her pull at his throat. He yields again with an irritated grunt.

"Duncan has invisibility too?" I ask.

"Not exactly," Gunnar answers. "See Duncan is a cheating bastard because he can teleport short distances. Sara has to physically move there. Duncan basically moves through space itself and comes out somewhere else. It makes for a great advantage, but is a pain to train against."

"Okay, but then how does Jade beat him over and over again?"

Duncan whips his head towards me and lowers his eyes into slits. *Okay, touchy subject I guess.* Jade and Duncan continue fighting as we talk.

"Jade's power isn't one that is necessarily seen. In fact, she doesn't have an official ability at all, since she was not born High Fae. Her father sat on the war council in SunSpark because of his brilliant battle strategies, but he was originally low borne. He drilled those skills into his daughter hoping one day she might live up to his impossible expectations. Jade uses predictive analytics. She can anticipate her opponent's next move based on body language, eye movement, and behavior prediction," Enzo says.

"She's amazing," I stare in awe, as Jade beats Duncan over and over. Finally he gives up and takes a seat next to Gunnar.

"Screw this, man. I'm not training with her anymore," Duncan huffs, blood crusted to his body from healed over wounds.

"I guess that leaves you two," Gunnar winks at me and Enzo.

"How do I know if I have a power?" I ask.

"I think it really depends. Sara says that the woman who approached her looked low borne, so the chances of you having any power at all are pretty small," Enzo says.

"Oh." I try not to sound disappointed, but it creeps into my tone anyways.

"But it never hurts to try. I mean the woman who met Sara also knew some pretty heavy spells in order to bond you two as Soul

Guardian. Who is to say she didn't have any other tricks up her sleeve?"

I know Enzo is just trying to be supportive, but it doesn't quite stick. Part of me feels less than everyone else now. They all have an ability and, once again, I have nothing. Even Jade is a master at what she does. They have been training their whole lives in fighting techniques and mastering their abilities, and I only just started a few years ago with Sara. I try not to let it get to me or to let embarrassment creep in. I hold my chin up high and take my stance.

You've got this, Aliyah. We trained for this. I know it was all just in fun then, but I was training you for this moment. Show them you can keep up with them. Abilities or not.

Sara's words bring a new sense of confidence to me. She's right. I can rise to their level.

"Here," Enzo reaches out and hands me three blades.

"Wha— Enzo, are these— are these the throwing knives from the bunker?"

A huge smile opens up across my face. I can't believe he brought these with him. I take them from his hand and feel the weight they carry from the crystal handles. I would have to adjust to their weight from my crappy knives back in Mareen, but these will be far more deadly with each throw.

Enzo smiles at me as I place one on each side of my thighs in the empty knife holsters. I keep one in my hand for the fight.

"Thank you, Enzo. Truly, thank you."

"You're welcome, little dove. I saw how much you admired them and figured you could use something from this kingdom to remember it by, and to remember our time together in the bunker."

"Stop flirting and get on with it, ZoZo! Though your flirting really could kill someone with how bad it is," Gunnar calls. I laugh and shake my head turning back to Enzo.

"Don't get too confident now, Aliyah. I still put you on your back in Mareen," Enzo says, throwing his first punch.

I duck right at the last second. *Dang, his hands are bigger than I remember them being the last time they were flying at my face.* He moves past me with his next punch, and I take the opportunity to land a slice of my blade in his side as he goes by. He turns and winces as he grabs his side. Seeing him in pain, I instantly feel bad and drop my hands.

Mistake. Enzo uses the opportunity to land a fist to my jaw. I stagger backwards, cupping my cheek.

"Never, ever, let your emotions for another douse your fire. They will exploit your every weakness," Enzo says.

Now I'm mad. He knows I don't want to hurt him, but the others didn't pull their punches. I need to anticipate when he will pull out his ability to use on me.

Enzo takes his stance and is bouncing on the balls of his feet. I take a deep breath and focus my mind. Don't think about the others, they aren't here. I run full speed at Enzo and drop, sliding between his legs before popping up and kicking him square in the back. He falls to the dirt before quickly hopping up, but before he can even turn I am throwing my knife straight at his back. I misjudge the weight of the knife and it goes sailing through the air past him.

Crap. It lands in the dirt behind him. He plucks it out of the ground and turns back to me. I pull another knife from my leg holster and brace myself for a knife fight.

Enzo is on me in a flash, swinging my own knife with lightning fast strikes. He lands a few to my cheek, leg, and upper arm. Not deep enough to damage anything, and I look down briefly to see my skin stitch back together on its own.

Well wouldn't that have been handy in Luar, I say quickly into Sara's mind.

Focus. Breathe, she says back.

"How do I try and access my power?" I ask bouncing on the balls of my feet.

"Remember all of those concentration exercises we did in Mareen? Use that. Imagine your heart pumping the magic through your veins. If it is there, you will be able to feel it coursing through you. Feel it in your heart first," Sara calls.

I take a moment to center myself. I take a few deep breaths and try and focus on my inner being. There is something— something is stirring in my chest, but it feels stuck. As soon as I feel like I have a good grasp on it, the feeling shatters inside me until it is gone.

Tears well in my eyes, but I bat them away quickly. Maybe their wasn't power at all, but that I wanted it so badly to be there, I imagined the whole thing. Focusing back on Enzo, he gives me a moment to collect my thoughts.

"Ready?" he asks.

"Ready," I say a little more choked up than I like.

Enzo moves to run at me again. I breathe out, and pull my arm half back before whipping the blade through the air, embedding it right into the shoulder that was coming at me. Enzo drops his blade and reaches for the hilt of the knife to pull it out. Before he can, I move to kick his knee to the side and as he drops, I land one swift kick to his balls and grip the back of his neck to connect my knee with his face.

"I yield, I yield!" he groans, falling into the dirt.

"Nice shot!" Gunnar yells, clapping his hands together, hooting and hollering into the night.

Jade claps too and a smile spreads across her face as I throw my arms up in the air in victory before bowing to signify the end of my stellar performance. Even Duncan smiles just a little. Sara runs up and wraps her arms around me.

"See! I told you if you just take a breath before you throw, you'll hit your target every time! You were going for his shoulder right?"

"Of course I was! I'm not trying to kill him or anything, at least not yet." I glance back at Enzo, still on the ground holding his crotch, and give him a little wink. He smiles back at me through the pain and winces as he stands.

"And you didn't even get the chance to use your powers on me! Take that!" I laugh. Everyone goes silent as I keep laughing.

"I would *never* use my powers on you, Aliyah," Enzo says, walking away towards his tent before disappearing inside. A confused look falls on my face before I turn to Duncan.

"What was that about? What did I do?"

"It's not you, Aliyah. Enzo doesn't use his abilities unless he absolutely needs to. Like, life or death, needs to."

"Why?" I ask. I don't want to feel bad for winning, but knowing that Enzo didn't use his full abilities kind of makes the sweet taste of victory turn sour in my mouth.

"That isn't our story to tell, but I wouldn't try approaching it right now. He can get really sensitive about it. Just give it a rest until another time," Gunnar adds.

"We should all get some rest. We have a long day ahead of us tomorrow," Jade instructs.

We all head to our tents for the night. I try to settle, but my mind keeps reeling about what happened in the training ring. I don't know what is so bad about his ability that he wouldn't even dare to use it for fun. I know he would never hurt me, so how bad could it really be?

As I toss and turn in my tent, I can't get comfortable knowing that Enzo is upset with me. I pull on my boots and open the flap on my tent. As I make my way over to Enzo's tent, a scuffle coming from the campfire gives me pause.

"I thought I told you to leave it be?" Duncan says, staring into the fire.

"I'm sure it can't be that bad. He will talk to me, just you wait and see." I pull Enzo's tent flap open and peer inside.

"Pst. Enzo, are you awake?"

He doesn't move, so I poke him in the thigh. "Pssssttttt. Enzo, wake up."

"Oh my Maker, Aliyah. What? What could you possibly need so badly that you couldn't wait until morning?"

"I want to talk to you."

Enzo huffs out a breath. "About what?"

I move into his tent and take a seat next to him. He turns to roll over so that his back is facing me.

"I want to talk about your powers. Why won't you use them? It can't be so bad that you couldn't even show me in demonstration."

"It is, Aliyah. Now go to bed."

"Oh come on. Talk to me. Why won't you use your powers?"

Enzo rolls over to face me and props his head up on his hand.

"My powers, they aren't a game. They aren't a fun party trick. My powers hurt people. *Kill* people. When I was learning to wield them as a child, the military, and my father, had me kill countless criminals to practice harnessing my ability. Criminals or not, those fae did not deserve to die like that. My power uncontrolled is horrifying and the military used it at their disposal. Do you know what that does to a child's mind? To make them not only witness these horrible acts, but to actually *perform* them. It breaks you, Aliyah. Every one of their deaths is on my hands. That is why I only use it in life or death situations. For protection."

I lay down next to him and scoot so that my head is laying on his arm. I bury my face in his chest, but he makes no moves to hold me.

"I'm so sorry, Enzo. You didn't deserve that. But you can use your power for good now. You don't have to kill people with them."

"There is no good in me when my powers are unleashed, Aliyah. It is only destruction. I used it that day in Mareen, when those Kalari were coming after us. You were horrified by what you saw."

"Enzo, I was horrified because I had no clue who you were, what you wanted with me, or where you were taking me. I thought you were a human. Humans don't have powers, so how was I to know that you weren't some monster."

"I am not a monster, Aliyah. But when I lose control, I am far worse."

I try to place my hand on his cheek to comfort him, but he snags my wrist before I can.

"I want you to leave now. I don't want you to ask me about my abilities ever again. Do you understand me?"

"Enzo—"

"Just go."

A tear slips from my cheek as I move to exit the tent.

"I didn't know who you were then, but I know who you are now. You are no where even close to a monster, Enzo."

I shut the tent flap behind me. Enzo doesn't say anything back. Several tears slip from my eyes on the way back to my tent.

"I told you."

"Maker, Duncan. I know, okay? I know you told me! But maybe I thought— I don't know what I thought, but I hoped he would let me in. That he would let me love him for every part that is him."

"You love him? Fully and with every fiber of your being?"

"I think I'm starting to."

"Then don't give up. Fight for him, even when he can't fight for himself."

With that, I crawl back into my tent and fall asleep to the sounds of a crackling fire and heartbreak.

Part III:

SunSpark Kingdom

Jane Rose Publishing, LLC

Chapter 34

ALIYAH

The following two days were a lot of the same thing. Riding, training, sleeping, repeating. Enzo continued to be in his foul mood and barely spoke to me the entire time. Trying to talk to him about his powers didn't work out the way I wanted to the first time, so I figured I might as well just wait until we got to SunSpark to try again.

Ever since coming to Olyrium I feel like I have learned something new every day. I always wondered how we constantly had food that just appeared out of no where. On the second day of our journey, I found Jade planting seeds in the ground that sprouted bread, fruits, cheeses, and even a few different kinds of meat. I was completely and utterly shocked at seeing a plant grow meat, but she explained that these were magical seeds only sold in SunSpark. You can buy or trade for them in the other Kingdoms, but Queen Starla of SunSpark creates them using her ability to harness plant life. In order to feed other kingdoms, like Krystal, where their primary growth is rocks, she creates seeds that can grow in any condition and produce certain foods.

It is nice to see Jade so connected to her home kingdom even though there has been such heartache there for her. "Are you excited to be going back to SunSpark?" I ask her.

"Not really, no. I don't really have anything I am going back to. I'm not even sure if I am going to be allowed back into the palace. Obviously, things didn't exactly end on the best of terms the last time I was there."

"I am glad you found a home here with Enzo and the others. We all deserve a family of our own, even if it is one that we choose ourselves."

"Thank you. I hope when we find out who your family is, they are better than my parents ever were. I hope they are honorable people who didn't want to give you away, but had to." Jade's face falls at the memory of her parents disregarding how their actions would affect her. If only they could see her now.

"Listen, when we bridge over the border from Krystal to SunSpark, it is going to take a few moments for your eyes to adjust, and probably your skin too. Once we get to the palace we can get you a cream that will protect your skin from the harsh sun. For now, just keep your long sleeve tunic on and wear this over your head to protect your face." Gunnar hands me a shawl from his bag and I wrap it around my neck, pulling the back up over my head like a hood. My long sleeve white tunic shirt is already starting to dampen with sweat, and it makes my skin feel slippery in my black leather pants.

"Is it getting hotter?" I ask, beads of sweat slipping down my back.

"I promise once we get there we will get you with Lil who is going to show you all the SunSpark fashion," Gunnar smiles.

As we approach The Bridge between kingdoms, my skin tingles in anticipation. I wish I could talk to Enzo about how I am feeling, but he has been hell bent on ignoring me since that first night. I just want to be there already so we can talk this out. Not talking to him has been torture for me. He won't even train with me anymore which is beyond frustrating. *You're being a baby,* I want to yell at him.

Jade and Reyla run ahead to pull the pillar from the ground that will allow us to bridge into SunSpark. She dismounts and Reyla runs off in the opposite direction. Jade lays her hand on the ground and speaks hushed words. Moments later, a large white pillar shoots up from the ground.

"This is where we leave the alicanto. They cannot bridge with us, and they can't fly, so they will remain here until we return. We need to bridge into the village outside the palace. Unfortunately, we can't bridge directly into the palace because of some stupid wards my parents insisted on putting up."

Mirage and the other alicanto run off together in their flock back towards the way we came.

"How are we going to get home again?" I ask.

"They come back, don't worry," Gunnar smiles at me. Everyone places their hands on the pillar.

"It feels good doing this willingly this time," I joke. Enzo doesn't say anything and the others just smile.

"Everyone imagine going into the village square. It should take you right there. On three," Gunnar winks at me.

The moment we cross into SunSpark the heat blazes down on us. My body suddenly feels like it is on fire and I squint my eyes as I look up at the blinding sun.

You lived here? I ask Sara.

Home sweet home, she says back, smiling at me.

How in the hell did she survive in Mareen, where all it does is rain, after coming from a place like this? We appeared in the village square, just like Gunnar said we would. The houses are surrounded by fields of sunflowers all in full bloom with brick walkways winding around the homes to make streets. Shops are bustling with people buying things and laughing while drinking ale on outdoor sitting areas. Everyone is so happy here. It makes me think of Korin and our night at Adryanna's. The sun is a dark orange by the time we make it to the front gates of the castle.

"Are you adjusting alright?" Enzo asks.

"Oh, so we are speaking again?" I say, a little more forceful than I intend.

"I know you were just trying to help. I want to tell you everything. I'm just not ready to pull those memories from the dark recesses of my mind yet. Just give me time."

"Now that I know I am fae, I have all the time in the world. When you're ready, I'll be here." I repeat the words he said to me and I give him a sweet smile before taking his hand in mine.

The SunSpark castle is even bigger than Citrine, which I didn't think was possible. I count the spires as we stand outside and there are almost double the ones in Krystal. The orange sun glints off the palace, making it look like it is glowing. As we make our way up the steps, the front doors fly open and out runs a girl with shoulder length, jet black hair and wispy bangs that blow in the wind as she runs. As she gets closer, I notice she has big ocean blue eyes and the biggest smile I have ever seen. She is wearing a rust colored orange dress that blows behind her as she descends the steps. She runs directly up to Gunnar and throws her arms around his neck and squeals.

"Oh, brother! Welcome home you big idiot! What took you so long to visit? Did you forget about us or something?" She laughs as she looks around to the rest of the group.

"Well aren't you going to introduce me to your new friends?" She places both hands on her hips, with one stuck out to the side, as if in waiting.

"Maker, Lil, calm down, we just got here. Aliyah, this is Liliana, Lil this is Aliyah." Gunnar smiles at his sister.

"Oh, brother. How I have missed you," Liliana says with a sneer. Liliana walks up to me and holds out her hand. I stare at it for a moment before taking it. Liliana pulls my hand towards her body and throws her arms around my neck.

"Hi! I'm Liliana, friends call me Lil. Maker, you are beautiful! I know she didn't grow up in SunSpark because she is paler than a ghost! Where are you from?"

"Jeez Lil..." is all Gunnar can say before she sees Sara.

"Well holy suns of fire, *Saraphena*? Is that really you? Maker! I thought you'd finally lost your mind and ditched my brother for good!" Liliana squeals as she throws her arms around Sara's neck.

"It's been too long, Lil. How are you? Still giving your brother crap I see," Sara smiles while hugging her friend.

"Obviously! I mean someone had to after you disappeared for what...like twenty- five years or something like that!" Everyone's eyes go wide at Liliana's forwardness about the situation. "Yikes, is that still a rough subject?"

Liliana pulls her lips down in a frown and her eyebrows shoot up like she can't believe that would be a sore subject.

"ZoZo, a pleasure as always to see you! I see you are still hanging around with a traitor's daughter."

"At the current moment, the only traitor here is your brother," Enzo cuts Gunnar a glare. Liliana winks at Enzo and a sudden flare of jealousy hits me. Gunnar and Lil start arguing over bringing Jade here, but I can't focus on anything they are saying.

Exactly how close are Enzo and Liliana? I ask Sara through the bond.

As it has been pointed out, I have been gone for the last 26 years. Last I knew they weren't close, but knew each other from the few times Enzo visited here with Gunnar.

Okay, it's fine. There is nothing to worry about. Enzo said he wants to tell me everything. That has to count for something. As if on cue, Enzo wraps his hand around my waist and pulls me into his side.

"Look, all I'm saying is that mother is going to be furious that she is back here. We will be lucky if she even makes it in the door without getting her head cut off!" Lil says blatantly.

"I will speak to mother. That was ages ago, and it wasn't Jade's fault. Just don't mention anything to her until I have time to see her."

"I will be sure to say nice things at your funeral," Lil gives him a smirk. "And who is *this?*"

"Lil, Duncan. Duncan, Lil," Gunnar rolls his eyes like he knows where this is going.

"Duncan, it is a pleasure to meet you." Liliana drops into a curtsy in front of him. "You're the prince of Twilight Kingdom, right? I have heard so many things about you from Gunnar," Lil says with a wink. Duncan cuts a look to Gunnar before Liliana blows Duncan a kiss and turns back towards Sara.

"If you don't mind, it is getting rather warm out here," Sara fans her face. I don't think Sara is actually warm, but just wants to end this conversation.

"Oh yes, yes of course! Mother and father are in a council meeting right now, but as soon as they are done I am sure they are going to want to see everyone. When I received your letter that you were coming to SunSpark, mother insisted on having a ball to welcome you home, but I told her that we needed something even grander than a ball, but she said since you aren't the first born, you'll just be getting a regular old ball. Kaleron will be out of his war council lessons soon and he is ecstatic to have his little baby brother home again," Lil says as she walks up the rest of the steps and into the front entrance of the palace.

Jade falls behind in the group as if nervous to walk in the front doors. I can't blame her. I wouldn't want to be here either if I knew the whole kingdom hated me. The rest of us follow Liliana and as we walk in the front doors, the air immediately shifts to a cool and refreshing temperature. *Thank the Maker.*

"So! Rooms are on the third floor. You each have your own, but if you'd like to share with anyone else in the group then my lips are sealed! I promise," Lil winks at us as she ascends the stairs, talking the entire time about the upcoming ball.

I let my hand trail over the golden railing as we walk up step by step. Each floor is grander than the last. The floors look like they are made of silver and gold ribbons with walls the brightest white I have ever seen. Why is it that I need to shield my eyes in this entire kingdom?

We finally reach the third floor and Lil shows us to our assigned rooms. As Liliana shows me to my room, she calls back for Jade and Sara to come in with us. Enzo glances back at me before entering into his room that is directly across the hall from mine. He gives me a quick wink, and closes the door behind him.

As if the room belongs to her, Lil walks over and throws herself onto the bed like she is ready for a night of gossip with the girls. I could care less about the bed situation as I take a moment to look around the room.

Everything is white and gold, and the bed is filled with soft, plush pillows. There is a small sitting area with two chairs and a couch that could sit three people comfortably. The fireplace roars with life, even though it is a million degrees outside, yet I don't feel any heat coming from it. I wonder to myself if it is just for show.

I turn to my left and see an adjoining washroom complete with a tub and a sink and rows and rows of bath accessories. *I will be trying all of those later.* We are all disgusting from our travels over the last three days and a working bath is just what I need.

"So ladies," Liliana claps her hands together. "Seeing as we are going to be spending lots of time together in the future, I suggest we put this whole traitor thing in the past." Liliana stares at Jade for a brief moment before continuing. "We need to talk dresses for the ball. It is going to be in two days, so we *have* to get our designs to the seamstress as soon as possible."

"Lil," Sara starts. "I think we just need a minute to settle in. Maybe have a bath...or three...before we talk about dresses. How about tonight after dinner we reconvene here over some wine and cheese?"

"You always were the smart one, Sara! I love that idea! We can talk about dresses, shoes, hair, make up, and *boys.*" Lil hops off the bed and walks over to the door.

"See you ladies at dinner! Ugh, I can't wait. This is going to be so fun! It is so nice finally having girls here! It was beginning to be male overload." Liliana exits my room and we all breathe out a sigh of relief at the quiet.

"She is gonna be a blast isn't she?" I laugh.

"Lil is honestly one of the best people I know. I knew her before Gunnar and I got together, since she and I are the same age. Gunnar was always just her older brother to me. When he returned from training ages later, we reconnected and the rest is history. But honestly Lil is so sweet. She is just her own ray of sunshine," Sara laughs. "But one thing I do know, she has *impeccable* taste in fashion, so any dress that she helps us create is going to be gorgeous."

"Before I can even think about a dress I need a serious bath. I am pretty sure my pants are going to just slide right off with how much I was sweating. Fingers crossed I don't get strangled in my bathtub by someone who hated my parents," Jade says.

"Let's get cleaned up before dinner. Jade, would you like to get ready in my room? I could use the company. If we are going to tackle the king and queen tonight at dinner, I am going to need at least three glasses of wine before we even enter the dining room." Sara smiles before getting up and exiting the room.

Jade follows her out and I am left in silence in the room. This bedroom is bigger than three of our apartments back home in Mareen put together, and I can't help but notice the feeling of emptiness without Sara living with me. I am happy she has Gunnar now, but part of me misses my roommate. Maybe a girls' night is exactly what I need.

Chapter 35

ENZO

After heading into the washroom to clean up after three days on the road, I finally feel myself again.

I pull out a pair of black leather pants from my bag and a dark green tunic and lay them on the bed. I slip on my pants and lay back on my bed, taking a moment to just breathe. I find it difficult to inhale as I think about Aliyah in this strange place, without me there to watch over her.

'If you'd like to share with anyone else in the group then my lips are sealed. I promise.' Liliana's words ring in my head as I think about my little dove. Would she consider sharing a room with me while we stay here?

I lay back on the bed and run my hands through my wet hair before stretching my arms above my head. My back cracks and it feels like heaven itself has descended upon my body. Maker I needed that.

A frantic knock at the door brings me back from my bliss. I rise from the bed and walk over to the door and crack it open, just in case whoever is on the other side doesn't have the best intentions. Clearly I was right...

Aliyah stands on the other side of the door in only a towel. The ends of her hair drip water onto the tile with little splashes. Her big blue eyes look panicked as she searches mine.

"Someone stole my clothes!" Aliyah whispers.

I peer into the hallway when I hear footsteps coming down the corridor. A guard approaches and his eyes go wide as he takes in the scene in front of him.

A low growl slips from my lips and my eyes darken as he stands there like a dead man, looking at Aliyah. Without breaking eye contact with the guard, I reach out to grab Aliyah's arm and pull her inside. What I fail to realize is I am pulling on the same arm that is holding up her towel.

At the same time I pull her inside, her towel is ripped from her hand and she stands there completely naked before me...and the guard. *I guess he'll just have to die now.* I quickly avert my gaze to give her privacy. I pull Aliyah inside and push her into the room and away from the guard's eyes. I see the heat flash in them and the flare of his nostrils.

I memorize every line on his face, every inch of his body. He quickly notices my perusal and scampers away in fear. I walk out of my room and to the room directly to the right of mine. Two sharp knocks on the door and Duncan opens it almost immediately.

"Guard. Brown eyes, brown hair. Scar above his left eye." That is all I have to say.

Duncan will know what to do. While I would much prefer to do this work myself, I have a frantic girl in my room to deal with. Duncan shuts his door behind him and walks off in the direction of the guard. I know he won't fail me. He never does.

I return to my room and find Aliyah sitting on the bed wrapped in the duvet, tears dripping from her eyes.

"Why are you crying, little dove?"

"He saw. He saw them, didn't he?"

"My dove, don't be concerned about that. Duncan will take care of everything. He will burn the image of your body from that guard's mind before making sure he never sees anything again."

"I don't care about that— I mean, I do, but I meant my back. He saw them. I know it. He must think I'm horrifying."

She is sobbing now with her knees pulled up to her chest and head buried in the duvet around her. The reflecting glass next to my bed reflects her exposed back. My body turns cold. The blood in my veins freezes and boils at the same time. Her back is torn to shreds. Scars, in multiple different stages of healing, line her back in long lines. I count each and every scar to make sure that when I find who did this, I can inflict the same amount of pain they have caused her. I'll add them to the list that seems to be continually growing since Aliyah came into my life.

When I saw that her back was hurt in Mareen, I thought it was from when I had pinned her to the ground. Not because of some previously obtained injury. Bile churns in my throat at the thought of what I did to her that day while she had already been dealing with those wounds to her back being split open again.

"Who did this to you?" I say, feeling my power swirl just below the surface. I take a few deep breaths, trying to reign in the beast clawing at my mind wishing to break free and slaughter whoever did this to her.

"Don't Enzo— just don't. Please, I'm begging you— just don't."

"Little dove—" I walk over to the bed and sit down behind her, putting my legs on either side of her body. I run my fingers over the scars on her back as her back heaves with each inhale between sobs. She tenses beneath my touch.

"Please don't look at them, Enzo. I never wanted you to see them. They are hideous. *I* am hideous because of them."

I don't have the perfect words for her, or any words at all for that matter, that will take away her pain. So I just pull her shoulders back and turn her so her head is on my chest. Her tears run down my chest. I stroke my hand over her wet hair and just let her cry. Her sobs finally stop and she looks up at me with glassy eyes.

"He's dead, you know. That day in the village. He was lying dead in the street when we were leaving. I never thought I would be happy to see someone dead, but after everything he did to me— does that make me a horrible person?"

"No, Aliyah, it doesn't make you a horrible person. I can't begin to imagine what you have gone through, or what you endured to survive. But what I do know is that every lash, every horrible thing you endured, has made you who you are today. I see the compassion in your eyes when you meet new people, when you care for Mirage, the way you understood Jade's past; you survived through all of that. You didn't let it define who you are. You, Aliyah, are beautiful, body and soul."

"When will it stop hurting? When will I forget about all of the things that happened in Mareen?"

"I can't answer that for you, my dove. What I can say is that no matter how long it takes, no matter how many eons pass, I will be here to replace every bad memory with a good one. I know you don't want to talk about it now, or maybe ever, but if, when you're ready, I want to hear your story. To hear all that you have endured so that you won't be alone in your pain."

"I'm just so tired, Enzo."

"Then rest. I'll be here the whole time."

I move to pick her up and place her under the blankets on my bed. Her smell of vanilla fills my nose as I place a kiss on her forehead before tucking her in further.

I glance one last time at the scars on her back and make a vow to myself that nothing, and no one, will ever lay a malicious hand on her again. She will never get hurt again as long as I can help it. I finish getting dressed and settle into one of the wing back chairs by the window. I hope wherever that bastard rots, he is thanking the stars he didn't die at my hand. I would *not* have been as gracious as The Kalari were.

Chapter 36

ALIYAH

As I wake in Enzo's room, he is asleep in the chair by the window. I know he said he would be there to protect me, but I am glad he was able to get some rest, too. I trust he would have awoken if anyone came in.

I slip from the bed as quietly as I can and pad across the floor, dragging his duvet with me. I slowly crack open the door and bolt for my room before anyone can see me. It isn't so much that I am afraid of anyone thinking we are sleeping together, but when he told me Duncan was taking care of that guard, something tells me he doesn't mean giving him a stern talking to.

As I shut the door behind me, I practically jump out of my skin as an older woman stands at the end of my bed. She is laying out, what is arguably, the most gorgeous dress I have ever seen in my life.

"Deepest apologies, milady! I wasn't aware you would be coming back so soon, but I wanted you to have something to wear tonight to the dinner with King Aramas and Queen Starla," the older woman says, blushing slightly at the fact that I am only in a blanket.

"Thank you. I really appreciate it. Um, if you could help me with some information actually that would be wonderful. My clothes seem to have been misplaced. I had a bag with an several sets of leathers in them and a few tunics. I can't seem to find them."

"Oh yes yes, Lady Liliana informed me that your clothes would not be suitable for your time spent in SunSpark, so she had me collect them while you were washing up. I apologize again, milady, I had no ill intentions."

"Oh, um it's no problem—" I stop. "Sorry, what was your name again?"

The old woman curtsy's low before adding, "Marigold, milady. I hope this dress is to your liking?" she asks, pointing to the dress on the bed.

"Marigold, please stop curtsying and calling me 'milady.' Please, call me Aliyah."

"Queen Starla insists that we call all her esteemed guests 'milady,' milady."

That is going to get old. I try not to roll my eyes.

"Okay well at the minimum, stop curtsying. At least while we are in private."

"Can I help you get ready for tonight's dinner? The other girls are getting ready in their rooms as we speak with their own chamber-maids. It would truly be my honor to help you."

"Um— yeah, I mean, I suppose you can. Do you mind if I ask you some questions about this kingdom while you help me? I'm afraid I am going to make a fool of myself at dinner with how little I know about SunSpark."

"I would be happy to share our history with you. Let's get you out of that duvet and into a robe before we start on your hair and make up. What can I answer for you?"

"To start, I'd like to know if I can get my original clothes returned. They are special to me."

"I will ensure they are back in your room by the time you return tonight."

"Thank you."

An hour later, Marigold helps me into the dress and had placed the perfect amount of makeup on my face. I asked her to not make me look like a common street wench, and she accomplished it perfectly. She used a black charcoal liner around my eyes, a light shade of pink on my cheeks to give me a sun-kissed glow and some sort of clear liquid over my lips to make them plump. My lips are tingling like they do after Enzo kisses me and I can't help but smile at the thought.

Marigold answered several questions about SunSpark's history, a few questions about the Queen and King's interests, and a few inquiries about Gunnar's older brother, Kaleron. I learned he is set to inherit the throne sooner than most think.

I asked her about Gunnar and why he decided to stay in Krystal instead of returning to SunSpark. Turns out he decided to stay in Krystal after he returned home and found Sara gone. Marigold seemed to be the gossip queen around here; being as old as she was, that doesn't surprise me. She knows everything about everyone in this kingdom.

"So, milady, what should we do with your hair?"

As I look into the reflecting glass in front of me, I take into consideration the low back dress I am wearing.

"Can we do something with my hair down tonight, please?"

"As you wish." Marigold starts at one ear and braids my hair across the top of my head to my other ear, forming a crown like braid. The rest of my hair flows straight down my back, covering the exposed skin there. Whatever dress I design with Lil will have to cover my back so I can wear my hair up in one of those pretty styles I saw in town today.

"Done." Marigold places one final pin in the braid and steps back to admire her work.

I stand and walk over to the floor length reflecting glass and stare into it in complete shock at the girl who stares back at me. The dress is a shimmering silver silk that hugs my curves perfectly with a looser layer of sparkling tulle over the top, giving a silhouette like appearance. There is a slit on the right side of the dress that comes all the way up to the top of my thigh. With each step I take, my entire right leg shows along with the edge of my lace underlings. Definitely need to keep aware of that. The top portion of the dress is the same material as the bottom; however, the front and back dip into a low v-shape that perfectly accentuates my cleavage. The straps are the same thickness as the pieces that cover my chest and down my back, exposing some of the side of my breasts as well.

"Isn't it a little— revealing?" I ask, Marigold.

"This is typical SunSpark attire, milady. Is it not to your liking?"

"No it's not that, I just. I wish it didn't show so much of the scar on my chest."

The bottom of the V stops right below the end of my scar. The raised tissue is still pink and I think it takes away from the beauty of the dress.

"May I make a suggestion?" Marigold asks.

"Always."

Marigold walks over to the vanity and pulls out a jar of black liquid and a small, fine pointed brush.

"With your permission, I can draw a design on your chest that will cover any skin you wish to hide."

"I think that is a wonderful idea. Thank you."

I push all my hair to the back to make sure those scars are hidden under my hair and push my shoulders back so she has clear access to the scar. Marigold dips the brush into the liquid and begins drawing swirls of black across my chest, completely covering the scar there and creating a beautiful painting on my chest. The center of my chest is clear of ink, but she followed the V shape of the neckline so it appears as if the swirls are coming off the fabric itself. It is absolutely breathtaking. I turn back to the reflecting glass and this time, I can't help but smile.

"One last thing, milady."

Marigold walks over holding a bracelet that looks like a pol-ished, dark gray color. She clasps it around my wrist. In a strange way, it goes perfectly with the dress, offsetting the light silver with the dark.

A knock comes at the door and Enzo walks in, stopping in his tracks as he takes me in. My heart stops in my chest. He is in a fitted black tunic that is tight around his broad chest and arm muscles, before tapering down to fitted, black leather pants. His hair has been styled back out of his face so you can clearly see the flecks of hazel in his normally brown eyes. SunSpark looks good on him.

"How come I have to wear a silver dress, but he gets to wear all black?" I smile at Marigold, before pointing my thumb at Enzo.

"Standing next to you, no one is going to give two craps what I am wearing. You are an absolute vision, little dove. If this is what you are wearing to a simple dinner, I can't wait to see what Lil comes up with for the ball."

I blush at his words as he takes my hand and pulls me into him. He gives me a deep kiss and runs his hand to the nape of my neck and pulls my hair back to tip my chin higher, deepening the kiss. His tongue prods at my lips and I immediately open for him. For a brief moment, I worry about my make up and the ink on my chest, but the groan that comes from his throat clears any thoughts from my mind.

I break away from the kiss before we go too far in front of Marigold, but as I turn to thank her for everything, I notice that she is already gone. I turn back to Enzo who has a heated look in his eyes.

"Let's skip dinner," he states.

"Enzo— we can't just skip dinner on our first night here. That would be rude to the people who are letting us stay here," I smile up at him.

"So, after dinner then?"

"Can't. I have a girls' night planned to discuss dress designs for the ball. Lil says we have to get our designs in as soon as possible. It feels kind of weird attending a ball when I don't even know anyone here."

"The only person you need to know here is me," Enzo says with a wink. His fingers trail up my exposed thigh and stop when reaches the bottom of my lace undergarments.

"I just need two more things and then we can go."

I pull away from his arms and immediately feel empty inside at the loss. I find my silver sandals that were left out and snag my thigh holster and wrap it around my exposed leg, slipping in one of the marbled knives Enzo gave me.

He cocks an eyebrow at my added accessories.

"What? Didn't you all say that just because people appear nice, doesn't mean they have nice intentions? I am just being prepared!"

"Seeing you with my gift strapped to your thigh really makes me want to skip dinner now. May I add your other gift to the ensemble?"

"Oh ZoZo, you wouldn't dream of the things I would do with this knife if we stayed. Of course you can," I give him a wink.

He walks over to the dresser and grabs the silver chain off the top. I move my hair over my shoulder so that he has access to my neck. He reaches around and claps the necklace around me. The feeling of his fingertips barely grazing over my skin sends a tingle to the bottom of my spine and my pulse kicks up at the contact.

"Does it take away from the dress? It feels a little silly wearing an ax necklace with such an elegant dress."

"Not at all. I think you look like the perfect combination of elegant, but deadly."

"And I think you might be a little biased," I wink at him.

I grab his hand and lead him from my room, shutting the door behind us. Time to meet the King and Queen.

I send a quick prayer to the Maker. *Please help me not make a fool of myself.*

Chapter 37

ALIYAH

As Enzo and I enter the large dining room, I take in my surroundings. The room has high ceilings, even higher than the
ones in Citrine. The floors are swirled marble of silver and gold like the
rest of the palace, but the walls in here are painted black with hundreds
of candles floating in the room and above the table.

The table could easily fit a hundred guests, yet it is only set for a
small gathering at one end. The plates are set upon a black table cloth
and everything is made of gold. Gold plates, gold cups, gold knives and
gold forks. One of these plates could probably feed all of Mareen for
a year. Part of me rages at the fact that these fae have so much, while
the people in Mareen are barely getting by. Something tells me the fae
here couldn't be bothered with one small village in Luar.

Already seated are Gunnar, Sara, Duncan, and Liliana, along with
a few others I don't know. At the head of the table sits an extremely
fat male, with a half- balding head, and fingers the size of sausages.
His huge belly barely fits behind the table and his fingers are already
grabbing at the meat and cheese plate in front of him. I'm going to go
out on a limb here and say that is the king.

Directly to the left of him is a beautiful woman who has short,
styled, dirty blonde hair with a glittering golden crown resting on the

top of her head. She has blue eyes and a flat affect. Best guess— that's the queen. How is it possible that these two people raised two of the most compassionate people I know?

To the right of the king stands a tall male. He has remarkable features, though nothing compared to Enzo. He has shoulder length brown hair with half of it pulled up into a knot at the back of his head, green eyes, and a jaw that could cut steel. He gives me a warm smile before sitting down. Was he standing while I entered the room? I scratch my wrist under the bracelet as I look around for where to sit.

Liliana motions for me to come over to her side of the table.

"Come sit by me, Ali!"

I move to sit down between her and the tall male, but Enzo pulls my arm back.

"I'm okay. I have your gift, remember?" I say, flicking my eyes down to my thigh.

He loosens the grip on my hand and lets me go. Enzo pulls out my chair for me and motions for me to sit, while holding eye contact with the male next to me the entire time. An unspoken warning passes between them. He moves to the other side of the table next to Duncan and takes his seat. I glance up to find a pair of eyes boring into my soul. The queen is just staring at me. I look down to find her gripping the golden knife so hard, her knuckles are blanched white. I lift my chin slightly higher to appear more confident, though I am anything but.

What the hell did you do to piss her off? Sara's voice fills my head.

I just got here. What could I have possibly done? I laugh back.

"What an honor it is to have my second born son back in his rightful home! And with the girl who left him heartbroken and in pieces no less!" The king laughs.

"Father— enough."

Gunnar lowers his brows at his father in clear annoyance. Sara pales next to him and casts her eyes down at the table.

Don't let him get to you like that. He has no idea what you went through, hold your head up high.

I send Sara some reassuring words. She lifts her head, and blinks away the tears brimming in her eyes.

"For those of you who don't know, this is my father and mother, King Mortaval and Queen Starla. Additionally, my eldest brother, Kaleron, heir apparent to the throne."

Gunnar nods in his brother's direction. Kaleron turns to me and grasps my hand before lifting my knuckles to his lips and pressing them slightly to his mouth in a kiss.

Something shatters at the other side of the table and all eyes flick towards Enzo, who has completely shattered the cup in his hand. He stares at Kaleron who is still holding my hand in his. I shake my head quickly, hoping he gets the message that I am fine, as I pull my hand from Kaleron. Enzo releases a breath before a servant comes over to collect his broken cup and replace it with a new one.

"It seems your guest still has quite the temper, Gunnar," the queen notes before sipping from her glass. "Please implore your guest to keep his temper in check during his stay here in SunSpark. I can't have my guards getting their eyes carved out and their throats slit every time someone looks at his plaything."

The queen's flat expression when she looks at me lights a fire in my chest.

"I am *not* a play thing," I snap back at her.

I scratch my wrist again, getting annoyed that this woman thinks she can insult me like that.

"You can play with me any time, gorgeous," Kaleron winks at me and bumps me with his shoulder. I whip my head in his direction.

"You'd be smart not to say such things to me. I'd like to believe you're better than that and your face is far too nice to be carved off to the bone," I glare at him flatly.

The doors to the dining room crack open and Jade walks inside with her head to the floor. She walks over to sit down next to Enzo and makes sure to not make eye contact with anyone.

"Jade," the queen starts. "Gunnar has spoken to me about your presence here. Let it be known that you must tread very lightly. If I hear even a *whiff* of you spying on this kingdom, you will face the same fate as your parents. Are we clear?"

"Yes, Your Majesty. Thank you for your grace in allowing me to be here. I am not my parents choices. You have my loyalty, as does all of Olyrium." Jade looks so defeated as she speaks. I wish I could do something to help the queen get over the atrocities from the past.

"Isn't it just so nice that we are all together again?" Liliana chimes in, clapping her hands.

As the servants place piles and piles of food in front of us, Lil goes on about the upcoming ball preparations. I wonder if they have balls often given how excited she is to have one. I'll have to ask her about that later so I can stop feeling like a witch every time I want to roll my eyes at her excitement.

Every so often, I glance up at Enzo to make sure he hasn't combusted into flames at Kaleron's attitude towards me. The rest of us eat in silence as Lil talks.

My plate is piled high with various meats and cheeses. There are vegetables I have never seen before that taste so good I might even consider eating vegetables more often. It's strange for me to have food at my disposal. There isn't a need to steal food to survive anymore. I wonder if the queen would consider selling any of her seeds to the villages in Luar. So many could benefit from having a steady flow of food. At the minimum, maybe she could donate some to the orphanages and poor.

I sip the wine in front of me and hints of cranberry and orange provide an interesting, but not unpleasant, flavor on my tongue. Taking a few more sips of wine for confidence, I decide it is time for a change in subject.

"Your Majesties, we have come a long way in search of my lineage. When we consulted the tome in Citrine, we were— well we were unable to discover anything we didn't already know. Gunnar mentioned visiting the Reflecting Pool here in your kingdom. I am requesting that we be able to visit the pool tomorrow."

"Yes, Gunnar mentioned in his last letter to Liliana that you are seeking your parentage. Unfortunately, from what he described, you are nothing more than a peasant's child," the queen states.

A flash of hurt crosses my face as I look to Gunnar. How could he describe me like that?

"Aliyah, that is not what I said. Mother, do not stir trouble where there is none to be had. I said that during our training we have not yet discovered if Aliyah has any powers," Gunnar corrects.

"My darling boy, that is the same thing. Fae who do not possess an ability are always known to be lesser than the rest of us. Isn't that right, Jade?"

Jade doesn't respond.

My wrist is killing me now. Maker what is this freaking bracelet made of?

Pssst. What are everyone else's abilities?

Well you already know the queen's from when Jade told you about the seeds, but she has dominion over all plant life. The king and Kaleron both hold the same power since it is passed down to the first born son. They both have Maker-like strength.

Looking at the king, I'm not sure I agree with that sentiment. I laugh in my head as I look at the overly sized king stuffing his face with pastries.

From what I have heard, the king believed that having Maker-like strength meant he could eat whatever he wanted to keep up with his ability. Before too long, things got out of hand, and he stopped using his power for anything other than lifting large containers of ale into his mouth. Hopefully, Kaleron is close to becoming king.

Sara is right about one thing, Kaleron is huge. I am surprised his shirt can contain his muscles. They are practically bursting at the seams. He flashes me a smile, while side eyeing me, as he sips from his wine. I quickly glance away, not wanting Enzo to get any more upset tonight.

What about Lil? I ask.

"I can feel another person's emotions, and when necessary I can siphon other's emotions to take them on myself." Liliana whispers next to me. I quickly glance at Liliana, eyes wide. Did I ask Sara that out loud?

"No you didn't say it out loud, but I could feel your shame when my mother brought up your lesser family. And just now I could feel your surprise when I answered your question. I'm not a mind read-er or anything, but other's emotions can be just as telling as their thoughts."

"Well that's— intrusive," I mutter.

Lil's smile drops as she looks at her hands, twisting her fingers around each other under the table.

"Sorry, I didn't mean to butt into your emotions. It won't happen again," she says.

"No, Lil I'm sorry. That isn't what I meant. I didn't mean to make it sound like a bad thing, just that I have never had anyone *actually* be able to read my emotions before. It took some adjusting to get used to the Soul Bond I share with Sara and having her voice in my head all the time."

"You're Soul Bonded with Saraphena?" the queen chimes in.

"That's right," I say.

"I thought all the Soul Guardians died off in the war? Killed along-side their bonded." Queen Starla looks quizzically at me. I feel like she is judging me for some reason.

"I— I don't know how it happened, I was just a baby then. I grew up in Luar. That is where Sara and I have been for the last twenty-six years. I only just came back when my village was attacked by The Kalari and Enzo brought me here."

I don't know why I feel ashamed of my story, or why I feel like the queen is picking apart everything I say.

"Saraphena, how did you become Soul Bonded to Aliyah?" she asks.

"An older woman came to me when I was in Citrine saying goodbye to Gunnar before he left for battle. She approached me and told me that Aliyah was important and that I needed to leave immediately, say nothing to anyone, and never come back here until the time was right. She didn't tell me when the right time was, but it seems we ended up here anyways. She did the spell for the Soul Bond and disappeared," Sara adds.

"Interesting." That is all the queen says, as she looks at me like I am a puzzle that needs solving.

"What is interesting about that?" Duncan asks.

"It's nothing. Just that there were very few people who knew the Soul Guardian spell. I am just surprised that a beggar woman would be able to perform such a spell without the proper research. Maybe there is more to you than just a beggar's child after all, Aliyah." The queen stands and pushes her chair back.

"If you will all excuse me, it is getting late and I do need my beauty rest if we are going to be hosting such an extravagant ball as my daughter has described. Aliyah, please recant my previous statement. Go to the Reflecting Pool tomorrow. I am interested to know what the pool will show you about your past, or better yet, your future."

The queen exits the room and everyone else stands to leave. Lil grabs my arm before I have a chance to get up.

"Let's meet in your room tonight for girls' night! I will sneak down to the wine cellar to snag a few bottles and bring them up. I'll see you there soon. Make sure Jade and Saraphena come too!"

Liliana skips from the room before disappearing and the rest of us move to head back towards our wing of the palace.

The queen's sudden change of heart is making me uneasy. Why does she want to know what the Reflecting Pool is going to show me?

Chapter 38

ALIYAH

Jade, Lil, Sara and I are all piled onto my bed after dinner. It feels nice to get out of that dress. It is still the nicest thing I have ever worn, but nothing compares to the soft sleep pants and tunic shirt that were waiting for me when I got back to my room. Marigold left a hair wrap for me, so I use it to pull my hair out my face. Just as I was finishing washing off my makeup, Jade and Sara came to the door already in their sleep wear. Lil had come in after Jade and Sara. She was carrying four bottles of wine in her arms, four glasses, a few pieces of parchment and some charcoal. She said it was so we could draw out our designs for the seamstress. Clearly she did not anticipate my lack of drawing skills.

I'm just thankful that I got that bracelet off my wrist. It is still a little pink as it heals, but by the time I got back to my room my wrist was raw and blistering. I'll have to ask Marigold what the bracelet was made out of because clearly I am having some sort of reaction to it.

"Let girls' night officially commence!" Lil clinks her glass with ours before taking a long gulp. A huge smile fills her face. I can't help but wonder if she has many friends? Her excitement over this night, and the upcoming ball, appear to consume every last one of her thoughts.

I begin drawing out the design for my dress. Sara is a beautiful artist. Her gown is perfectly sketched down to the last detail. I just hope the seamstress would be able to bring her vision to life. Jade described her dress to Sara, who took the liberty of sketching it out for her. Liliana, having clearly done this with all of her gowns, was sketching away like a mad woman, drawing up over ten different designs in the time that it took me to draw one.

"How's it going over there, Ali?" Sara asks.

"Ummm, it's— okay I guess." I stare back at the page in front of me. I turn my page around and all the girls collectively burst into laughter. My cheeks heat at my level of embarrassment. I'll blame it on the wine. On my page is a straight line with two lines near the top for arms, a circle for a head and some squiggly lines for hair. The dress is a basic triangle bottom and a square top with two lines for straps.

"Okay you guys, clearly I need some help," I laugh.

"Here, let me." Lil takes my drawing and crumples it up before tossing it to the floor beside my bed. She starts sketching something on a new piece of parchment. The rest of us sip our wine and chat while she works. Several moments later, she turns the page around. Each of us collectively gasp at what Lil has created. "Lil, it's—" I start.

"Amazing," Jade and Sara say in unison.

"I will get these sketches to the seamstress as soon as we are done having girls' night!" Lil beams, clearly proud of her work. "Can I confess something?" she asks, seriously.

"Of course," I say, sensing the seriousness in her tone.

"I've never really had friends like this before. It's hard for others to be around me and feel like they can be themselves. Because of my— ability— they never know which are their real emotions or what might be fabricated by my ability, even though I have complete control over it. I think that is why I try to be happy all the time, so that people want to be around me," she confesses.

"I know we have a complicated past, but that seems like a really crappy thing for those fae to do. It isn't your fault you were born with your power. We like you just the way you are," Jade looks at Lil with sincerity. I'd like to think I softened Jade up a little back in Citrine but, in a way, she kind of reminds me of Ruby. Threatened by those who threaten what she loves most. I can't exactly fault her for that. If someone threatened Sara— hell, if someone threatened any of my new friends— who knows what I would do to them.

"So, on to something less depressing," Lil's chipper attitude returns. "Let's talk boys! Sara, obviously I know about you and Gunnar, and *yuck*. I *don't* want to know about your love life with my brother, but *Aliyah*," Lil turns to me. "You and *Enzo*?! Who knew that male even had a heart to share!"

My cheeks flush at the mention of Enzo. "Yeah, um, it's new. He initially brought me here against my will and almost got me killed, but somehow I think that just brought us closer. Now, I can't imagine what life would be like without him."

"Rumor in the kingdoms has it that he is amazing in bed! Have you two—?" Lil wiggles her eyebrows at me, in question.

"Whoaaa, no no no, we have never— we made out a few times, but nothing more than that. I haven't told him this yet, because honestly I don't think it is in the stars for us, but I never wanted to have relations with anyone until we were married. That plan changed slightly with an incident back in Luar, but if anything, that just solidified it even more for me.

"I'm sorry for whatever happened in Luar. But you can't deny that Enzo and you wouldn't make beautiful children!" Lil winks at me.

"It's no rush, Aliyah," Jade says. "You can love someone without rushing into marriage. It happens all the time." Some part of me gets the feeling she isn't talking about a stranger, but rather someone in particular. Something still feels weird talking about Enzo and me as a couple in front of her, so I decide to steer the conversation in another direction.

"What about you, Lil? Any suitable males around here? You are a princess after all," I ask.

"Not really," she sighs. "But that one with you, Duncan, his emotions are impossible to read. If anything that makes him even more appealing because I won't know if he likes me back or not. Is he with anyone?"

Jade, Sara and I share a look with each other. Duncan has never talked about a love life with us before. I think back to that night at Adryanna's tavern and recall him sitting alone at the table while the rest of us danced. Even Jade found herself someone to be with. Duncan just sat there the whole night brooding.

"I don't think he is with anyone. I'm not sure he is really looking for anyone either," Jade adds.

"Hm." That is all Lil adds. "You know what would be fun?"

She gives us a huge smile before grabbing a bottle of wine and heading for the door. She cracks the door and looks up and down the hallway. She turns and waves for us to follow her. We each look at each other in question before shrugging our shoulders and getting off the bed. I am sure whatever Lil is about to get us involved in is going to be far more interesting than gossiping about males all night.

Chapter 39

ENZO

Duncan, Gunnar, and I sit around the library fireplace, each with a crystal glass of amber. We sit in silence, wrapped up in our own thoughts.

My mind keeps wandering back to Aliyah earlier— both in her towel and in the magnificent dress she had on at dinner. I can't think too long about dinner though. The way Kaleron was touching her, looking at her, breathing the same freaking air as— I can't go there. My blood starts to heat at the thought.

Tomorrow we will take Aliyah to the Reflecting Pool, hopefully find out her past, go to this Maker-forsaken ball, and then get the hell out of here. I want to take her back home to Korin, where she belongs. *And away from Kaleron.*

"I wonder what the girls are up to tonight?" Gunnar finally breaks the silence.

"Probably just sitting around braiding each other's hair, gossiping about the latest fashion and drinking wine. Nothing as fun as what we are doing," Duncan says with a flat face, eyes never leaving the fireplace.

"Well aren't you just a ray of freaking sunshine, Duncan. What's next? You going to shoot rainbow crystals out your backside?" Gunnar laughs, before throwing a pillow at Duncan's head.

Without even turning he catches it and tucks it behind his head, laying back and closing his eyes. I smirk at the two and sip my drink. I look out the window of the library and see the deep orange sun still blazing in the sky. I miss Krystal. The moon would be up by now, casting light down on the mountains creating that beautiful ribbon of color in the sky.

"So, you cut the guard's eyes out, huh? Did he beg for his life?" I ask.

"Don't they always. He swore he didn't see anything, but the amount he was sweating told a different story," Duncan answers, not opening his eyes.

"Next time you gotta invite me for that stuff, Duncan. I know you are Enzo's go-to guy for that, but I am ready and willing if you ever need back-up. You know, just in case you can't handle it," Gunnar winks.

"Can't handle it? You're the one who has gone soft on us since getting back with Saraphena!" I taunt.

"*Soft?!* I am anything but soft, brother. Bring it on!" Gunnar yells.

"Mind if I join in on this little fight?" A voice comes from the other side of the library, and I hear footsteps coming towards us. Kaleron appears before us with a drink in his hand and a smirk on his face.

Finally.

"Why not?" I say, finishing my glass of amber. "I have been itching for a chance to fight you since dinner. That is, if you think *you* can handle it?"

"Oh, I think you will find I am capable of handling *anything* I choose." Kaleron smirks at me.

That's it. He needs to go. I'm confident I can make it look like an accident.

"Don't kill him, ZoZo. He is just trying to goad you," Gunnar whispers to me.

I grind my teeth together.

"It's working, but because he is your brother I will try to refrain. But one more comment about Aliyah and he's done."

Duncan and Gunnar move the furniture out of the way, making a circle in the library big enough for us to fight without breaking too many things. I crack my neck from one side to the other, and then pop my knuckles. It is going to feel so good to have my fist connect with his stupid, smug face.

"Everyone for themselves?" Gunnar smiles.

"Is there any other way to do it?" Kaleron asks. "Just like old times, huh little brother?"

"Yeah, except this time you're old enough where I don't have to hold back. No more pulling my punches or risk getting in trouble for *hitting the future of SunSpark,*" Gunnar mocks his mother's words. With that Gunnar throws the first punch at Duncan, hitting him square in the jaw.

"That's the only hit you're going to land tonight," Duncan growls at Gunnar.

They are a blur of fists, fire and frustration as Duncan keeps disappearing and reappearing. I set my sights on Kaleron. He still has that smug smile on his face.

"I'd apologize for any pain I inflict on you tonight but, honestly, you deserve every second."

I throw the first punch and hit him in the stomach. He doubles over, but recovers quickly. Knowing that he has increased strength, I need to adjust my approach.

Usually, I can overpower someone with my own strength, but he will have a significant gain on me. With that in mind, I shoot for agility over power.

Dodging some of his blows and landing a few quick jabs of my own, Kaleron and I are dripping sweat after only a few minutes of fighting. Blood is crusted over the parts of my healed body from the few punches he did land, but the fury doesn't cease.

"Your punches are soft, Enzo," Kaleron taunts. "Just like Aliyah's skin beneath my lips."

Blind rage takes over. It is like I am outside myself looking onto the scene below. I stop pulling punches and let my full rage take over.

"How *dare* you let her name fall from your mouth. You will *never* touch what is mine again. Aliyah belongs to *me!*"

My vision goes black and the next thing I know Gunnar and Duncan are pulling at my arms and shoulders. When I snap back to reality, Kaleron is on his knees gasping for air, but I'm not touching him. My power took over and is cutting off his air supply by my thoughts alone.

Normally when my abilities take control I feel sick and horrified at taking someone's choice away, but now— now I just feel satisfaction.

The furniture in the room is completely destroyed, shattered into pieces. Books are strewn about, pages floating down from the ceiling after being ripped out of their spines. *That's gonna be a pain to clean.*

I release my mental hold on his throat and step closer so that I am towering over him while he is still on his knees. He looks up at me, tears streaming from the corners of his eyes, but anger is etched into his face.

"Let's get one thing clear. You are not dead right now because you are Gunnar's brother, but make no mistake, I would do *anything* for Aliyah. If you so much as even *think* about her, I will not hesitate to rid this realm of your blackened soul. Is. That. Clear?"

Gunnar and Duncan try to pull me back, but my gaze holds firm.

"I make no promise that—" he starts.

"Is. That. Clear?" I ask again.

"Perfectly." Kaleron gets to his feet and places a hand on his neck, rubbing slightly. "Though if my king or queen commands it, I must obey, as is my duty to the realm."

His smirk returns to his face. Before I can get my hands on him again, he exits the library without another word. Anger settles deep in my chest. I can't wait to get out of this kingdom.

"Come on. Let's get to bed. We have a long day tomorrow and I think we all could use some sleep." Duncan shoves me towards the door and I glare back at him as I move towards the exit. Gunnar and Duncan follow behind me, exiting the library.

As we make our way down the hall to our rooms, something feels off. I'm not sure what, but something isn't sitting right in my chest. Suddenly a guard comes running down the hallway trying to flag us down. A look of pure panic is on his face.

"Your Majesty! Come quick, the girls— they've been attacked."

He turns signaling for us to follow him. The three of us take off after the guard. Panic seizes in my chest. *Please be okay little dove.* How can this keep happening? Why am I never there to protect her when I should be? I told her I would keep her safe. How will she ever forgive me after this?

As we round the corner to our wing of rooms, the guard pushes open the door to Aliyah's room and the three of us push inside.

Splat. Something sticky hits me right in the face, followed by something soft smacking me in the head. White feathers are flying everywhere around us and giggles fill the air along with them.

Gunnar, Duncan and I stand there completely stunned and as I turn, I see they too are covered in jam and feathers. The girls are on the ground clutching their stomachs and kicking their legs, while silent laughter pours from them.

"You have *got* to be kidding me!" Duncan growls, before exiting the room without another word.

Gunnar walks right up to Saraphena and pulls her from the floor, carrying her like a rag doll in his arms back to his room. She is still laughing as his door shuts behind him and I hear a high pitched squeal before turning back to Aliyah.

"You should have seen your face! In fact, you should see your face right now! You look like you'd fit right in as one of the Alicanto!" she says between inhales and laughs.

"I hope you're happy. That guard is going to die now for being involved in your little prank. His blood is on your hands, little dove."

Her face falls completely flat, all signs of laughter gone.

"Enzo, please no. It was just a joke."

She pleads for his life, but it is no use. His fate had already been sealed the moment he made me believe that Aliyah was hurt.

"You should have thought about that before you involved him."

My tone is completely void of emotion. Liliana stands to say something, but I cut her off before she even gets the chance.

"Don't bother, Lil. I can only assume this was your idea to start with. Be lucky I am letting you walk out of here right now. I suggest you go before I change my mind."

She exits the room with Jade quickly, and quietly, before turning around and giving Aliyah an *'I'm sorry'* face. Aliyah is certainly going to be sorry for this. I'll make dang sure of it.

Chapter 40

ALIYAH

"Enzo seriously–" I start.

"Oh I am *very* serious, little dove. I do not take kindly to pranks. Especially ones that involve your safety."

Enzo's eyes darken as he stalks towards me, like a predator about to pounce on his prey. I want to be afraid. Part of me is, but it's really hard to take him seriously with the way he looks right now. I stifle a laugh as he looks down at me covered in jam and feathers.

Liliana had led us down to the kitchen after we left our room and asked the cook for two large buckets of strawberry jam. Being the princess of SunSpark, the cook didn't even question it. He provided two large batches of jam and we carried them upstairs back to my room. Liliana laid out the plan for us: Jade and Sara were going to throw the jam at them as they entered the room, taking them by surprise. Then Lil and I would hit them with the feather pillows. We had ripped them open at the seams so we were certain the feathers would fly.

The only hiccup in our plan was how we were going to get them all to enter the room at the same time. That is when the guard happened to walk by. Liliana said that he owed her a favor for not ratting on him when he was late to his post one evening. He would inform the guys that we had been attacked, that way we knew they would all come running. What we didn't anticipate was them being as mad as they were.

"I'm sorry, Enzo. We really didn't mean anything by it. Please, the guard was just following orders. He doesn't need to die," I plead.

"You're not as sorry as you are going to be, Aliyah. If you don't want the guard to die, what are you willing to do in exchange for his life?" Enzo's eyes heat and his nostrils flare.

"What's the price?" I ask in a whisper, making my biggest doe eyes at him.

"To start, you are going to clean up the mess you made."

In one swift motion, Enzo picks me up and throws me over his shoulder. My sleep shirt rides up and I feel the jam from his chest and neck sticking to my exposed skin. Enzo walks me across the hall into his room, right into the adjoining washroom and sets me down in front of him.

He stands before me, that stern look still plastered to his face. *Along with the jam and feathers.* I am really trying not to laugh in this situation because I know it will just make it worse for me.

"You infuriate me sometimes, little dove," he says.

I blink up at him, but smile. I run my fingers under his tunic and feel his abs flex as I run my hands over his abdomen. I let my hands caress up his chest and he lifts his arms for me as I pull the tunic over his head. I stare at his bare chest and note the marred skin beneath the curls of chest hair.

"We didn't mean anything by it, Enzo. It was just supposed to be a fun prank," I say.

I kneel before him and unlace his boots before pulling his foot from each one. I suppose the least I could do is make sure that all the jam and feathers comes out of his hair.

He moves to get into the stall and turns on the water. It rains down over his body, but the feathers won't budge. Apparently jam and water don't mix well. I stifle a laugh as I walk over to the wash basins across from the stall. I hop up on the counter and watch as Enzo tries to wash the jam from his hair. I place my hand over my mouth to hide my smile.

"Ugh! That's it. Get in here and help me."

I slowly slide off the counter and make my way over to the stall. We both stand there in the water fully clothed, not caring that water has begun to splash all over the tiles.

I pull my bottom lip in between my teeth to try and stop myself from laughing. Enzo is still covered in jam and feathers. Memories of that powdered, jelly-filled pastry flash through my mind.

"Aliyah. Stop smiling. This isn't funny," Enzo says.

He hands me a small container filled with purple liquid. I pour some into my hands and rub them together. It smells of rain water on a crisp fall day. I reach my arms up to rub the suds into Enzo's hair, but I strain to reach his head properly.

Sensing my discomfort, Enzo begins to lower himself to the floor. Kneeling before me, Enzo wraps his arms around my legs and lays his head on my stomach. He begins those soothing circles again on the back of my legs.

"Wash, Aliyah."

He continues holding my body as I run my hands through his hair, washing away the jam and feathers. They float towards the drain at the other end of the stall and slip beneath the surface of the stone, eliminating any evidence of our prank. I let my eyes slip closed as the feeling of Enzo's hair returns to all its silky glory. I let the water wash away the suds and use my hands to cup his jaw and tilt his head up to look at me.

"Enzo."

"Yes, little dove?"

"Thank you for bringing me here. To SunSpark. To Citrine. To Olyrium as a whole. You truly have changed my life forever."

He stands up in front of me and when he looks down at me, water drips off the ends of hair and lands on my cheeks. Enzo leans down a breath away from my lips. I close my eyes waiting for his kiss, but it never comes.

"Apologize."

"What?" I can barely get the word out in my love induced haze. My body is on fire for his touch, waiting for every nerve to explode.

"Apologize for the prank. Apologize for making me think you were hurt. Apologize for making me think I failed in protecting you...again. Apologize for it all, Aliyah."

I open my eyes to look him so he knows I mean it. "Enzo, I know you will always protect me. I know you will always do whatever you can to keep me safe."

"Say. It."

"I'm sorry, Enzo."

With that, his lips crash to mine. His body pushes up against mine and even fully clothed, I feel like he is seeing my soul bared to him for the first time. I want this with him. I wish we could be married so that I can truly know him in that way. I wish our fates could be aligned forever. But I know the Maker has bigger and better plans for Enzo. Our stolen kisses is all we will be allowed in this life.

Before I can do anything else, he picks me up and I wrap my legs around his waist. He starts to lead us out of the stall and walks towards the bed. He sets me down and walks over to his dresser. Pulling out an oversized tunic and soft linen pants, he hands them to me and turns around.

"Change," he commands, turning around.

I strip out of my clothes and quickly change into the dry ones.

"I'm done. You can turn around now," I say.

He walks over to the head of the bed. I watch his movements like they are my favorite painting and I never want to look away.

"Get in. You're sleeping here tonight, and you're going to like it."

"But wait— where will you sleep? This is your bed. You should sleep here."

"Who said I wasn't sleeping here? Now get in, shut up, and sleep."

He moves to the other side of the bed and climbs under the sheets. He pulls me close so my back is to his chest and I feel his nose nuzzle into my hair.

"Enzo," I whisper. "Please don't kill the guard."

"He lives. For now," he replies, and then darkness pulls me under.

Chapter 41

ALIYAH

"H ow far is the Reflecting Pool from here?" I ask as we make our way to the front of the palace.

"Not far, but we can't make it there on foot," Gunnar says.

"So how do we get there?"

Gunnar just smiles at me before leading us out of the palace. Liliana decided to join us on the journey today saying that she wanted to get out of the palace for a while. Personally, I think she just wants to spend more time with Duncan.

Queen Starla saw us off this morning after breakfast, reminding me to inform her of what the Reflecting Pool shows me. I want to ask Gunnar why she cares so much, but at the same time, they all warned me there might be trouble in SunSpark and I don't want to upset Gunnar by accusing his mother of anything.

As we walk, I overhear Lil talking to Duncan. This morning at breakfast Sara told me that she overheard Liliana in Duncan's room last night. I guess she had gone to his room to apologize, but he shot her down real quick. Apparently, Marigold had overheard Liliana telling Duncan that the feathers weren't the only thing stuck in places he didn't want them. He still has a grumpy look on his face today, but at least he is allowing her to talk to him. Every so often I catch the slightest hint of a smile grace his lips, but Makerforbid he let anyone see. Maybe Lil is good for him. He needs someone who is a ray of sunshine to his dark cloud.

Outside the palace is sweltering hot compared to the cool interior. When I went back to my room this morning Marigold was waiting to help me get ready for the day.

She put my hair in two braids starting at my forehead and ending about the middle of my back. She told me that I would want my hair out of my face today, for whatever reason. She also had laid out a short sleeve, white tunic that has ties crisscrossing over my chest and black leather pants.

Initially, I complained about the leather pants, as the last time we came here it was far too hot for them. She insisted I would want them on today. After I laced up my boots and headed for my bedroom door, she handed me a black leather jacket that zipped up at a diagonal.

I told her that I wouldn't need it in this heat and left without it. She must have blabbed to Enzo, because when we left this morning he had it tucked under his arm.

Sara and Gunnar walk hand in hand at the front of the group, with Jade not far behind them. Lil and Duncan somehow switched from her laughing and him grunting in response to them arguing over which kingdom has the best food. Apparently the Twilight Kingdom is winning. Duncan may be slightly biased in that regard. Enzo and I bring up the back of the group, taking our time. He takes my hand and I look up at him and smile.

"We are even now. You locking me in your room and me covering you with jam and feathers. Truce?" I say, winking at him.

"Oh are we now? If I remember correctly, my actions served a purpose, while yours were just cruel. I will agree to a truce as long as you promise no more pranks," he smiles back.

"It only seems fair." I bend my leg up to the side to kick him in the butt as he walks. He laughs and puts his arm around my shoulder tucking me into his side.

"Enzo, how are we getting to the pool?" I ask.

"The Reflecting Pool is not easily accessed, which is why the queen was so angry that you would even ask to go there. It is a very secluded and private space. It floats in the sky high above SunSpark. The pool sits in the middle of a large floating rock formation. The only way to get there is by sphinx. They are matched to those of SunSpark like the alicanto are to the people who live in Krystal, but sphinx are much kinder to those who are not matched with them."

"So does Gunnar have a sphinx and an alicanto?"

"Gunnar had a sphinx back when he was a child, but I am not sure if it is still alive. They have longer lifespans than alicanto, but Gunnar is 704 years old, and most sphinx only live to about 200. I am sure it has passed on by now."

"Gunnar is 704 years old?!" I say with an exasperated tone. "How old does that make you?"

"Oh, I am significantly younger than Gunnar," Enzo smiles. "I am only 702 years old."

He laughs so hard at my wide eyes and wide open jaw. *Holy. Crap.* I am only 26 years old.

"Since I am technically fae, does that mean I am going to live to be over 700?" I ask.

"Little dove, you are going to live far longer than 700 years old. I will make sure of that myself."

He plants a kiss to the top of my head. I reach up with my hand and interlink our fingers with the hand that rests on my shoulder.

"Who's ready to ride a sphinx?" Gunnar yells back in excitement. I think the only two who are excited are Gunnar and Lil.

"We will have to ride in pairs since none of us other than Lil are matched to one," he adds.

"I'm good to ride alone. I grew up around sphinx even though I never matched to one," Jade states.

We are approaching a large field with a fence around it that does absolutely nothing because standing in the field are giant sphinxes. They have a body that looks like the lions I have seen in books with large manes, thin swishing tails, and massive paws.

I wish I could say that was the scariest part of this whole thing, but it is suddenly dawning on me why we need to take them to the Reflecting Pool.

Protruding from their backs are two massive, white feathered wings. The sun reflects off them, casting a bright light into my eyes. Gunnar and Sara walk up to one of them and it immediately drops down onto its front paws, allowing them to climb up.

Sara grips onto its large mane. Gunnar puts his arms around Sara's waist as the sphinx shoots into the sky. Sara lets out a scream followed by laughter, as she spreads her arms out like she is flying too.

Lil puts two fingers in her mouth, blows out a patterned whistle and calls out. "Molly! Come on girl!"

A sphinx comes bounding over to her. For a moment I think it is going to attack her by the way it leaps into the air, paws outstretched, landing on top of Lil. Its huge tongue licks her face before getting up. Lil laughs and takes ahold of Duncan's hand clearly not giving him a choice before pulling him up behind her.

He rolls his eyes as she takes his hands and places them around her waist, telling him to hold on tight. She gives the sphinx a light kick and it takes off into the sky. For a second, I swear I see fear in Duncan's eyes. I laugh as I walk over towards Jade.

"So what do I do? Just pick one?" I ask.

"Yup! So just walk up to one, maybe give it a little head scratch just for good measure, and hop on!" she says.

"You sure you are going to be okay to ride alone?"

"Absolutely. When I was younger I would make my way over this field from my village and watch the sphinx play and graze. I always wished I could ride one." She rubs the head of one while she talks and I hear it purr under her touch. "I used to imagine I was flying through the sky. I was never allowed to match with one because I am not High Fae. Today, my wish came true." She wipes a tear away, before climbing on the back of the sphinx, and taking off into the sky.

I smile as I watch her fly away. *I'm glad you got your wish, Jade.*

I turn to find Enzo already on top of one. He reaches down and pulls me up onto it, sitting in front of him. I grasp onto the mane and hold my breath as it shoots into the sky.

I close my eyes when I start to see little black spots, but when I open them back up— We are high above the clouds soaring through the sky. The others aren't far ahead of us, and I can hear the hoots and hollers in the wind as they fly. Their sphinxes perform dips and swirls, clearly having as much fun as they are.

"Do you want to try?" Enzo asks, placing his chin on my shoulder.

"I'm scared," I admit.

"Anything that is worth doing in life is always a little scary. Hold on tight," he says, moments before we suddenly drop from the sky.

The sphinx tucks its wings and begins spiraling like a corkscrew through the sky. A scream rips from my throat as a sudden rush of air stops us. Spreading its wings, we glide over a large body of water with a glassy surface.

The sun reflects off the water like glistening starlight. My braids whip back behind me with our gaining speed. The sphinx tips to the side, dipping the tip of its wing in the water creating a wake behind us.

I risk letting go of the mane and allow my hand to touch the water that splashes up. It races past my fingertips in powerful waves. I close my eyes and let the warm breeze caress my skin and feel the sunshine on my face. I feel *free*.

A few tears slip from my eyes from both the force of the wind and from this feeling in my chest. It's like nothing I have ever felt before. There is no impending doom over when my next beating will come. No pressure pushing down on my chest at the thought of when I will eat next. I just. Feel. Freedom.

Enzo's arms tighten around me as he places his chin back on my shoulder and I tip my head to the side to rest it on his. For the first time in my life, this feels dangerously like home.

The sphinx pulses its wings in harsh beats and takes us back above the clouds, joining the others. They are ascending further now, approaching the floating island of rock above us.

My moment of bliss is gone and is replaced with dread, as I remember why we are here. What if I don't get answers? What if the answer I get is not what we are looking for? What if–

"Stop. Relax. Everything is going to be alright, no matter what we find here," Enzo speaks as we land on the rock's surface.

It is almost as if he could feel my head spiraling into panic.

"How do you always do that?" I laugh.

"I have spent hours upon hours staring at you Aliyah. I *know* you."

He presses a kiss to my neck and slides off the sphinx. Helping me down, he grasps me around the waist and lifts me up before planting me safely on the ground. My knees give out a little after being in the air, but he is there to hold me up. I turn and give the lion a scratch behind the ears. I lean closer to its head and whisper.

"Thank you for what you did." I'm not sure if it understands what I said, or if it understands the gift it gave me, but I owe it a thanks nonetheless.

I turn to find the pool sitting in the middle of the rock formation. The water is turquoise reflecting the sky above us. There are a few large rocks around the outside of the pool and some green moss that grows on the outside ring. The rock isn't huge, but big enough for everyone to sit and wait for me to get this over with.

The rock sits above the clouds, so the sun is blazing down on us. Thankfully Lil gave me some protective lotion before we left or I would be completely red right now. Sara and Gunnar are already seated on a rock and of course Sara is sunbathing, getting about two shades darker with each moment that passes. *Lucky bastard,* I think to myself and laugh under my breath.

Jade sits next to Lil and Duncan at the edge of the water. They are talking idly about Lil's sphinx, Molly, and how she became her matched. I try to swallow the worry sitting in my throat, but it is met with a large knot that makes me feel like I am choking on the pressure.

What if I brought everyone here for nothing? I gaze at the water and start walking towards it. Sitting down at the edge, I begin unlacing my boots. I should have brought a change of clothes.

"Enzo." I look at him with tears in my eyes as he sits down next to me, taking out an apple from his pack and biting into it.

"Tell me how this works again." I start to unbutton my pants, but Enzo stops me.

"Everyone turn around," he commands.

"It isn't anything that we haven't seen before, Enzo," Gunnar smirks at him, clearly goading him.

"You will all turn around right freaking now if you want to still have eyes by the time we leave here. You are my family, so I will spare your lives, but you will *all* lose your eyes if even one of you turns around."

Everyone shifts to turn around before settling back down. I hear Gunnar mumble under his breath. "Guess all the sphinx are losing their eyes then."

Sara laughs next to him and hits him in the arm. Right as Gunnar is laying back to relax on the rock, Enzo chucks the apple at the back of his head, hitting him. Everyone bursts out into laughter as Gunnar reaches behind to rub his head as he picks up the apple and takes a bite of it.

"Disrespectful, ZoZo. Dis—re—spect—ful," he taunts.

It feels nice to laugh again before this. If there is one thing this group can do it is break the tension with a joke.

With everyone now turned around, I pull my tunic over my head and place it next to my boots. I unbutton my pants and fold them nicely, leaving me in my undershirt and lace underwear.

I stand there in front of Enzo and take in his heated eyes. His hands are flexing at his sides, like he can't help but want to touch me.

"Problem?" I ask.

"Get in the water, Aliyah," he grits through his teeth.

"Maybe I'll just take one more moment out here in the sun to warm up before I go in," I wink at him.

"Aliyah. You're playing a game you will not win."

I move to sit down on the shore and stretch my legs and arms out letting the sun wash over me.

"Ahhhh. Isn't this nice, Enzo?"

Without another word, Enzo is picking me up over his shoulder and gives my butt a hard smack. I yelp at the contact, but I can't deny the leap that occurs in my heart. Enzo walks us right to the edge of the water and stands there.

"Can you ever just follow directions the first time, little dove?"

"And if I don't, ZoZo? What will you do? You're just a big ol'—"

Suddenly I am flying through the air and a scream rips from my throat. Water engulfs my entire body and I have to kick my way up to the surface.

"You'll pay for that later, Enzo!" I call back, swimming out to the middle.

The water is crystal clear beneath the surface. I turn to float on my back, keeping my head out of the water. I kick my legs out in circles and try to relax.

"How do I see the vision of my past or future?" I call back.

"Go out to the middle of the pool and just relax. Give yourself over to the water. Let it flow around you, making you one with it," Gunnar calls out.

Relax. Great. The one thing I suck at most. I can do this.

Aliyah, I believe in you. I know that relaxing isn't your strong suit, but you're safe here. We all have you.

Sara's encouragement is what I needed to help slow my racing heart. I feel calm, fully at peace with myself, like all my anxiety has suddenly been completely taken away. If it is Lil taking the edge off my emotions, I am thankful she decided to come. I lay my head back in the water and close my eyes. I breathe in...out...in...out. *Nothing.* Nothing is happening.

"I don't understand what I am supposed to be feeling." I yell towards the shore. "What is it supposed to—"

My air supply is cut off as water fills my mouth. My eyes fly open and see the surface of the water above me. I'm being dragged down by something. I look down to try and see what has its hold on me, but I see nothing. Oh my Maker, I think I'm being dragged down by the water.

I start to panic. I try kicking my legs towards the surface, but whatever has a hold on me isn't letting go. I open my mouth to scream and water fills my mouth and slips down my throat.

Sara help! I can't breathe! I try calling out to her, but I hear nothing back.

My arms scramble above me, like I can claw my way to the surface. Right as my vision starts to fade in and out, a bright light flashes beneath the surface in front of me, and a booming voice ripples through the water.

"Aliyah." The voice is so loud that I have to reach up and try to cover my ears.

"A strong name, for a strong girl. One whose name means to ascend to great and mighty things. Let the sky be your limit, Aliyah. Rise from this realm and into the next."

The voice cuts out and an image appears in glowing light. There, before me is an image that looks like a door, but it has no handle on it. I can barely make out the thin lines of light coming through the slats. The water around me turns cold and my skin pebbles in response.

Just as quickly as the vision appeared it blinks away, leaving me at the bottom of the pool fading into nothing. I inhaled too much water. My vision slacks and I see nothing but darkness.

Chapter 42

ENZO

I stand on the shore watching Aliyah paddle out to the middle.

"How do I see the vision of my past or future?" She calls back.

"Go out to the middle of the pool and just relax. Give yourself over to the water. Let it flow around you, making you one with it." Gunnar yells back.

She is not exactly skilled at relaxing. I laugh to myself and shake my head. She yells something back at us, but I don't quite catch what she says, my mind still clouded from the haze her presence induces on me.

Suddenly, she disappears under the water. My eyes flash to Gunnar to see if this is normal, but his back is turned to the pool.

"Enzo!" Sara yells at me, standing and running towards me. Okay, obviously this isn't normal.

"Enzo, she's in trouble. I can't get through to her, but I can feel it in here." She places a palm over her heart. "Enzo, she needs help."

Without hesitation I run into the water, taking a deep breath, before diving under the surface. I pull on the water hard. I swim deeper and deeper. Thank the Maker the water is crystal clear. She's there, right at the bottom of the pool, *not moving*. Panic surges in my chest at the sight of her still body. I swim as fast as I can towards her.

When I reach her, I put my arm under her legs and one around her back, pushing off the bottom towards the surface. About halfway into our ascent, a bright light casts out through the water, opening up an image before me. A voice, louder than anything I have ever heard before, ripples through the water around me. I want to reach up and cover my ears, but I refuse to let go of Aliyah.

"Enzo." The voice sends a chill through my spine. "One born with the meaning of home to those who love you. You will feel great loss, but fear not, for all who are lost can be found and brought home again."

The voice washes away with the ripples in the water. I blink to make sure I am not just oxygen deprived, but clear as day I see a vision of me on my knees covered in blood. I hold something in my arms, but there is nothing there but a bright, golden light. In the vision, I'm crying and shaking whatever it is I am holding, before lifting my chin to the sky and screaming into the abyss.

I blink and the vision is gone. I look down at Aliyah, still not moving in my arms and put the vision into the back of my mind to deal with later. I kick my legs hard, finding I am able to move towards the surface once again. As soon as I break the water line, I spin onto my back and place Aliyah's body out of the water on top of mine. *Why is she always dying on my watch?*

I make it to where I can stand again, and pull her into my arms, racing as fast as I can from the water. Sara stands on the shore, hand covering her mouth in shock and tears pouring from her eyes as she sees Aliyah limp in my arms. Everyone else is still turned away from the pool, but they are all standing now.

"Will one of you freaking help me?" I yell.

"Will we get our eyes gouged out if we turn around?" Gunnar quips.

"Maker Gunnar, help me!" I growl.

Everyone turns now and races toward us. I lay Aliyah down on the ground and start shaking her body. This can't be my vision. She can't be the one I was holding in my arms. I will die here and now if that is my fate. I shake her hard one last time before my mind is made up on what I need to do. I pull on my power and bring it out of the depths of my soul. I place my hand on her chest and imagine her lungs forcing the water out of her body. She convulses beneath me, water comes flying out of her mouth, coughing as she does.

"Thank the Maker," Saraphena says, kneeling down next to me.

She pushes the hair out of Aliyah's face and lays her head in her lap. I hold Aliyah's hand and kiss her lips as her eyes open and find us all kneeling around her.

"Well that was...eventful." She smiles up at us, like she didn't just drown.

"Don't you *ever* freaking do that again," Saraphena says, looking down at her. I can't say I disagree with her command.

We all smile and disperse as I pull Aliyah into my arms and give her a deep kiss. I run my fingers through her wet hair and pull her as close as I can to my body. It still doesn't feel close enough. If I could crack open my chest and stuff her inside so she can never be harmed again, I would.

"Enzo," she says. "Um, I'm a little cold. Do you mind if I get dressed now?" She smiles softly up at me.

"Please do. I gave them all a pass to help me when you weren't breathing, but I still don't want them seeing you undressed," I smirk.

Helping her stand, she slips on her leather pants and white tunic shirt. The sun dried us both off pretty quickly, but her hair is still soaking wet. I walk over to the sphinx and grab her jacket off the back. Marigold came to me before we left and told me that Aliyah refused to take it, but that she knew Aliyah would need it after her swim.

Helping Aliyah slip it on, I zip it up for her and watch as she shutters at the warmth the leather provides.

"Don't tell Marigold she was right," she laughs.

"So?" Jade asks. "What did you see? Past or future? What was the vision?"

Everyone stops and looks at Aliyah now. Tears well up in her eyes.

"I– I didn't see anything really. All I saw was what looked like a door with thin slats that let light in. I don't remember anything like that from my past, so it must have shown me my future, but I don't understand any of it. This gave me no more answers than that stupid book in Citrine."

"What did it show you?" Duncan asks me. Now everyone's eyes are on me.

"Nothing. It didn't show me a vision. I probably wasn't in there long enough, nor was I very relaxed," I smirk, and laugh it off.

They don't need to know what I saw. Whatever that vision was, it is *not* my future. I won't let it be.

Chapter 43

ALIYAH

The ride back is unbelievably cold. I don't know what I would have done without the jacket Marigold insisted I bring, or the heat from Enzo's body.

We don't speak the entire flight home and as we make our way back to the castle, the energy of the group is somber. Enzo holds my hand as we ascend the steps to our rooms. Standing outside my door, I turn to him before I go in.

"Enzo, I'm sorry about today," I say.

"There is nothing to apologize for. We knew we were taking a chance with the Reflecting Pool, but it was not a loss. We may not understand what the Pool showed you, but I know we can figure it out together."

"Thank you."

"Would you like me to come and keep an eye on you while you ready yourself for the evening?" Enzo says trying to lighten my mood.

"No, that's alright. I think I need some time to myself. I'll see you later." I close the door behind me and take a few deep breaths before heading towards the washroom. Filling up the tub with warm water and lavender soap that creates bubbles on the surface, is just what I need to relax.

I watch the water fill almost to the edge of the tub and something pinches in my chest. I stare at the water rippling on the surface as the bubbles pop. My mind flashes back to that moment being pulled down below the surface. My breath quickens and I feel my heart racing in my chest.

I try to take a deep breath, but its like my chest won't expand. *I can do this. I can do this. I can do this.* I repeat this to myself over and over to try and build my confidence. Pins and needles bombard my face and my vision wavers as panic claws at my mind. I move to step into the tub, but freeze midair.

A knock sounds at my bedroom door. Relief washes over me knowing that I don't have to get into the water. I exit the washroom and find a robe to throw over my body. I have just finished tying it as I open the door.

Kaleron? He is leaning on the door frame, one ankle crossed over the other and hands in his pockets. I glance around him to the door across the hall that leads to Enzo's room.

The door is shut, and I suddenly wish I had accepted his invitation to watch over me. My cheeks flush at Kaleron's presence, and the fact that I am completely naked, asides for the robe.

"Um, hi. Can I help you with something?" I ask.

"May I come in?" he says, a smile gracing his face.

"I'm not sure that is the best idea. I was just about to step into the bath."

"Oh, what a shame I interrupted that," he smirks. "I just wanted to see how the Reflecting Pool was? I heard you had quite the experience."

"If you heard, then why are you here asking me?"

"Mother's orders, I'm afraid. She wanted to come herself, but I offered in her stead. She wants to hear it directly from the source."

He moves to step into the room and I quickly grab one of my throwing knives from the table next to my door. I tuck it behind my back as I move further into the room, putting some distance between us.

"The pool didn't show me anything of note," I snap. I don't know why I am getting defensive about what the vision showed me, but I'm really not in the mood to answer a ton of questions about why I didn't see anything that can help us.

"Interesting." He says, before quirking an eyebrow. "I will be sure to let the queen know that you saw nothing of importance. I must admit, I have an ulterior motive for coming here. As you know we have the ball tomorrow night, and it would be my greatest honor if you would accompany me. What do you say?"

"I'm not sure that Enzo would like that very much. Nor would I for that matter."

"Please keep in mind that here, I am a prince. Enzo is a soldier. Nothing more. To refuse me could result in dire consequences."

"What could you possibly do? The king and queen are the ones who rule, not you."

"You've seen the king. You tell me if he is fit to rule. All he does is stuff his face and sleep his days away. *I* am the one pulling the strings. My mother takes my recommendations very seriously. You wouldn't want me to tell her to stop providing those little seeds that feed all of Krystal, now would you?"

My blood is boiling. How dare he use this against me just to go to a simple ball with him. *How bad can one night really be?*

"Fine. I'll go to the ball with you."

"Excellent!" He claps his hands together, and a broad smile fills his face. "I will pick you up here tomorrow night then. Please, do let me know if you have any other *desires* during your stay." He moves to exit my room before stopping at the door and turning towards me.

"Oh and Aliyah, don't mention this conversation to anyone. It will be our little secret lest there be dire consequences." Challenge flashes in his gaze.

"Oh please, Kaleron. You're nothing but a prince with a silver spoon shoved up your—"

"Test me, Aliyah, and I'll have to make sure your party leaves here with one less."

"You wouldn't dare touch Enzo. He would never let that happen," I snarl.

"Who said anything about Enzo?" He exits and shuts the door behind him. Rage bubbles up in me and tips over the edge. I scream and throw my knife, embedding it into the door frame.

"Well, that was certainly enlightening." A voice comes up from behind me, and I almost jump out of my skin, as Sara materializes out of thin air.

"Maker Sara!" I put my hand on my chest. "You scared the crap out of me. When the hell did you get in here?"

"Sorry," she laughs. "I was heading back to my room when I saw Kaleron walking towards yours. I hid myself and waited behind him, just in case he tried anything shady, and when he pushed himself in here I slipped in behind him. I can't believe he threatened the entire Krystal Kingdom. Without those seeds no one would have the ability to grow food."

"I know. And to say that all with a stupid grin on his face too. I can't believe that's Gunnar's brother!"

"Trust me, they are nothing alike. Kaleron has been raised to be a ruthless leader. He was taught to do whatever it takes to keep his kingdom alive," she says.

"If I ruled a kingdom, I would certainly not rule with fear. Respect goes much farther," I say, rolling my eyes.

"Are you going to tell Enzo?"

"I don't know. I don't want anyone to get hurt, but at the same time, he would be so angry if he found out and knew I didn't tell him. I feel like we are in a good place right now, and I don't like the idea of hiding things from him. But you heard what Kaleron said. It isn't just about Krystal. He threatened everyone I care about. How can I just sit back and let that happen?"

"You don't. He screwed up in the deal he made with you. Kaleron said *you* couldn't tell Enzo. He said nothing about me."

"Tell me what?"

Enzo's voice fills the room. Anger flares is in his eyes and his hands are clenched into fists at his side.

"I can't tell you, but Sara can. Let's just hope Kaleron isn't a stickler for semantics," I say, stepping into the washroom and shutting the door behind me.

I hear muffled talking on the other side of the door as I sit on the edge of the tub, my feet in the water. This is as far as my body would let me go without panicking. Something shatters and a door slams.

He knows. Good luck. Sara's soft voice fills my head. Great, he knows *and* he's pissed.

"No way in hell is that happening, Aliyah!" Enzo yells on the other side of the door. I hear him jiggling the handle, but I locked it knowing that he was going to be mad.

"I swear if you don't open this door right now, I'll—"

"Not until you calm down," I say, swinging my feet in and out of the water watching the droplets roll off my skin.

Suddenly a large crash sounds to my right and I whip my head around to see that Enzo has broken down the door and it lays in splinters on the ground around me.

"Or you can do that too," I roll my eyes. Even though Enzo is angry, I know he would never do anything to actually hurt me. Enzo walks over to me and pulls me by the back of my neck out of the tub and slams me up against the wall completely ignoring the fact that I am only in my robe.

"Maker Aliyah, what were you thinking?" he yells, only inches away from my face.

"I was *thinking* about Krystal! I was *thinking* about *your* kingdom! It is one night. How bad can it possibly be? You will be right there the entire time! There is nothing he could do to me that is anything worse than what I have already survived!" I yell back, frustrated now that he doesn't understand the position I was in.

"I'll kill him for this. I warned him once. That is all he gets." Enzo releases my neck and storms out of the room.

"Enzo, wait," I call back.

He stops in the washroom doorway, his back facing me. I walk over carefully to avoid the splinters and wrap my arms around him from behind.

"Please don't go. I want to take a bath but— I can't."

I feel the rapid beat of his heart under my palms and the air in his chest as it rises and falls in short breaths. He reaches up and grabs my hand. Slowly I feel his breathing settle and his head hangs down. I turn my face and lay my head on his back.

"I can't let this go unanswered, Aliyah. Its not who I am."

"I'm not saying you have to let it go, I am asking you to trust me. I can do this. And if he does anything you don't like, you can be right there to protect me."

"If even a single hair on your head is out of place by his hand, I will not hesitate again."

"Understood. For now, will you stay with me?"

Enzo turns and looks down at me. "I will *always* stay with you."

He turns and lifts me off the ground so I don't step on any of the splintered wood. I wrap my legs around his waist and put my hands around the back of his neck as he carries me over to the tub. I run my nails over the base of his skull in soothing circles and his skin pebbles in response.

Setting me on the edge, he lowers himself next to the tub. Reaching for my hand, he takes it and helps me step into the tub. He closes his eyes as I take off the robe. I sink down into the tub and pull the bubbles around me so that I am covered. I wait for the panic to creep up my neck, but the longer I sit here staring at Enzo, I never feel it come.

"You saved me today...again," I say.

"You almost died today...again," he says back, opening his eyes.

I snort out a quick huff of laughter.

"That's what? Twice now?" I joke. It doesn't land.

"I don't know what I would do without you, Aliyah. I don't know who I would *be* without you. My entire life I told myself that I would never need love, but then you walked into my life and I can't let you go." He grips my hand, almost painfully so as if he lets me go, I will never come back.

"When you brought me here, I was *so* angry. But now...now I can't imagine my life without you. I hope I never have to know a world without you, Enzo. But if the time comes, I want you to promise to let me go. Even though you are my world, I know I cannot be your future."

"Aliyah—"

"Promise me, Enzo. If there ever comes a time when our journey together comes to an end, I need you to let me go. Even if it hurts."

"I cannot make a promise I have no intent on keeping. No matter what comes our way, I will be by your side. I can never let you go, because if I let you go, you would take what is left of my soul with you. I would have *nothing* to live for. I would be a shell filled with darkness and destruction. So, no, I will never let you go."

He kisses me deeply, pulling me closer by the back of my neck. I want him to promise me that he will move on, but I can't bring myself to break our kiss. I need this. I need him.

He runs his hands up my shoulder, moving to caress each scar on my back. I move to pull away from his touch as he traces them, but he holds firm.

"Be proud of your scars, Aliyah. You survived. You *lived.*"

I try to let his words settle into that space in my heart where my shame lives. I want to be proud of the things I have survived. I don't want them to hide away in my mind forever. I want to know that when I look back at my life, I know that it meant something. That *I* meant something to someone in this world.

Enzo has taught me so much. I know there will never be a way to ever repay him for the person he is helping me become. The only way I can think to truly show him how thankful I am for all he has given me is to become the person he thinks that I am. I know he accepts me, flaws and all, but I want him to know that for him, I will keep trying to let my past go.

"Have you ever thought about marriage?" I ask.

"Not until very recently," he smiles at me.

"Are fae allowed to marry someone who is not their mate?"

"While it is not common, yes, there are people who marry that are not mates. Finding a bonded mate is a beautiful thing, but not everyone is lucky enough to find theirs. Some are even from different kingdoms or they lost their loved one to death. They will go on to marry someone whom they love, but do not share that bond with. However, it does not make the marriage any less special."

"Do you hope to marry your bonded mate?"

"There is only one person I am interested in being married to. Bonded mate or not, there is no one else."

I blush at his comment and try not to let his words get to my head. As much as I want this, I am still so uncertain of our future. I know what I want, and he may say he wants the same with me, but if he finds his bonded mate, he should be with them.

"Aliyah," he starts.

"Let's not ruin this moment with talk of things that can never come to pass. I just want to enjoy whatever time we have together. No one's future is ever secure," I smile softly at him.

He smiles at me before standing and turning around.

"What are you doing?"

"Waiting for you to finish washing up. You'll be staying with me again tonight. I don't want a girl covered in pond water sleeping in my bed however," he laughs.

I finish scrubbing my body while trying to keep thoughts of what could have been out of my head.

Chapter 44

ENZO

I hold Aliyah in my arms with my head resting lightly on top of hers. The tips of my fingers run up and down her back, and this time, she doesn't pull away.

"Enzo, will you tell me a story?" she says, sleep pulling at her voice.

"A story? What kind of story?"

"Any story."

"Hm. Alright. Once upon a time there was a beautiful woman. She had long, dark brown hair—"

"Hey! I don't want to hear a story about another woman you've been with!"

"Hush little dove, and listen to the story."

She settles in as I continue.

"She had long, dark brown hair and bright green eyes. Her favorite thing in the world was baking pastries. Her father was a baker, you see, the best one in town.

One day, a group of young soldiers came into her shop and one male in particular caught her eye immediately. He approached the woman and asked for her finest pastry. She handed him a chocolate cupcake with raspberry flavored frosting on top. As he went to pay for the item, the woman refused the money.

Stunned, the male asked if she would join him for dinner that evening as a way of paying for his food. She agreed, reluctantly.

That night when they met at one of the local establishments, she was swept off her feet by the male's charm and humor. They walked around for hours after they ate and told stories of their childhoods.

As time went on, their love grew. But one day, he was called away to serve the realm. He didn't want to leave the woman, but he had no choice. She promised to wait for him, no matter how long it took and he promised to come back to her. So she waited. Time passed, but she waited. Years went by, and still she waited.

Every day for the last several years she would look up when the bell on the door rang, hoping it would be her love coming home. One day, she was working in her shop when that familiar sound carried through the air. In the doorway stood the love of her life.

The moment they laid eyes on each other, a bright light broke through their chests and an invisible tether formed between them. Even after all those years of waiting, their love was so strong, the mating bond awoke. Her years of missing him, not knowing if he was alive or dead, were all worth it now that he was her mate.

Soon after that they married and had a baby boy. Years passed, and time became a blur. Every day, the woman and her mate grew more and more in love. The little boy knew he wanted a mate of his own after seeing the love his parents shared.

But the woman became ill. The male searched high and low across the realms for a cure. The little boy took care of his mother the best that he could but, she was withering away like a fading rose. The male was gone for several months before he finally returned. He hadn't found a cure, and he was too late. The woman had died holding the boy's hand not days before.

The man was crushed with regret for leaving his mate and vowed never to love again. Seeing the man turn to monster, the little boy became hardened to love. He never wanted to experience what his father went through. He let his heart turn black. Until a woman came into his life hundreds of years later. Now, the little boy's heart doesn't seem so black anymore."

As I look down, I see Aliyah fast asleep. I stroke my fingers through her long blonde hair and place a kiss to the side of her head. I will never move on from her. Even in death, I would wait for the day we find each other again. You're my forever, little dove.

Chapter 45

ALIYAH

L ight streams in from a crack in the curtain over the window. I blink away the sleepiness from my eyes and I find Enzo awake in the chair by the window. He is reading a book and sipping from a small cup of tea. It's such a strange sight to see him simply lounging by a window sipping tea. A smile creeps across my face the longer I stare at him.

"Good morning, my dove, are you ready for the ball today?"

Crap. That's right. Memories of last night come flooding in. Kaleron, that bastard, is making me go to the ball with him.

"Enzo," I start, "can we— can we talk about the ball tonight? You cannot kill Gunnar's brother."

"I won't," he pauses. A breath of relief whooshes out of me. "That is unless he does something that is worth killing him for. Fair warning, Aliyah, he is already on the edge of that line."

"We can't solve everything by killing the problem," I roll my eyes. Tension returns to my chest.

"*We* can't. *I* can." He walks over and places a kiss to my cheek before laying down next to me. I roll in his arm so that I am facing him. His eyes are settled on mine and he gives me a soft smile.

"Enzo, I'm serious."

"So am I, little dove. Kaleron dies if he does anything you don't like. He has had far too many warnings at this point."

"You've only given him two warnings." I give a soft laugh.

"Two too many."

"I'm sorry I fell asleep during your story last night. How did it end?"

"I'm not yet sure how it ends, but I'll let you know when I do."

Before I can ask what he means, the bedroom door bursts open and Enzo grabs me, pushing me under him so he is covering me completely.

"Time to get up sleepy heads! We have a ball to get ready for! Ali, let's go! The girls are already in their rooms with their ladies maids getting ready!" *Liliana.*

Her cheerful personality is brighter than the sun during the highest point of the day, but it is far too early for that level of cheer. Enzo lets out a growl, that even I am slightly shocked at.

"Liliana, get the hell out. Aliyah will be over when she is ready."

Lil stands there with her hands on her hips and a smirk on her face.

"ZoZo, you don't scare me, not even a little."

"Gunnar!" Enzo yells. We hear chuckling from the hallway as Gunnar passes Enzo's room.

Lil smiles as she walks over to the bed and grabs my hand to pull me away. Enzo moves to pull me back, but I give him the *I'm fine* smile and he lets me go. She leads me out into the hallway and we cross back over into my room.

"Lil, I don't understand, why are we getting ready so early?"

"Early? Girl, you slept till mid-afternoon. I know yesterday was exhausting for you, but we are already behind schedule!"

"Mid-afternoon?" As we walk into my room across the hall, the curtains are pulled back and the setting orange sun blazes across the sky. Four dress bags hang on four long mirrors that have been brought into the room.

Lil walks over to a small rolling table and pours me a glass of wine and hands it to me. Jade and Sara are sitting with their lady's maids discussing hairstyles to try with their dresses. Marigold walks up to me with a smile.

"Come on dear, let's get you cleaned up!" She ushers me into the bathroom and begins filling the tub with water. Anxiety claws at my throat thinking about getting into the bath again. My heartbeat races and my palms begin to sweat as I rub them together. As if on cue, Sara comes walking into the washroom.

"Marigold, would you be so kind as to fetch us some more wine? It seems Lil plans to get us all so drunk that we have no choice but to party all evening," she smiles, excusing Marigold.

"Of course, but milady needs to bathe. Please ensure that happens."

"I'm all over it. Thank you." Sara smiles at me.

"Thank you—" I start, but Sara walks over to me and wraps her arms around me in a tight hug.

"You never have to apologize for not being okay. Being your Soul Guardian means protecting you from more than external threats. Sometimes it means protecting you from yourself." She pulls back, looking me up and down.

"I feel like I have been kind of a shit Guardian these days, but honestly sometimes I'm afraid Enzo will tear me to pieces if I get in his way of saving you," she laughs.

"We both know he could try, but you wouldn't go down without a fight."

"You know me so well," she winks. "How about I stay with you while you bathe? We can chat, catch up, the usual stuff. I feel like I haven't seen much of you since I got back with Gunnar and you and Enzo started things up." She wiggles her eyebrows at me.

"We are in desperate need of girl talk," I say, stepping into the tub and sinking up to my neck in water.

A crushing pressure pushes on my chest and I grip the sides of the tub. I let my eyes slip shut, trying to picture being anywhere but here.

In...out...in....out. Sara's voice fills my mind.

I follow her words with my breathing. I can't do this. I can't. Panic overwhelms me and I shoot up from the tub. Water sloshes over the side and onto the floor. My whole body is shivering, but not from the chill in the air. My skin feels like there are a thousand needles sticking in it and the overwhelming need to vomit rises in my throat. Sara races over with a towel and wraps it around me. She rubs my arms up and down to try and warm me up. Tears spill from my eyes.

"What's happening to me, Sara?"

"Sometimes the things we experience leave more than just physical scars. Sometimes, it is the invisible wounds that take the longest to heal."

My friend stands there in the tub with me, holding me and stroking my hair. I cry into her shoulder in heavy sobs. For a moment, we just stand there and I feel like for the first time I am back in Mareen. When it was just Sara and me. She moves to let go, but I stop her.

"Please don't go yet. Just another minute," I plead.

"Take as much time as you need."

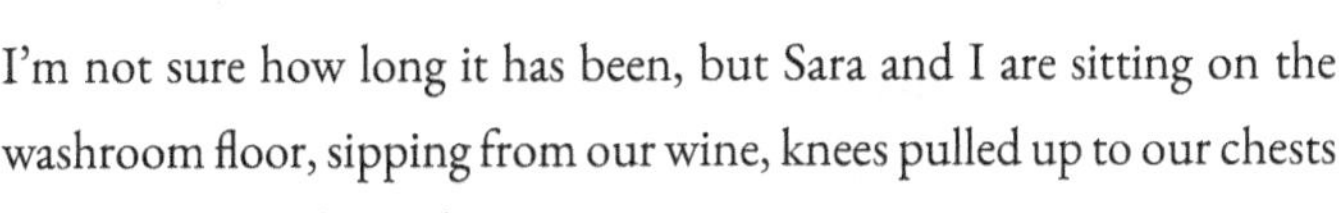

I'm not sure how long it has been, but Sara and I are sitting on the washroom floor, sipping from our wine, knees pulled up to our chests and heads tipped together.

"Sara?"

"Yeah?"

"You're so much more than just my best friend, you know that right? You're– you're my family."

She reaches over and interlocks her fingers with mine.

"And you are mine. No matter what happens, no matter where we end up in this life, we will always be together."

I look down at the moon shaped scar on my arm and the sun scar on hers. Two things that without each other would never be truly complete.

"I'm sorry you had to leave your family for me," I whisper. She rubs her thumb over the back of my hand.

"I wouldn't change any decisions I made about you back then or in the future. I'm with you till the end."

"Well, we should probably get up before Lil comes in here and finds us not getting ready," I laugh.

"I won't tell Marigold that you didn't bathe if you don't rat me out that I didn't make sure it happened." She reaches out her hand to me, pinky finger raised.

"Promise," I say, wrapping my pinky around hers.

We stand and move towards the door to go back into my room. On the other side, Lil and Jade are laying on my bed in silk robes, sipping from their wine and laughing at a story Jade is sharing about Duncan. My three best girlfriends, all in the same room together. I smile and take a run at the bed before diving in between them, sloshing wine over the sides of their glasses with my impact.

"Ooooo. Marigold is gonna *kill* you, Ali," Liliana laughs.

"Maybe you should have held your glasses tighter," Sara yells, mid-air as she jumps onto the bed with us. Lil and Jade laugh, happy tears dripping from the sides of their eyes.

"So what are we talking about?" I ask.

"Jade was just sharing how Duncan once bet Enzo that he couldn't break into their local armory, completely drunk, and be undetected. Needless to say, Enzo lost, mainly because of Gunnar's stupidity, and now owes Duncan a favor to be collected whenever he wants," Lil giggles to herself.

"Speaking of which, Duncan and you really seem to be hitting it off," I wink at Lil.

"Honestly, I'm fairly certain he hates me, but every once in a while, I siphon off a little of that dread that seems to circle him constantly. It's in those moments I get a glimpse of his smile. Please don't tell him I told you that. I just want him to have a little joy in his life, even if it is brief." Lil lifts one corner of her mouth and her eyes are soft with emotion.

"Duncan deserves some happiness in his life. If you can give that to him then we will take this secret to our graves!" Sara says.

She rolls onto her back to look at the chandelier hanging above us. I do the same, and so does Lil and Jade. We lay there together, heads all touching in a circle. It feels nice to just have fun for once.

"Girls!" Marigold comes into the room, scolding us for laying around when we should be getting ready. We all pop up and scramble towards our mirrors. Sara sits in the chair to the left of me, Lil is on my other side, and Jade to the right of her.

The other lady's maids come back into the room and start working on our hair, pulling it up into beautiful up-do's. I chat with Marigold as she curls my hair. It dawns on me that I forgot to ask her what that bracelet was made out of before we left yesterday.

"Marigold, what was that bracelet that you gave me to wear for the dinner with the king and queen made out of? I had a horrible reaction to it."

"Oh dear, I'm so sorry. I had no idea. It was made of iron, milady. I will make sure all jewelry in the future is not made with that material. Apologies, again."

"It's fine, Marigold. I would appreciate that though," I smile at her.

"If you don't mind me asking, what kind of reaction did you have to the bracelet?"

"Just a strange burn where it sat on my wrist. It has healed over now, but it was really red and blistering that night. It began to fade away as soon as I took it off."

"Interesting. I have never heard of that happening to anyone else before. Either way, I will make sure you are never given that again. Your hair is done, milady."

We all look in the reflecting glass and gape in awe of what the women have created. Sara's hair is in a beautiful, full braid down her back with smaller braids woven into the main one. Jade has her hair pulled up into some sort of twist in the back and a few face framing pieces in the front that hang down and curl around her chin. Lil has half of her hair pulled back and the rest is down and curled, her wispy bangs perfectly styled just above her eyes.

When I look into the glass in front of me, Marigold has pulled my hair into a large bun at the base of my neck with some strands pulled through the bun to give it a flowing look. She styled the front pieces of hair out of my face in large braids tucked behind my ears and pinned into the bun at the back. It is truly a work of art.

As the ladies start on our makeup, Sara reaches over and takes my hand. We sit here, arms stretched across the space between us. I reach over and grab Lil's hand who grabs Jade's in turn. Smiling at each other, I know it is going to be an unforgettable night.

Chapter 46

ALIYAH

"Lil, this dress is gorgeous!" I spin in the mirror in front of me. The dress is a mix of black, white, red, and orange wispy feathers. The straps hang just off the shoulder, and creating v-shape that ends at the bottom of my scar. The dress dips down all the way to my lower back, showing off every single one of my scars. I thought I would be embarrassed, but I remind myself of Enzo's words last night. *You survived. You lived.*

I let that fuel me into being proud of my scars. The feathers make up the entire skirt and flare out at the bottom, making it appear as if I have a trail of feathers behind me.

"How did you think of this?"

"I'm not really sure! When I saw how much you were struggling to draw a dress I just kind of let inspiration flow. It must be something my ability is picking up from you. Maybe something inside you is just waiting to come out and this is what it looked like in my head," Lil smiles next to me.

"Well, I absolutely *love* it. Thank you," I say, taking her hand.

Lil is wearing a fitted white gown with invisible looking material over her stomach and down her legs, with white silk wrapping around her body covering her chest, butt, and groin area. The invisible material has a dusting of glitter over it, making it shimmer when she turns in the light.

Jade has on a deep purple, silk dress that hugs every one of her curves. The straps are thin and run over her back in crisscross formation. It looks like a bucket of purple ink was poured over her in the best possible way.

Sara twirls in the mirror, elated at the dress she has on. It is a strapless dress, and is absolutely gorgeous on her. The bodice is see-through except for the exposed corset- like boning. The skirt is a layering of a few feathers near her hips before it poofs out into a huge ball gown of white and blue feathers.

"Sara, that wasn't the dress that you initially sketched out. How did you change your designs after Lil gave them to the seamstress?" Jade asks.

"She didn't," Lil pipes in. "I had the designs altered after I designed Aliyah's gown. I figured since they were Soul Bonded, it was only appropriate that they match a little."

"I absolutely love it. Thank you, Lil." Sara gives one last twirl.

A knock at the door cuts off all excitement in the room. Marigold walks over to it and opens the door, revealing a smirking Kaleron in the doorway. He is wearing an all black suit save for the bright red flower that is pinned to his chest pocket.

"Well, don't you just look like an absolute dream." He says, drinking me in. His eyes roam up and down my body. "Do a little spin for me, baby."

"Oh gag, brother. Don't be gross. I don't even know why she agreed to go with you in the first place," Lil says, rolling her eyes and pushing past her brother, bumping him in the shoulder as she goes.

Lil told us while we were getting ready that she convinced Duncan to escort her to the ball tonight, so hopefully she is on her way to rally the troops for the evening.

I'm just going to go find Enzo and Gunnar. Let me know if you need me. Sara says into my mind as she exits the room, giving Kaleron a death stare as she goes.

Jade squeezes my hand and gives me a nod as she leaves the room to join the others. Hopefully Enzo will be in his right mind enough to escort Jade to the ball. I would hate for her to have to go by herself, even though I know she doesn't need an escort. She is strong all on her own.

"My mother wants to see you before we head down to the ball. Walk with me, won't you?" He offers out his arm. I roll my eyes, and loop my arm through his.

"You're sick, you know that?" I snarl, as we walk down the hallway.

"Did you keep our little secret?" He smiles down at me.

"If I didn't, you would already be dead."

"Well, I would hate to find out that some little bird let it slip. The blood spilled would be on your hands." He winks at me.

I swear I grit my teeth so hard I feel a tooth crack. We walk in silence the rest of the way until we are outside of the queen's chambers.

"What does she want? I thought you already told her about the vision? Not that there was much to share."

"I told her, but she wanted to see you anyway. I'll be waiting just outside if you need me."

He leans against the far wall and crosses his ankles over one another. A group of girls go walking by and he stares at their backsides as they pass. *Grotesque.* I knock once on the door and it opens on its own.

"Hello?" I call.

"In here, dear. Come and sit with me. You look lovely."

The queen is in the far back corner of her large room. Despite being in SunSpark, her entire room is filled with rich, dark blues and blacks. There isn't an ounce of light in the whole place, except for a few candles lit here and there. The four poster bed is painted black and deep blue. Lush, silk sheets adorn it. The floor is black marble, but the ceiling is what really catches my eye.

The entire ceiling is covered in tiny crystals that are spread out to look almost like stars. The candle light reflects off them, making it appear like a night sky. It makes me miss Krystal.

"It's beautiful, isn't it?" she says, now turned to face me.

"Yes, very much so. But why is it so dark in here when you live in SunSpark?"

"It reminds me of home," she says, looking up to the ceiling with a soft smile on her face. Her hands are clasped in front of her.

"You aren't from SunSpark?" I ask.

"No dear. I grew up in the Twilight Kingdom, though my family is not of royal blood. My father was a duke and served the previous king, King Olivar's father. I grew up in that castle with King Olivar, though there is no relation. Then, as a young woman, I was sent here to this kingdom that is forever in sunlight. Not a drop of darkness to be found. The alliance was advantageous for our kingdom, but there is little consideration for the female in the bargaining. I was able to bring some things with me from home though. It makes it feel not so far away."

"I'm sorry. I know how difficult it can be to leave the only place you have ever known."

"You know nothing of the sacrifices I have had to make." Her face resorts back to one of royalty and not of a normal fae. A cold, distant look. Anger flares in my chest. She has no idea what I have been through either.

She continues. "It doesn't matter now. I have something for you." She walks over to her vanity and opens a small drawer on the right side. She pulls out a small black box, tied with a white ribbon. Handing it to me, I take it with reluctance.

"What is it?" I ask.

"Something you must need."

She gives me a soft smile, breaking that cold look on her face for just a moment. I pull the ribbon on the box and let it fall to the floor. I take the lid off and inside sits a black oval ring set in silver metal that is made to look like flowers on a vine. The black stone has small flecks of silver in them, matching the ceiling above me.

"Thank you, it's– beautiful. Why are you giving this to me?" I ask, slipping the ring on my middle finger.

"I took that ring from my kingdom long ago as something of a comfort. I used to wear it all the time, thinking one day I might have a use for it. But the years went on and I learned to tolerate my life here in SunSpark. I find that I no longer need it, but I think one day you might."

I look at the ring shining on my finger.

"I'm not sure how much good a ring will do me, but I appreciate the gesture."

"It is not about the gesture, girl," she snaps. "It is about what the ring means."

"I don't understand. It's just a ring." Queen Starla doesn't respond, but simply walks over to her vanity and continues putting her make up on.

"What do you think my vision meant? I know that Kaleron told you about it."

"The Reflecting Pool can be fickle. Sometimes the vision is only part of a larger picture that remains to be seen. I would not worry yourself over the details of something many of us cannot comprehend."

"Have you ever been to the pool?"

"Yes, a very long time ago. It was part of my initiation to this kingdom. It was to see if I would get a glimpse into how I would be as a queen."

"What did you see?" I ask.

She turns to face me, and pins me with her usual cold heartless stare.

"I saw you."

Chapter 47

ENZO

I pace the hallway outside Aliyah's room. I know she already left with Kaleron. Sara came to find me after the other girls left. Jade leans against the wall, waiting with me.

"She's going to be fine," Jade says.

"She has almost died too many times on my watch. I can't afford to keep letting harm come to her," I snap.

"She can handle herself, Enzo. Give her some credit."

All I can do is grumble at her. "ARGH! Where is she?" I am growing impatient. We have only been here for a few days. She doesn't know her way around the palace or how to navigate the vultures that live here picking apart other's lives like a dead carcass. I know she can handle herself. It isn't her I don't trust, it's everyone else.

"Maybe she is already downstairs."

I push open her door and find the room empty. Not like I expected anything different. I look around and see her throwing knives are all still on the desk by the window. *Of. Freaking. Course.* The one time I want her to have a knife strapped to her body, she goes and leaves without them. I hear footsteps in the hall and rush out to see if it is her, but I am only met with Gunnar and Sara.

"She's with the queen. I'm not sure why so don't even ask. That is all I know," Gunnar says.

"Well let's go then." I start walking, but Gunnar grabs my arm.

"Enzo, she is fine. It isn't like my mother is going to behead her without a public show. It just isn't her style."

"That isn't the comfort you think it is," Sara whispers to him. "I haven't heard anything through the Soul Bond or sensed that she is in danger, so I have to believe that she is okay."

I snarl and slide down the wall to sit on the floor. I run my hands through my hair and drop my head between my knees. *Please be okay.*

"Let's head down to the ball, I am sure she will meet us there when she is done. It's all going to be okay," Jade says. I stand and start walking towards the sound of the music playing. If she isn't there after two more songs I'm going to find her, respect for the queen be damned.

Jade laces her arm through mine as we walk. I am glad that she and Aliyah are getting along so that I don't have to blatantly reject Jade to her face. Jade knows were my heart lies. With each step away from Aliyah's room, trepidation settles in my chest. I regret ever agreeing to let Aliyah go with Kaleron.

Two massive doors open leading to several stairs descending into the ballroom. Each step down is a step away from Aliyah and it is killing me. Jade smiles with her arm linked through mine, but my eyes are scanning the crowd. Hundreds of fae line the dance floor or are grazing at the tables of food. The king is, of course, stuffing his face with food while completely ignoring his guests. Liliana was right when she said it was going to be grand. Tables are adorned with lavish bouquets of flowers and enough food to feed an entire kingdom for a year. The musicians play an upbeat melody that has every couple spinning in each other's arms.

"Let's dance," Jade says. "It'll take your mind off things."

She takes my hand and pulls me out to the dance floor. Jade has to lead the dance as my eyes roam around the room waiting to spot my dove's head of blonde hair. Jade grabs my hand and spins herself around before tucking her back to my chest. My hand finds her hip out of instinct, but I am looking over her head at the front entrance we came through. My eyes catch on Sara's dress and I see her and Gunnar sipping wine with some nobles.

Liliana and Duncan are on the dance floor with us. Duncan looks at Liliana with an actual smile on his face. I can honestly say, I don't think I've seen him smile like that since— well since ever. Rage is starting to boil in my chest. Kaleron is too unpredictable and after the way he threatened our friends and my entire kingdom— I'm done.

"I'm going to find her," I say to Jade.

"Enzo, wait. I'm sure she will be here soon. If you barge into the queen's chambers you will be starting a war that Krystal is not prepared to win. Aliyah is strong. She survived in Luar without you for 26 years. I am sure she can survive one night," Jade says.

I know she is right. But every part of me is screaming that something is wrong. I can feel it. It's like the change in air right before a thunderstorm. I grind my teeth at the reminder that Aliyah *had* to survive without me all those years. She may be able to survive one night without me, but I cannot survive one without her. I move to push out of her grasp when the front entrance doors open. There, standing at the top of the stairs, is my little dove– and her arm is laced around that of a dead man.

Chapter 48

ALIYAH

"You– you saw– me? Why? How? I wasn't even alive then," I stammer.

"As I have said, the Reflecting Pool is a fickle thing. Everyone believes it shows random visions, but in my experience with listening to others share their visions over the years, it has always been what they needed to know most about their life," Queen Starla answers.

"Then why didn't it show me who my family are? That is the whole reason why we are here in the first place," I practically yell. My fists clench at my sides in frustration.

"Maybe finding out who your family are, is not what you *need* to know most. When I saw my vision, I had no idea who you were, or what you would be to me. All I saw was this moment. The vision was of me, handing you my ring. To be honest, I assumed you would have been my daughter, but to my surprise you are nothing more than a lowborn fae. But the vision shows what the vision shows. While I may not know your intentions with the ring, I must follow what the vision shows."

"It's just a stupid ring," I shout. "Why would it show you this moment?"

"Much like you, the ring is more than meets the eye," she says, cryptically. *Add that to my freaking list of questions.*

"If it's all the same to you, I'd like to go to the ball now. I am sure my friends are waiting on me."

"Of course. Please enjoy the ball. I hear it is going to be quite a *memorable* evening."

I give the queen one last quizzical look before storming out of the room. When I whip open the doors, Kaleron is still standing there waiting for me to come out.

"Well, how did it go?" he asks.

"Choke and die, Kaleron," I say, giving him an obscene hand gesture with my new ring. I storm down the hallway, at a much faster pace than my heels can carry me. *I should have worn my boots.*

"I take it that it didn't go well?" he laughs, to himself. I flash him an angry look.

"Look, I just want to get this night over with alright. I'm tired. I've had a long day and frankly a long freaking life." I huff out a breath trying to calm myself down.

"Tell you what, I'll drop all talk of my mother and any threats, if you can promise to have a memorable night with me. Drinking, dancing, general merriment, and all that."

"Oh good, another deal with you. Surprise, surprise." I roll my eyes. "Fine. One night and then I never want to see your face again."

"That can most certainly be arranged," he winks at me.

He takes my arm in his and we walk towards the front entrance to the ballroom. When the set of double doors opens, the ballroom below us is in complete bliss.

Everyone is dancing, drinking or laughing together. Music fills the air and there's an upbeat melody that people spin in and out of their partner's arms. Guards are stationed at every corner of the ballroom dressed in their finest armor. It's nice to see that the guards can have a night of fun.

My eyes instinctively scan the crowd for my friends. They find who I am looking for almost instantly. Enzo is wearing a deep burgundy suit with a black undershirt and a black dahlia flower on his chest pocket. His hair is pushed back out of his face and his eyes are in thin slits, most likely at the sight of Kaleron and me. He agreed to this, so he can't even be mad right now. *Like that has ever stopped him.*

I smile down at him as we descend the stairs. He doesn't make a move to come up to us. I asked him to keep his distance as much as possible tonight, so that he doesn't rip Kaleron's head off for just breathing the same air as me. I can see that his fists are clenched at his sides.

Jade stands next to him, and while we are on good terms, I can't help the flare of jealousy that she gets to spend the night dancing with him. I spot Lil and Duncan at the edge of the dance floor and much to my surprise, Duncan has a smile on his face as he talks with Liliana. Her bright smile shines and she is laughing at something Duncan said. I had no idea Duncan was funny.

Where are you? I ask Sara, through the bond.

By the food table. Don't worry we have all eyes on you, our group and practically the entire ballroom.

She's right. Everyone is staring at the prince as we descend the staircase. It makes sense that they would all be looking at him. He is the prince, and I'm suddenly nervous I am going to trip and fall on my face down every single one of these steps. Maker that would be embarrassing.

My heel skids across one of the marble steps and I tip forward a little too far. *Son of a— I knew this crap was going to happen to me.* Before I can catch myself, Kaleron wraps his arm around my waist and holds me steady.

"Falling for me already, Aliyah?" he whispers in my ear. Bile rises in my throat.

To everyone else it must look like he is whispering sweet nothings into my ear and the red on my cheeks, from rage, could easily be passed off for blushing. I elbow him lightly in the stomach as we reach the bottom step, but he just chuckles next to me. He turns to me at the base of the staircase, with everyone watching us.

"May I have this dance?" he asks.

I hold back the eye roll this time, since I did agree to try and have a good night with him. I curtsy in front of him and take his outstretched hand.

He walks us into the middle and the other guests part for him, so it is just us on the dance floor.

I spot Enzo at the edge of the circle of fae around us. His jaw is so tight and the grip he has on his wine glass causes his knuckles to go white. I can't imagine how hard this must be for him. I know he hates Kaleron, but I have to do this. For my friends and for his kingdom.

Kaleron bows at the waist and places a kiss to my knuckles before meeting my eyes. The musicians begin another song and Kaleron leads me in the dance. I do my best to follow his footsteps, even though I have never danced like this in my life. Every eye is on him.

Being barefoot would be better than these stupid heels.

"Their eyes aren't on me, tonight," Kaleron says, as he spins me around. My feather dress flares around me as I twirl.

"You are their prince. I am a nobody," I say back.

"On the contrary, Aliyah. Every male in this room wants to be me, and every female wishes they were you. Relish in it, my dear. Get used to the feeling of everyone worshiping you. I imagine your future is bright with adoration." He spins me back towards him and presses my back to his chest. Kaleron leans down so his mouth is a breath away from my ear.

"Why be with a soldier when you could be with a prince?"

"Enzo is twice the man you will ever be. He doesn't have to threaten an entire kingdom just to get a date."

"If that is true, then Enzo will have no problem with me kissing you."

My eyes widen and before I can respond Kaleron's lips are on mine. I try to pull away from his grasp, but his hold on my throat and waist keep me locked in place. I don't stand a chance with his strength ability.

I hear a loud crash and commotion coming from behind me, but I am unable to see what caused it. Enzo is a lot of things, but being patient with other males is not one of them. I'm not sure I will be able to do anything for Enzo in exchange for Kaleron's life.

Kaleron's tongue prods at my lips and a low groan falls from his throat. I open my lips for him allowing his tongue to enter. When I get his bottom lip in between my teeth, I bite, hard. The taste of copper floods my mouth and Kaleron pulls away from me. Disgust lines my face, but Kaleron just smiles at me before taking my hand and spinning me again.

"I did always love a good challenge. Unfortunately, I fear our time together is coming to an end, for now," Kaleron says.

"What do you mean? We just got here," I say, confusion setting in.

"Eager to spend more time with me, Aliyah?"

"I would rather be thrown from the back of a sphinx into boiling water than spend any more time with you. But I don't understand, why did you say our time is coming to an end?"

Kaleron pulls me in close, wrapping an arm around my waist, and holds my other hand in the air with his. His mouth is right next to my ear, so his words are only for me.

"Tell me, Aliyah," he whispers. "Do I strike you as someone who lives and dies by his word?"

"You do."

"Then why is it that you spilled the secret about our deal for this night?"

My eyes go wide. He couldn't possibly know that Sara was in the room that night, or that Enzo found out.

"I don't know what you're talking about."

"Oh really? I am set to rule this kingdom one day soon, Aliyah. I have spies *everywhere*. I know that Sara was in your room that night, which means she is the only one who could have told Enzo about our little bargain. Pity too, I always did like her."

I push away from him. "You wouldn't dare!" I shout, and start punching him over and over again in the chest.

"I'm sorry, Aliyah, but I did warn you and I am a prince of my word. What's done is already in motion. I cannot stop it even if I wanted to. I wish things could have been different between us, Aliyah. I have a feeling our lives will be intertwined for some time to come. I have confidence you will be able to move past what happens here tonight." He smirks at me before catching my wrists from beating on his chest.

Enzo is by my side in a flash, ripping me away from Kaleron. He shoves me out of the way with his power and I fly through the air. I hit my head on the floor with a hard crack.

Spots cloud my vision and I blink to try and clear them. I reach my hand back to feel where I hit the floor and when I pull my hand away, it's covered in blood.

"Aliyah!" Enzo yells. "Aliyah, I'm so sorry! I didn't mean to hurt you! This is what I was afraid of happening. I'm so sorry," Enzo pleads.

"I'm alright. It'll heal, promise," I smile at him.

"Look what you've done, Kaleron! This is your fault!" Enzo yells. He helps me back to my feet and holds me until I steady myself.

"I'm alright, Enzo. It isn't your fault." I try to calm him down.

Enzo's eyes turn dark as he spins and punches Kaleron in the face. Kaleron's head snaps back, but he is ultimately unaffected by the impact. Remembering Kaleron's words, my eyes frantically search for Sara and Gunnar. Liliana and Duncan push their way through the crowd.

Okay, they are fine. Jade comes up next to me, grabbing my hand.

"Where are Sara and Gunnar? I can't find them anywhere."

"Let's get out of the center of the room. I am sure they are here somewhere." Jade pushes people out of the way as we make our way through the crowd.

"There! I see them! Sara—" My eyes find hers through the crowd. A tear drips from her eye and she has her hand to her neck.

A scream rips from my throat as I push my way through the crowd. Just when I reach her, I fall to my knees as blood drips from her nose. Tears slip from her eyes as she falls into Gunnar's arms.

"No, no, no, no, no!" Gunnar yells. "Sara please. Please don't leave me again. I won't let him do this to you."

Gunnar, now seeing me with her, rushes towards his brother still fighting with Enzo. Duncan joins them in the center of the dance floor in an instant as he appears out of nowhere.

The four of them unleash a fury of fists and abilities, lighting up the ballroom with flames and objects being thrown at Kaleron from across the room. Jade moves to join the fight, but I can't leave Sara's side.

Everyone is running panicked at the chaos ensuing around them. I see Liliana being pushed out the doors by the crowd trying to escape the fight. Tears drip onto Sara's face as I look back down at her.

"Just keep your eyes open, Sara. It's going to be okay, I promise. I'm here now. I'm not going anywhere without you. Till the end remember? You said you'd stay with me to the end. Please, don't leave me," I sob.

Sara's eyes open weakly and she looks up at me. Her tears replaced with blood running from her eyes.

"You are my best friend, Aliyah. I would do it all again for you...I would do it all–" Her eyes slip shut and her hand goes limp in mine.

"Sara? *Sara!* Please, come back to me. I can't do this without you. I need you."

The world around me goes quiet. It's just me and my best friend. Suddenly, someone is throwing me back, away from her. *What the heck?* Marigold is over Sara, pouring something into her mouth.

"Marigold, what the hell is going on here? What did you give her?" I wipe the tears from my face.

"Aliyah, go back to your room. I packed you a bag. Grab your pack and get out of this palace, now. Run as far and as fast as you can. Take a sphinx if you must. I will get the others to find you. No matter what you do, leave this castle. Do not come back for anyone."

"No, I'm not leaving her," I say back.

"Aliyah, listen to me right now. It isn't safe for you here. I've got her. Now, go. Run towards The Bridge. It will take you into Krystal. If you are able to take a sphinx, it will be able to fly across the ocean without needing to bridge. That is the safest option right now. After that, keep going. Do not stop. I will send the others that way when I can, but you need to go now. Slip out with the crowd."

I look down at Sara laying on the cold, marble floor. I don't want to leave her, but dying here and now won't let me avenge her death either. I stand there a moment more.

I look over trying to get Enzo's attention, but more guards have joined the fight. They knew. They knew that this would happen so Kaleron made sure they were there. How could I have been so foolish as to think they were there to have fun?

"Aliyah. Bag. Bedroom. Run, now!" Marigold scolds. I kick off my heels and fall into the crowd exiting the ballroom.

"Aliyah!" Enzo yells.

His eyes find mine for just a moment, but the distraction is all Kaleron needs to land a blow to Enzo's head. It knocks him to the ground and he is out cold. Jade, Gunnar, and Duncan still fight on, but Kaleron is ruthless and determined to kill them.

I try to push back into the ballroom to get back to Enzo. I can't lose him too. The crowd is a stampede now, pushing and shoving. The screams from those who have fallen down rise in the air as they get trampled. I can't get back into the ballroom. Guards run towards me, swords at the ready.

I quickly duck and run beside a woman with a hat so large it could hide an entire alicanto behind it. The guards must have lost me in the crowd because I don't see any following me.

I have to make a decision. Do I go back and try to get Enzo and the others out, or listen to Marigold and flee, knowing they will find me again?

I have to trust Marigold. She has helped me thus far. I have no reason not to trust her. I hesitate for one more moment before turning and sprinting towards my room.

I turn down several hallways before making it back to our wing. I close my door behind me and find a pair of leather pants and a long sleeve tunic laid out for me, next to my boots. I quickly slip off my dress and leave it in a pool of feathers on the floor. Part of my heart breaks that I couldn't wear it longer. I slip into my pants and tunic and quickly lace my boots.

The pack that Marigold said would be there is ready by the door. I don't have time to check the contents, so I hope she packed me everything I might need. I quickly sling it on my back and crack open my door. Several fae are running through the hallway, including many guards, most likely looking for me. *Okay, too risky to go out the front.*

Sara...what do I do? What would you do?

I try to reach out through the bond, but I know I won't hear anything back. Tears start brimming in my eyes at the thought of doing this alone, but I wipe them away quickly. This is no time to cry.

I turn and face the window before opening it to look out. On the outside of the palace there are rows and rows of vines crawling up the side. I look down at the drop. It is at least a couple hundred feet. If I fall it is at minimum a broken leg. *Or worse.* Take a deep breath Aliyah. You can do this. It's what Sara would do.

I step out onto the window sill and place my foot on the first branch I can reach and push down hard to make sure it can hold my weight. It doesn't give way, so I move onto the next branch. I work my way down the side of the palace and before I know it my feet are hitting cobblestone.

Well, that could have been a close one. I turn and look at the dark orange sun. There are not a lot of shadows to hide in here. I'm never going to be able to make it on foot to The Bridge.

Marigold said I could take a sphinx. Hopefully she tells the others so they know how to follow me. Maker, even if I do make it across the border, how are they going to know which part of Krystal I am in. *I* barely know how to get there. I take a deep breath before running in the direction of the field where the sphinx graze.

I hit the fence line just as my legs are about to give out. I walk up to the first sphinx I see and rub my hand behind its ear. It purrs under my touch and nuzzles my chest.

"Alright, alright. No time for snuggles. We've got to get going." I climb on its back and give it a light kick with my heels. It shoots off into the air, flapping its large white wings as it carries us higher and higher into the sky.

"Can you take me across the Krystal border?" *Please understand me.*

The sphinx makes a wide turn in the other direction, and I pray to the Maker who I know is listening the sphinx knows where the border is. As we fly high above the palace, I look down to see a whole section up in flames. *Please have gotten my friends out, Marigold.* Tears spill from my eyes from the force of the wind and I turn my back on the palace.

Leaning down on the sphinx's mane, I bury my face in the soft fur and let the tears pour out of my eyes. At least in the safety of the air, I can finally let them all out.

Chapter 49

ALIYAH

I must have fallen asleep at some point during the flight because when I open my eyes, I am freezing my butt off and we are gliding above crystal mountains. *Thank the Maker.* I pat the sphinx on the neck.

"Thank you," I whisper. It soars down to an open patch of land and glides to a stop. Hopping off, my legs nearly buckle as tingles run down them from the lack of feeling.

"Well, now what?" I look to see what is around me, but there is only endless crystal mountains. The sound of flapping wings fills the air and I turn hoping to see the others.

"You found–" I cut off my sentence when I see it is just the sphinx flying away from me. I'm officially alone now.

"What the hell am I supposed to do now?" I scream into the sky.

It echos back at me off the mountains, and I swear it comes back in a mocking tone. I push the heels of my hands into my eyes until I see stars.

"Okay, you've got this." I say out loud to myself like a crazy person. "Just start walking. You've got some daylight left. Just walk until you reach something that looks familiar."

I head off in the direction that I think is north based on the sun setting to my left.

As the sun begins to set low in the sky, I find myself standing in front of a rapidly flowing river. I look around to see if there are any large rocks that I can use as stepping stones to cross. No such luck.

"Crap," I say to myself. "Okay, new plan."

I walk several paces up river. This way when the current carries me down stream I won't get too far off course. Not wanting my pack to get wet, I pull it from my back and hold it above my head. Walking up the waters edge, that feeling of a thousand bricks crushing my chest sweeps over me. Panic claws at my spine and my nerves light up trying to manage the strain.

"I can do this. I can do this. I *need* to do this." I close my eyes and take a deep breath. When I open them, a vision of Sara appears standing next to me holding my hand and smiling. I step towards the water and walk as far as I can before my feet no longer touch the bottom. Trying to keep my head above water, I kick as hard as I can trying to make it to the other side. I hear Sara talking to me from the shore line.

You can do this Aliyah. I'm right here with you. Don't give up. You didn't come this far just to drown in a freaking river.

Even as I swim for my life, I laugh at the words Sara says to me. I'm so close to the other side. I have moved down stream farther than anticipated, but I can correct that later. I reach my feet down trying to find purchase on the rocks below the surface. Right as I find my footing, a current swirls under me and knocks my feet out of place.

I remember Sara's words as panic claws at my mind again. *I'm with you. Til the end.* My hands grip some rocks as the water begins to lower. Pulling myself up onto the shore line, I turn over on my back and inhale deep breaths, reminding myself that I am no longer in the water.

"I'm safe. I'm alive and I'm safe. I made it. Thank you, Sara." I look around to see if Sara is still with me, but she is nowhere to be found. Tears well up in my eyes and I fist the ground beneath me as angry sobs pour from my body. Sara should be here. She promised me she would be with me until the end. I scream at the sky letting all my rage and fury pour out of my lungs.

"Please, Maker above, please bring her back to me. I can't do this without her," I pray to the heaven above. Wiping my tears I stand, now soaking wet, and do the only thing I can in this moment. Put one foot in front of the other.

The worst part about being alone all the time, is being trapped with your own thoughts. You start to rethink every decision you have ever made, wondering if you did something different, would your future have changed? What if I had escaped Enzo that day? What if I didn't survive that ax to the chest? What if... what if... what if. Two little words that, separate, mean nothing. But together they can spiral you deeper than you ever thought possible.

I feel like I am locked inside my own mind. It's maddening. This is all my fault. I brought Sara here. I asked her to stay with me in Krystal. It was at my request that we went searching for my family. Why couldn't I just have been happy with the family I had? Sara was all I ever needed. Then I met Enzo, Jade, Gunnar, Duncan, even Liliana and they became my family. Why couldn't that have been enough for me?

I don't know how long I have been walking at this point, but the sound of rushing water fills my ears again. As I clear a large crystal formation, another river sits in front of me. I have barely dried off from the last one.

"You've got to be kidding me."

When I get into the water this time, I don't find myself panicking as much as I did before. I let my anger over having to cross another stinking river fuel me to get to the other side. Luckily, this river isn't as deep and is not flowing as fast as the last. I make it to the other side and pull myself onto the shore line once again. This time when I start walking again, I'm just mad. I'm soaking wet *again,* and I have no clue where I am going. I hope Enzo and the others find me soon.

I walk for what feels like hours. I spend most of my time mumbling to myself about nothing in particular just to fill the silence around me. The problem with crystal mountains is that they all look the same after a while. My pack starts getting heavier and heavier with each step. I set the bag down on the ground and open it. Inside there are two water sacks, a loaf of bread, four food seeds, a small mat, and a blanket. Okay, so no shelter. That's fine. It will be like I am back in Mareen sleeping with my scratchy blanket and no pillow. I think coming to Olyrium, having consistent food, and soft beds to sleep in has made me soft.

I wish she had packed me at least a small pillow, but I am sure Marigold did the best she could. I roll out the mat on a piece of land that has the least amount of crystals jutting up from the ground. I sit down and pull the blanket around my shoulders. I should have grabbed my leather jacket on the way out. It's so much colder here than in SunSpark. I reach into my bag to see if there is anything else left that might help me. My hand hits something that feels like parchment, and I pull it from the bag. In my hand is a folded up letter with my name written on the front. Opening it up, I begin to read the words:

Dearest Aliyah,

By now I hope you have made it across the border and are somewhere safe. I overheard some of the guards talking in the hallway about the impending assassination attempt on Sara and how things were most likely going to get ugly. They spoke about having orders from the prince to capture your entire group for being a threat against the realm. The queen backed her son's decision. As soon as the coast was clear, I ran into town to meet with a trusted herbalist who gave me every antidote they had. By the time I made it back to the palace you had already left for the ball so I had no time to warn you. I hope the contents of this pack hold you over until Enzo can find you. I know he would burn heaven and hell to get back to you. I will do what I can for Saraphena, but I apologize now if I cannot save her. I am sure once the queen learns I have helped you escape, I will be tried and executed for treason. If that is the case, then might I say it has been a pleasure serving a woman such as yourself. You are too good for this world, Aliyah. Know that all who have met you here love you and will stand by your side when the time comes. In all my years of service I have never met a more fierce, confident survivor such as yourself. Make this world a better place than we left it, Aliyah.

Yours, Marigold

P.S. As you know, rumors are my trade. Long ago there was a rumor that the late Queen Dione birthed an heir before she left for battle. Find the heir and bring peace back to Olyrium. Bring peace to all the realms.

Holy crap. The Queen of Citrine had an heir? There would finally be someone to rule in Krystal and could help unite the kingdom's again. I tuck the letter back into the pack. When I see Enzo again I will have to show him what Marigold wrote. I hope she gets away alive. I lay back on my mat and gaze up at the stars. The ribbons of light dance across the black, night sky.

"I'll find you again, Enzo. I promise. And when I do, we will avenge Sara's death together. This whole time we have been trying to figure out who my family is, but I'm starting to realize I knew who they were all along."

My eyelids are heavy and my eyes drift shut as sleep pulls me under. I hope my dreams are better than my reality.

Chapter 50

ALIYAH

I know this place. The grassy field, and the wildflowers growing at my feet, blow in the warm breeze. I'm wearing a tattered old dress that flows behind me. I look around, but I don't see the man I once saw before.

"Hello?" I call out.

Silence. Typical. I put my hands to my mouth and cup them around my lips to help my voice travel further.

"Hello!" I yell this time.

"Aliyah?"

I spin around and am face to face with my tall, handsome man.

"Oh my Maker, Enzo! Please tell me you are alive and I am alive and I didn't freeze to death in this wasteland of crystals."

I rush up to wrap my arms around him, but some invisible barrier stops us from being able to touch. He places his palm on the barrier, and I place my hand over his.

"No, little dove, you aren't dead. Where are you? I need to find you."

"I'm back in Krystal. Somewhere in the mountains. I'm trying to head north back to Korin or Citrine City. Whatever I hit first I guess."

"What do you see around you? Describe where you are in as much detail as possible."

"I'm surrounded by mountains on both sides. I crossed two rivers heading north."

"What color are the mountains around you?"

"Um. Purple on the left and green and red on the right. But Enzo, all these mountains look the same to me. How can this possibly help you?"

"I know exactly where you are, little dove. You're in the Krystal Mountain Pass. It is a straight shot north that ends at The Bridge to Twilight. I'm coming for you. Just keep walking north. Call out for Mirage. She will find you, no matter how far away she is, she will hear you calling, I promise."

"Enzo, how is Sara? Is she alive?" Before Enzo can answer I am being pulled back away from the barrier and he is nothing but a dark spot in the distance.

My eyes shoot open. It's still dark out. The ribbons of light still run through the sky. And I'm still alone. I hope that dream was real and Enzo really does know where I am. Please let them all be alive.

I sit up and reach for my pack, pulling out some of my bread, I take a few bites before returning it to the bag. I stand and roll up my mat and blanket and tuck them back into the pack. Slinging it over my shoulders I decide to use the light in the sky as my guide. Enzo said to keep walking north. So I will walk as far as I can, for as long as I can.

I yell out to the sky for Mirage, calling her name over and over again. She will find me. At least, I hope she will. I look up at the stars and imagine myself on that rooftop with Jade, sharing in our memories and bonding through a lifetime of trauma. I remember all those nights with Sara out on the streets before we were able to find our apartment. We would stargaze for hours before falling asleep under the moon. I remember the night at Adryanna's Tavern in Korin with Gunnar and Duncan. I could have danced all night with Gunnar trying to convince Duncan to join us, until he finally relented. And I remember Enzo. Every kiss, every touch, I remember. I let these memories fuel my body to keep walking. They are my family and we will find each other again.

Chapter 51

ALIYAH

I sit on a large crystal in the blazing sunlight. I've eaten through the bread I had and the seeds to grow food ran out three days ago. I walk all day and continue for as long as I can through the night. I only rest when I absolutely have to, but I can feel my body getting weaker with each passing day. I haven't been able to cover as much ground as I did before.

I am completely out of water. I should have done a better job rationing it. It's been at least ten days since I left SunSpark, without a trace of seeing anything I recognize. I have blisters growing on the backs of my heels that open and close as my skin tries to keep up with the healing.

My pack rubs against my back and shoulders causing my skin to rip open faster than it can heal. I know if I carry on much longer like this, my body won't be able to heal itself anymore.

My lips are so dry and my skin is burned and peeling off from being exposed to the sun for so long with no shelter. The silence is driving me mad. The only sounds I hear these days are my feet hitting the ground and the heaves of my breath. I can't even talk to myself any more, my throat is so dry.

I let the pack slip off my back and I drop to my knees in exhaustion. I lay on my back and stare up into the sky watching the clouds drift by and the sun beat down on my face. My throat strains against my voice.

"I'm sorry, Sara. I'm sorry for everything. You could have lived a happy life. A life filled with love. Maybe even had children with Gunnar. He would have made a great father. I'm sorry I took all that away from you." A tear rolls down my cheek and I swipe my tongue out to catch it. It is the only water I have had in days and it tastes like heaven itself.

"And I'm sorry I'm failing you now. I should have stayed with you. I should have never left you to die in such a horrible place. I should have never left Enzo. I would have rather died next to him in that fight than out here alone. I'm not going to make it back to Enzo. I'm going to die here in this freaking mountain region surrounded by nothing but my own blood, sweat, and tears. I'll never get to avenge your death. I hope you can forgive me. I'm coming for you Sara. Save me a seat next to you in heaven. I'll see you soon."

Tragically, now I finally feel like I have something to live for. To honor Sara's memory by living, but it seems fate has other plans for me. I want to live for Enzo and the others, but I know they will be alright. I knew Enzo and I couldn't be together forever. It just wasn't in the stars for us. I just thought we would have a little more time. I'm okay dying like this. I'll drift off to sleep and never wake up. I remember the days I begged for that in Mareen, but I thought for a brief moment, I wouldn't have to wish for it again.

At least I don't have to worry about Sara grieving my death. We will find each other again. Maybe when Enzo finally passes, we will have our chance together in heaven. I close my eyes against the sun and allow my breathing to slow. "I'm coming, Sara. I'm coming home now."

I must be hallucinating because I hear shuffling across the crystals to my right, but I'm too tired to get up. *It's just in your head, Aliyah. Nothing, and no one is there.*

The shuffling stops right in front of me and a huge shadow is cast over me. Shade. I have shade. I crack open my eyes and standing before me, feathers spread wide above me, is Mirage.

"Are you real?" I ask reaching my hand up towards the alicanto. "If you are, thank you for finding me. Thank you for not letting me die alone."

"I'm telling you the stupid bird ran this way. I know it did. Doesn't it know that we don't have long legs like it does?" *Gunnar?*

"Shut up, Gunnar. Just keep walking. We are going to find her eventually. Stop complaining and lift your feet up. They keep dragging on the ground." *Jade?*

"Will you both just stop talking for once in your lives! This has got to be the most painful trip we have ever taken." *Duncan!*

"I think I'm getting a headache from all of you bickering so much." The sound of Enzo's voice fills the air and brings tears to my eyes.

"Honestly, I'm just happy to be here! I mean what an opportunity! Seeing other realms, going on an adventure with my best friends. Best. Adventure. Ever." *Liliana.*

"I'm over here! I'm here," I try to call, but my voice is drowned out by the strain on my throat.

"When we see her, I'm getting the first hug, you hear me?"

I burst into tears at the sound of Sara's voice carrying above the rest. My family comes walking around the side of a giant crystal.

There I am laying in the freaking dirt, too tired to get up, but they all run to me. Tears stream down my face as Sara throws her arms around me and lifts me up.

"You're alive." That is all I can manage to say.

"Till the end..." she says, stroking my hair. Everyone moves around me to pull me into a giant group hug. Even Duncan joins us. Everyone breaks apart but Enzo remains. He kisses me deeply and runs his hands over my sweat matted hair.

"I told you I'd find you," he smirks at me.

"Can we do the I told you so later, please?" I whisper. "Do we have any water?"

"Here! You can have some of mine!" Liliana brings me over her water sack and I immediately down the entire thing.

"Sorry," I say, finally finding my voice again.

"Don't sweat it! I stuck a few extra water sacks into Duncan's bag before we left," she smiles at me.

"Is that why my pack weighs more than everyone else's?" Duncan says.

The group starts comparing whose bag is heavier than whose, but my eyes fall to Sara. She walks over to me and takes me over to sit against some crystals.

Mirage follows us and spreads her wings wide again, giving us a nice shaded spot.

"Sara, what the hell happened back there? How did you get out? How are you even alive?" I ask, taking her hand in mine.

"Kaleron found out somehow that I told Enzo about your deal. Apparently he does care about semantics." She shrugs her shoulders as if she didn't just come back from the dead.

"When I was brought back from the brink of death, Marigold was above me telling me directions about where you were going and how to find you. After that, while all hell were breaking loose in the castle, your lady's maid set off a bomb in the ballroom."

"That was the fire I saw."

"Yeah, the whole room caught fire, but it bought us time to get out of there. She had packs waiting for us in the servants entrance, so it was easy to slip out during the chaos. Unfortunately, by the time we left, guards had swarmed the field where the sphinx were so we were forced to make it on foot. It took forever just to make it to The Bridge. Once we got into Krystal, we called for our alicanto and just kept walking, knowing they would find us eventually.

"On our way, Mirage ran over Enzo at full speed, clearly on a path to you. It was so funny, Aliyah. Enzo got clean knocked on his butt. He was so furious, but it knocked some sense into him because he figured we should just follow Mirage and hope it would lead to you. Now, here we are!"

"Oh, Sara. I was so worried I lost you forever. Do you know what happened to Marigold?"

Sara's smile drops and her eyes fill with sorrow. "I'm so sorry, Ali. As we were fleeing the ballroom, the guards got ahold of her. I tried to go back for her. I owed her for saving my life, but she shouted at me to keep going. That I needed to find you and that everything we needed to know was in the letter. I have no clue what letter she was talking about, but we hoped you would know. That was the last thing she said before— before they cut off her head. I'm so sorry, Aliyah. I know she was important to you."

Tears slip down my face knowing that the last thing Marigold did was help my family escape the castle. I need to survive now. I need to survive for her.

"Your skin is already looking better." Sara tips my chin back and forth looking at my face.

"It's a miracle what a little water can do for the soul," I laugh, wiping the tears from my face. The others walk over now to where we are sitting, clearly done fighting about whose pack is heavier.

"So," I start, "where do we go now?"

Chapter 52

ENZO

"We can't go back to Korin. That is the first place they will look for us," I say, looking down at my little dove. I was so scared I had lost her for good. If we hadn't run into– well, if Mirage hadn't *literally* run into me, we might not have found her in time.

Maker she looked so broken when we rounded that corner. Her skin is looking better since getting some water in her. Luckily, fae heal very quickly when given the right amount of nutrients to their body.

"I know where we can go," Duncan says.

"No way. We can find another way. We don't have to do this, Duncan," Gunnar speaks up.

"Where does he want to go?" Aliyah asks.

"To the Twilight Kingdom," Duncan says. "It is the last place they will think to look. No one has heard anything from Twilight in ages. If my father won't give us refuge, maybe my brother will."

"Duncan–" Liliana walks over and grabs his hand.

"It's okay. We need to keep this family together. We need to keep everyone *safe*. That takes precedence over everything else. My past is my past. I can only look towards the future now," he says looking at Liliana. *Dang, she's making him go soft.*

305

"How do we know it will be safe there if no one has heard anything from Twilight in ages?" I say. "I won't bring Aliyah somewhere where she will be put in danger again. I won't bring *any* of you into danger."

"Enzo, right now it might be our only option," Jade says.

"Fine, but one whiff of trouble and I'm calling it. I will take our chances back in Korin, on our own turf."

"Deal," everyone says in unison.

"Let's rest now and keep moving tonight. Might as well get used to walking in the dark. There is barely any sunlight in Twilight," Duncan adds.

"I think I'm okay with no sunlight for a while," Aliyah laughs, and the others huff out a laugh around me.

"Hey listen, before we break up to rest for a while, I need to show you the letter that Marigold left me. We might need to add a task to our list of things to do on our journey." Aliyah motions for us to all sit down.

Everyone moves to gather around her as she pulls the crumpled parchment from her pack. She reads it aloud for everyone to hear. Liliana sheds a few tears in remembrance of Marigold, but when she reads the end, everyone's jaws gape, and a few choice words slipped out of some.

"Hold on a second, Queen Dione had an heir? Since when?" I ask.

"Marigold said it was just a rumor, so it could be nothing at all. But if it is something, and this heir can bring peace between the kingdoms, isn't it worth a shot to find them?" Aliyah adds.

"There is no harm in looking, but right now our biggest priority is evading the SunSpark guards who will inevitably be looking for us," Jade notes.

"Agreed. We can look for the heir after we land somewhere safe," I add.

"Okay, I just wanted you all to know. Maybe someone in Twilight will have a better idea or might have heard the rumor as well," Aliyah says.

"Everyone get some rest. We are close to the Twilight Bridge, but it is still a distance to the castle," Duncan says, rolling out his mat to lay down.

Liliana rolls hers out next to him and they both talk quietly to themselves. Jade has settled down with Mirage who curls around her. Gunnar and Sara sit against a crystal together sharing some bread. I guarantee he is never letting her out of his sight again. *The feeling is mutual, brother.*

Aliyah walks up to me, puts her arms around my waist and hugs me tight. I press my nose to the top of her head, and even beneath all that sweat and grime, I can still smell that hint of vanilla.

"Aliyah," I say.

"Yeah?" She lets out a small sniffle against my chest.

"Are you okay?"

"Honestly, no. I was so afraid I would never see any of you again. For a minute there I really thought I was going to die out here all alone. I was prepared to die out here."

"If you were going to die, little dove, I would make sure I died too. Right alongside you," I smile down at her.

"That isn't exactly comforting, Enzo," she laughs.

"I missed that laugh."

"It's only been ten days."

"Every moment away from you is like having my heart rip out of my chest to chase after you. After everything, I'm never letting you out of my sight again."

"You know, you keep saying that, and yet I keep having to leave you," she laughs.

"At least you know I will always come after you. Come on, let's get some rest. I don't want you falling behind tomorrow." I wink at her. She elbows me in the stomach and unrolls her mat.

"Aliyah," I start. "One last thing." I reach into my pack and pull out her three knives. She turns and sees them in my hand.

"Oh thank the Maker of above and below!" she squeals, before tipping her head back and letting out a breath. "I thought I lost them forever. I didn't have time to grab them on my way out."

"I found them in my room and figured you might need them."

"Thank you, Enzo."

She tucks them into her pack and puts one in her thigh holster. I roll out my mat next to her and pull her in close to my chest. This time, this is where she will stay.

PART IV:
TWILIGHT KINGDOM

Chapter 53

ALIYAH

"What the hell happened here?" I ask.

Our group stands at the edge of a small village outside the palace in the Twilight Kingdom. There is no sun, which makes what lies before us that much more bleak. The small village is in complete ruin. Every house is burnt to the ground. Skeletons and charred bodies lay in the streets. There isn't a single live fae in sight. It is completely abandoned. Duncan kicks some debris around him looking for anything that might still be alive.

"This didn't happen recently," he says.

"How long ago do you think?" Enzo asks.

"Who knows. At this point, I don't really think it matters. Something isn't right. We need to find the king and queen and my brother, Aramot. They will know what happened here," Duncan adds.

We make our way through the village, kicking up ash and soot along the way. As we approach the palace, there are no lights in the windows. It looks almost as abandoned as Citrine. The only problem is that this castle shouldn't be abandoned.

We walk up the crumbling front steps and find the front doors to be broken open.

"I'm getting a not so good feeling about this, Duncan," Liliana says, taking his hand.

"Me either," he says. "Weapons out everyone. We need to be ready for anything." Everyone draws their weapons and prepares for whatever might come out of the darkness.

"King Olivar! Queen Araleia! Aramot! Hello! Is anyone around?" Duncan yells. *Silence.*

"Do you smell that?" Jade asks.

"You mean the smell of rotting flesh and bones? Yeah I smell it. I think it's burned into my nose at this point," Lil says, placing her hand over her nose to try and block the smell.

Bile churns in my stomach and threatens to come up. The smell gets worse as we walk deeper into the castle. There is no one here. Cobwebs hang from the ceilings and a layer of dust has collected on the window sills.

"Duncan, what do we do now?" Sara asks.

"*Shh.* Do you hear that?" Enzo silences us.

We all stop our movement and listen. The chattering of voices fills the air in the distance. The sound of something beating against the ground in a rhythmic beat has us all eyeing each other.

"Crap," Duncan says. "Follow me. I know exactly where that sound is coming from."

We follow him out the back side of the castle. The smell of rot grows stronger the farther we walk and the sound of war cries hits my ears in loud rumbles. When we crest over the top of the hill, what lies in wait for us is something I don't think any of us expected to find, nor are prepared for.

Chapter 54

ALIYAH

Across the glade of burnt grass and ashes I see a tall male, clad in a black armor helmet with two metal antlers protruding from the sides. The sword sheathed on his hip is almost as big as me. He is waiting on top of a large boulder looking over the horde of Kalari, waiting for his command. Some of The Kalari are made of pure black skeleton, but others wear skin that appears too loose, like ill fitting clothing. Most of the skin around their faces and arms are rotted away. Now I know where the smell comes from.

"We've been expecting you, brother." His voice booms across the field and the chattering of The Kalari cease at his words. "Our spies in the south sent word of your treasonous acts against the SunSpark Kingdom. I have called upon my army to wipe you off the face of this realm."

"We are not the traitors here, Aramot. You have aligned yourself with the Banished Kingdom. You are the only traitor standing here, today. Where are mother and father? Why have they not stopped you from dishonoring our home?" Duncan calls back.

"*Our* home? Brother, do you forget that you left us after father killed your low borne lover? *You* brought shame upon our house by neglecting your royal duties, and for what? Father did everything he could to protect you, to keep you from being sent away to the military. But when he put you in your place, you did what you always do...you ran away. Turns out, in the end, mother and father were just as weak as you are. They lacked...vision. They couldn't make the hard decision to do what is best for *all* the realms. They had to go."

Out from the horde of The Kalari walks two figures. The skin is rotted in multiple places and sags around the eyes, revealing a black skeleton underneath. A crown is placed on top of each head, but they do not wear royal clothes. They are dressed in armor and strapped with weapons. Duncan's jaw shuts so tight, I swear I hear his teeth crack from here.

"Enzo," I whisper. "Who is that?"

"When The Kalari want to appear as part of the living, or just for sick pleasure, they wear the skin of another. The bodies in the village were most likely skinned and then burned so The Kalari could have a new skin sack. The two wearing crowns are the king and queen. They must have died a horrible death," Enzo answers.

"We don't want to hurt you, brother," Duncan calls back. "Be reasonable. This is not the way. You can still make the right decision."

"We are far past reasonable, *little brother*. For years we have banished The Kalari to rot in a prison they did not deserve. They were trying to unite the kingdoms under one ruler! To bring order to the realms. What is so bad about that? Olyrium needs a leader and I shall be the one to carry out the Banished King's work in his name. It is time to embrace the change. When the holes started to appear in the barrier, it was just too good of an opportunity to pass up. We had researched how to fix a broken pillar to open The Bridge to the Banished Kingdom. I am happy to report we were successful in our endeavor. I have been slowly sneaking The Kalari out of the Banished Kingdom and providing refuge here. The Maker has blessed my endeavor by opening fourteen tears at once, allowing several hundred Kalari to join me here today. While the plan was to continue building my empire until we were strong enough to take on the entire realm, I take pride in knowing that any lives lost today will be in service to cleansing this realm of your souls."

"Unite the kingdoms by slaughtering thousands? Murdering the innocents? How does that make a ruler fit to lead?" Enzo roars across the battlefield.

"This is your last chance. You can either join me and be a part of the change, or you can die a traitor's death at the hands of my army."

"I think I speak for all of us when I say we are not joining your army. Death is not a good look on me," Liliana shouts next to me. She spins her dual swords in her hands, staying loose for the coming fight.

"Agreed," I say.

"So be it. I'll see you in the depths of the below, traitor. At least there you will get to spend eternity with your one true love," Aramot mocks his brother.

"Alright, this is it. Last chance to back out," Duncan says, just to us.

"Not a chance," Gunnar states plainly.

"We are agreed. We either fight and win, or we die trying," Enzo says. "Jade, battle strategy, please."

"If we can kill him, maybe the rest of The Kalari will retreat. But right now it is seven against hundreds," I say. *Not great odds.*

Our group stands in a circle, backs to each other as Aramot's army circles around us. If we had time to prepare more maybe we could have rallied more soldiers. *Not that anyone knew we would be facing this.* But instead I stand here with my family knowing that if I die today, I will at least die around those I love. Out of the corner of my eye I spot Enzo and for the briefest moment I wish I could tell him I love him, but he doesn't need that distraction right now. I can tell him when this is all over and we can live out our lives peacefully in a small cottage somewhere in Korin.

"We need to take them in sections," Jade yells. "Everyone break off and take a quadrant. Duncan and I will take the north. General Enzo, think you can handle the south?"

"It's been a long time since you've called me that, but don't ask stupid questions, Jade," he smiles at her.

"A title well deserved. Okay, Lil and Aliyah, you take the west. Gunnar, Sara, you take the east. Everyone ready?"

"Let's kill the bastards," Gunnar smiles, like he has been waiting for this moment for ages. I let myself smile picturing Gunnar grinning like a child during battle.

"Listen up, Aramot's power draws from the moon. He uses the light to bend it into weapons. It may just be light, but it can kill. So watch your backs," Duncan yells to us.

Focusing back on the army of rotting corpses, I take one final breath before unleashing a war cry that has to be heard by all the realms and unsheathe my knives in both hands. I run straight into my section and plunge one of my knives into the neck of the first Kalari I meet. His bones turn to dust and blow away in the wind. I turn to the next, and the next, and the next until I find myself far away from my family who are all focused on their own circle of Kalari.

Lil is using her swords to cut the heads off any Kalari who dares to come too close. She is pushed back further away from me until I lose sight of her in the battle. Enzo uses his powers to incinerate and throw the enemy back, but using all of that at once will drain him too quickly. He needs to rely on his strength, as well. Jade and Duncan fight back to back. Duncan is disappearing and reappearing, taking them out one by one. Jade and him must have found a system, because she matches their moves hit for hit, while backing them up towards Duncan.

I look around the glade to try and find Sara and Gunnar as I continue to clear my quadrant. I can't lose my best friend again. We need to all walk out of this battle alive, or none at all.

Sara and Gunnar have a system of their own. She leads them towards her before disappearing, and Gunnar blasts them with his fire. I can't say that the smell of burning, rotting corpses adds a pleasant aroma to the battlefield.

I need to focus back on the enemy. I have to trust that my family will survive this. A corpse comes running at me with a spiked ball swinging from the end of a chain. It doesn't seem like the most effective weapon, because every time he swings it, I am able to dodge out of the way. It seems they don't have much skill, but there are hundreds of them and that is what makes them dangerous. They are disposable to Aramot. I spin and land my knife in the temple of the Kalari's skull.

Another one comes at me from the right. He holds a nine strand whip in his hand, with the ends pointed with metal. *I'm so sick of whips.* I didn't get to kill Cyrus, so I'll just have to settle for this instead.

He snaps the whip and I move out of the way as fast as I can, but two of the points connect with my thigh. I'm lucky it didn't cut through my pants, but it hurt like a mother. On the next snap of his whip, I risk reaching out and grabbing one of the strands. I catch it in my hand and wrap it around my forearm before pulling on it hard, bringing The Kalari closer to me. As he fumbles over his feet, clearly not expecting me to grab the whip, I plunge my knife right into his sternum, eviscerating him.

Liliana comes into view running straight towards me.

"Ali! Ali! We have to take out Aramot, this might be our only chance! We need to clear a path!" she shouts, over the collisions of swords and weapons.

"I will make sure you get there," Enzo says coming up on my right. His brown hair is soaked with sweat and the rest of his body is torn to shreds. I nod once, and take one last moment to look at him.

I love him. After everything we have been through, everything he has helped me through, I know that without a shadow of a doubt, I love Enzo. My ZoZo. When this is all over, I am going to make sure he knows it.

"Okay, let's go!" I shout, but as I do, Kalari are thrown back, clearing a direct path to Aramot. I turn to see blood dripping from Enzo's eyes.

"Run Aliyah, run," he grits through his teeth as he falls to his knees in the dirt, gasping for breath.

I can't let this opportunity pass. I break out into a sprint, Lil running right next to me. Suddenly, a sword juts out from the reforming line, slicing Lil in the thigh and she falls.

"Keep going! I've got this handled," she smirks, as she quickly rises, hobbling on one leg.

I don't hesitate. This needs to end now. I keep running until I have cleared the last line of The Kalari and am headed straight for Aramot.

He jumps down from the rock, confidently walking towards me with that fucking smirk on his face. He thinks I am going to be cut down like a blade of grass. *If I'm going to die, I'm going to make him work for it.* I take a moment to catch my breath.

"Do I take your breath away, little one?" Aramot smirks, standing there waiting for me to recover like he has all the time in the world. His hands are on top of his sword, resting as the tip digs into the ground. *Cocky bastard.* All I can see are his black eyes looking at me from behind his helmet.

"I'm going to plunge all three of these knives into your chest. Then we will see who is gasping for air."

I narrow my eyes at him and charge. He casually picks his sword up, but on his first strike against me, I stagger back from the force. He has strength on me, but I am smaller than him and have to use that to my advantage. He brings his sword down, arcing towards my neck. I thank the Maker I had been training with Sara for the last eight years or I wouldn't have been able to dodge his blows at all. Huffing out a breath, I regain my footing.

Aramot starts to get frustrated at his continued missed hits. He grits his teeth and his eyes go dark as he kicks his leg out hitting me square in the chest. I go flying back into the burnt grass and cough trying to get air in as fast as I can.

Wearily getting to my feet, I charge at him with everything I have. He steps out of the way at the last second and as I pass him, he cuts across my back. *Great, another scar on my back.*

I scream out in agony. I am so done with his games. I turn and exhale a breath, throwing my knife hard, burying it in his right shoulder. He staggers back and moves his sword to his left hand. He moves to take a step again, and my other knife sails through the air, hitting him in the left shoulder.

He drops his sword and rips the dagger out of his shoulder before throwing it to the ground.

"You're going to regret that," Aramot staggers as he picks up his sword.

While he finds his footing, I dare glance across the battlefield to make sure Enzo is safe. His eyes find mine and something in my chest explodes. Enzo's eyes go wide. My arm is burning and I look down to see my moon scar burning bright red before disappearing.

Sara? Sara? Can you hear me? I need you.

Silence.

Aliyah, behind you!

Enzo? Enzo! I can hear Enzo in my head! But that would mean—Enzo is my—. I don't even have time to process all this information before I am turning to duck as Aramot swings his sword wide, nearly missing my head. He is not as skilled with having two injured shoulders, but he is still stronger than me.

I go to reach for my third and final knife on my ribs, when a searing pain shoots through my leg, causing me to stumble. As I look down, I don't see a wound, but I hear Enzo roar in the distance.

Do I...feel his pain? I try to regain my focus. Gripping my blade, I slash and slice at Aramot, landing small, but not fatal, strikes to his body. Pain radiates up my arm, but Aramot is no where close to me.

Enzo, what is going on? Why do I feel what you are feeling? How do I turn it off? I plead, but there is no response.

Aramot keeps coming at me no matter how many strikes I land. *Why doesn't he just give up!* Bright streaks of light come flying towards me with the intent to kill. I drop quickly to the ground, but another wave of light shoots past me, slicing through the side of my ribs.

Maybe I can wear him down? He can't pull from his power forever. But he is also a much stronger fae. This would all be so much easier if I had a freaking power. While dodging his strikes, I try to find that piece of me that Sara was talking about. I search my body and mind for any flicker of hope that I have an ability, but all I feel is that broken piece of my soul that won't function. Any power I might have clearly doesn't want to come out.

The light blades stop coming at me and Aramot grips his sword harder now. Another blow across my back— no, Enzo's back— sends me stumbling forward. All I feel is pain. Blow after blow. Ribs...legs... cheek...I can't keep this up. I can barely hold my own against Aramot, without Enzo's injuries slowing me down too. I can't keep this up forever. I need to strike smarter, not harder.

On his next blow I quickly drop to a squatting position and slice for his legs. Hitting my mark and cutting straight across his knee caps, ripping the tendons from his body. It may not be his chest, but I'll take it. He screams in agony and falls to his knees. I take the hilt of my sword and hit him in the side of the head, knocking him out cold. *This kill belongs to Duncan.*

I turn to face the battle still raging behind me. More and more Kalari are cut down as my friends slice through them. Lil is back up on her feet with part of her torn shirt tied around her leg wound. Jade has several cuts on her arms and legs. Duncan is all focus as he rips heads right off bodies with his bare hands. Gunnar and Sara are back to back clearing the rest of their section in a blur of fire. I can't believe it. We might actually win! Once the rest of The Kalari see that their leader has fallen, they will have to retreat.

My eyes meet Enzo's. *My mate.* I can finally breathe again, knowing this is going to be all over soon. Enzo cuts through the last Kalari in his quadrant and a smile graces his face as he runs towards me, eyes locked on mine. The rest of The Kalari are starting to retreat after seeing their leader fall. My eyes brim with tears. I can't believe Enzo is my mate. Something I didn't even know I could have is suddenly now all I want.

His eyes go wide and I start to walk towards him. He starts running towards me.

"Enzo," a lump in my throat starts to form. "Enzo, I love—"

Agony. So much pain in my chest, but I look at Enzo and he has no wounds on his chest. I don't understand, why does my heart hurt so much? I look down and see a blade sticking out of my chest. Tears drip from my eyes and onto the blade as it disappears.

The sound of blood thumping in my ears is so loud. I swear I hear Enzo yelling, but I can't focus on anything he is saying. He reaches me right as I fall to my knees, but they never hit the ground. His strong arms come around me. *I can't believe that bag of dicks stabbed me.*

Chapter 55

ENZO

Aliyah did it! She was able to take out Aramot and The Kalari will retreat, not knowing what to do without orders. Aliyah is my mate. For so long I wanted what my parents had. When that went away, I thought I would never want love in my life. I didn't want my life tied to someone else in that way. But with Aliyah, I can see a future with her. Since that moment back in Mareen when she first held that knife to my throat I just knew. I knew she was going to change my life forever.

Aliyah starts to say something over the battlefield. I don't have time to make out what she is saying because Aramot is already moving too quickly behind her. I pull for my powers to stop him before he can hurt her any further, but I have nothing left. I burned it all out fighting for our lives, and now I don't have the strength left to save my dove.

I try to yell to her to turn around or to move, but it's too late. The sword cuts through her back and out her chest. *No!* I break into a sprint running towards Aliyah. The cut is clean through her heart. Right as I reach her, she falls into my arms. Duncan materializes behind his brother, sword drawn and cuts off his head.

I kneel in the soil and lay Aliyah down on the ground in front of me. Her wound is pumping blood out across my fingers as I try to stop the bleeding. She can't die. I just found her and now I am losing her. Her eyelids are heavy and her hand wraps around my forearm.

"Enzo...Enzo stop." Her voice is so weak.

"No. Aliyah you can't die. You're not going to die. I've got you. I'm here now," I plead.

"Enzo." She tips my chin up so my eyes meet hers. A soft smile graces her lips and her eyes shine bright with tears. "Enzo...I love you with all my heart. Well, what's left of it now." Even in death she tries to comfort me with a joke.

"Enzo," she continues. "I need you to remember your promise to me." She coughs and blood starts dripping from the corner of her mouth. "Promise me you'll move on. Promise me you'll be happy."

"Shhh. It's okay. There is time for that later. Right now we just need to get you patched up. You're going to be just fine."

"Enzo, because of you, I don't feel so broken anymore."

My tears begin dripping onto her cheeks below me just like my blood did that first day that we met. I should have left her in Mareen. I never should have brought her here. This is all my fault. I will never forgive myself if she dies.

I grip her hand in mine, holding tight. Her eyes slip closed. *No. No. No.*

"Aliyah, wake up. Aliyah, keep your eyes open. Stay with me...please...stay with me!" I lean down kissing her lips trying to get her to open her eyes. I need to see her blue eyes, to know she is okay.

"Enzo...you...were always my...home." Her soft voice in my head is all I hear before her hand goes limp in mine, and her chest stops moving.

A roar rips from my mouth as I tip my head up to the sky. I begin to sob, tears flowing freely now. I shake her shoulders trying to get her to wake back up.

I need you. I am nothing without you. I try to push the thoughts down the bond, but the tether is no longer there.

"It's time to let her go, Enzo. She's gone." Gunnar comes up behind me and places a firm hand on my shoulder. Sara stands close, holding Gunnar's hand, before turning into his chest. I hear her silent sobs as she mourns her best friend.

"The rest of The Kalari have retreated," Duncan says. "Take whatever time you need." He backs up to stand next to Liliana.

"We will stay for as long as you need. Come on, let's give them some space." Jade guides everyone away so I can lay here with Aliyah for just a little longer.

I lay down next to her, and put her arm around me, as I lay my head on her chest. I feel her blood coating my skin. This is the last I will ever feel of her. Those few moments of the bond are gone. Shredded into nothing. I feel *nothing*.

I am not sure how long I lay there with Aliyah, but the moon fades and the light of dusk grows brighter. Her body has gone cold, and I can feel her blood drying on my cheek. I stand, feeling an ache in my heart knowing what I need to do. I pick her up and cradle her in my arms. It's time to take her home.

EPILOGUE

S tanding on the grassy hill I look out over the ocean. Aliyah would have loved it here. Seeing the sun shining on her face, hair blowing in the breeze, it would have been perfect.

I know that Luar was never truly home for her, but having her in Olyrium is too painful. My fingers graze over the chain around my neck and the small ax feels cool beneath my touch. I couldn't bury it with her. I needed a piece of her to remind me that even though she is not by my side, a part of her will always lay over my heart.

As I kneel down in the grass, I place a single rose on the fresh soil atop her grave. It is marked only by my sword. I promised to protect her...and I failed. I will carry that burden with me all my life. I leave my sword with her now, to guard her in the afterlife.

I pray to the Maker that she is without pain and without sadness. I hope, even now, she can find happiness without me. I can't keep my promise to Aliyah. I will *never* move on from her.

I never had the chance to tell her that I love her. I told her there would be time for us. Time to share in that love. To show her everything that being my mate could be. We could have built a home together. I thought we had forever. I let my heart turn good once. I let it turn good for her.

I will never make that mistake again.

Jade waits patiently close by, giving me room to say my final goodbyes. Jade has been by my side since Aliyah died. I think that Jade and my dove grew close over those last few days with each other. In the end, I think Jade was her friend.

Jade had wanted to come with me so I wouldn't have to bury Aliyah alone, and yet that is all I feel now...alone. My life is nothing now. I will let the darkness take over my heart once again and I will not allow even the smallest bit of light back in.

I look out across the ocean one last time as I feel a single tear drip down my cheek and land on Aliyah's grave. I will never come back here.

Luar is on it's own now to fight the Banished if they return here. Aramot is dead, but he took orders from the Banished King.

When Gunnar arrived back in Krystal, he received word from the loyal spies in Krystal that The Banished Kingdom found a way to pull down the barrier for good which either means they have one hell of a weapon, or the queen's spell had a loophole.

There had been no reports of any Kalari trying to escape, but I know they are planning an uprising. If Aramot is to be believed, the Banished King isn't done yet. With The Bridge fixed between realms, it is only a matter of time before the Banished King returns to Olyrium.

I stare down at Aliyah's grave and say my final goodbyes.

I love you Aliyah, may you find the happiness I could never give you.

I turn from her final resting place and start walking with Jade back to The Bridge. I am a shell of a man. I told Aliyah that my soul would go with her if our journey together ever ended. And I was right.

My only purpose now is burning The Banished Kingdom to the ground. If anarchy is what they want, that is exactly what they are going to get.

ACKNOWLEDGEMENTS

I'd like to start by saying a huge thank you to my best friend, Jacque, for endlessly supporting me through this process, creating this world with me, and countless hours on FaceTime going over plot points and ideas. You helped bring this world to life through your graphic design, and I couldn't be more proud of the things we have accomplished together. I never imagined that eight years ago you would walk into my life and become everything that you are to me. Our love for books has brought us closer than ever in these last few years, and I cannot wait to see where this journey takes us next.

To my family who has endlessly supported me throughout this process. You all have heard me talk for hours about how excited I was to create this world, and all the dreams I have for this book series. A huge shout out goes to my dad for introducing me to the world of fantasy as a child, reading "The Hobbit" and giving every character their own voice. You helped form my overactive imagination that helped me envision this world, and bring it to life on paper.

To my husband for putting up with me these last few months as this all came together. Every TikTok post, no matter how silly, you supported and even helped film at times. You accepted my crazy and helped make this all possible. Thank you for bringing me food when

I refused to leave my desk because I wanted to get "just one last thing" done. Much like Enzo is Aliyah's home, you are mine. Do not ever change.

Lastly, to all you readers. Thank you for your constant belief in me during this process. The comments on TikTok encouraging me to keep writing and pursue my dreams mean more to me than you can ever know. I hope this story speaks to you in a way that empowers you to fight your inner battles, knowing you will come out stronger on the other side. I can't wait to take you on this journey with us into the next few books...and who knows after that.

ABOUT THE AUTHOR

These are the faces behind "Jane Rose." Just two best friends sharing their love for books and writing along the way!

Find us on social media to follow our story and writing process for the next book!

TikTok: JaneRose_TheBookBesties

Instagram: janerose_thebookbesties

Website: janerosepublishing.com

www.ingramcontent.com/pod-product-compliance
Lightning Source LLC
Chambersburg PA
CBHW061333160726
47995CB00001B/15